Dangerous Boundaries

Evelyn Burroughs

Copyright © 2024 by Evelyn Burroughs

All rights reserved.

No portion of this book may be reproduced in any form without written permission from the publisher or author, except as permitted by U.S. copyright law.

Contents

1. Chapter 1 — 1
2. Chapter 2 — 12
3. Chapter 3 — 20
4. Chapter 4 — 29
5. Chapter 5 — 37
6. Chapter 6 — 50
7. Chapter 7 — 65
8. Chapter 8 — 76
9. Chapter 9 — 88
10. Chapter 10 — 100
11. Chapter 11 — 116
12. Chapter 12 — 128
13. Chapter 13 — 138
14. Chapter 14 — 151
15. Chapter 15 — 161

16.	Chapter 16	171
17.	Chapter 17	183
18.	Chapter 18	196
19.	Chapter 19	205
20.	Chapter 20	214
21.	Chapter 21	225
22.	Chapter 22	233
23.	Chapter 23	244
24.	Chapter 24	257
25.	Chapter 25	273
26.	Chapter 26	284
27.	Chapter 27	301
28.	Chapter 28	306
29.	Epilogue	314

Chapter 1

Everyday is a new beginning. Rethink, Restate, and Rebuild! This was what Avni Mehta told herself every morning. She was not the kind of person who would dwell much over what it could have been & had always focused on what can be. Probably that was why, even after having a huge headache induced by a supposedly happy hour hangover, she downed the very definitely not appetizing tonic to help her get through the day.

She was not someone who was high on parties but having a best friend who would celebrate all of Avni's ups & downs didn't really keep her away from adventures like these every once in a while. Quickly grabbing a toast and stuffing it inside her mouth, she did a last check at herself in the mirror before leaving her apartment for the day.

London was as cold as it had always been in its January winters. Chilling wind blew on the rather deserted street, turning Avni's nostrils & ears red because of the cold. Walking up to the subway, she almost ran to board the metro as she pressed her fingers against her forehead while trying to stop herself from thinking about the last night at the club. It was her last day at work at her then job and she was supposed to go for a meeting today for her new job. Avni would have chosen to curl up inside her blanket and watch some murder-mystery but as always, her bestie Hazel Anderson convinced her to let loose by going out and party at some club she had been wanting to explore. The night started with trying all the exotic dishes in the menu and drinking the most expensive cocktails on the bar. But by the time both of them figured that they actually were not very great with handling the alcohol, it had been too late.

Avni's head throbbed and cheeks turned pink out of embarrassment when she remembered how last night took a wild turn when she had ended up grinding herself against a complete stranger - a very hot one though! That was the only fact that was keeping her sane. At least he was good! And man, those hands! Oh, let's not even start about the way he smelt. He felt like danger coated with a thick layer of charm & control.

Avni's thoughts came to a halt just like her body-wrecking makeout session had last night, when the metro stopped. Realising that it was her stop too, she got down the train and briskly walked out of the subway.

She put a hand on her chest as she tried to catch her breathe once she had finally reached her destination - The Khanna Mansion. She quickly watched the time on her wrist watch and finally breathed in relief when she figured that she still had fifteen minutes in hand. Avni had always had this habit of being awfully punctual. She hated it when she was late.

The guards let her in when she showed them the official mail that she had gotten from her potential employer, some Mr. Neil Khanna. Avni looked around the mansion as she walked through the pathway which was carved out as a road midway between a huge lawn. She smiled at all the different flowers that they had planted at the sideways, the tonic finally showing its effects as she could feel her headache subsiding.

The maid who received her at the door was generous enough to greet her with a bright smile and have her seated in the outer lobby of their huge mansion as she moved away to inform her boss about Avni's arrival. Avni bit on her lower lip as the jitters started taking over and she felt nervousness coursing through her. She smiled at the house-help who brought her a different variety of fresh-fruit juices, tea, coffee and some snacks to go with.

Her caffeine addicted self definitely wanted to grab some hazelnut cappuccino but she wisely decided against it as she waited for Mr. Neil Khanna.

Guess someone else was awfully punctual too, her supposed employer entered the lobby just when the clock ticked the 10 a.m. mark. Hearing the firm footsteps, she looked up at the man as she blinked. And all of a sudden, the headache that she thought had subsided, came back rushing to her with a magnitude ten folds higher.

What in the freaking cheese-marshmallow fondue!? She had basically attempted to grope her potential employer? Definitely not a potential anymore! He would probably throw her out the moment he looks at her and recognises her whiny-horny self from the last night.

All the events of the last night flashed in front of her eyes as she tried to blink her eyes fast as if that would help the situation.

Man, this stupid world is a small place thing sucked! Why him out of all the people? Was the embarrassment from last night not enough?

She recalled the way she had stumbled her way up to the bar to get herself some water as she felt thirsty among all the dancing with Hazel. Gulping the whole glass down, she turned to go back to the dance floor but before she could do so, she stumbled on her footsteps again. Sure that she was going to hit herself against the floor and make a fool out of herself, she closed her eyes shut as she mentally prepared herself for the fall, however that never came. Instead, she felt something cold enveloping her but even then she felt hot.

Unstable as she was because of the cocktails she had downed, she blinked her eyes open as she tried to get a hold of the situation. Avni had to blink her eyes a few times before she could see him clearly, the alcohol was messing with her senses and also the fact that she was wearing contacts instead of her regular glasses didn't really help much. But once the haze was clear and she looked into his whiskey like brown eyes, she couldn't look away. They were intoxicating just as the colour of his orbs suggested. She could feel herself wrapped around the whiff of his smell that resonated with that of something similar to rich spices and open countryside air.

Her foot stumbled again because of the dizziness she felt and in an attempt to steady herself, she held on to his arms while he kept holding her with his arms around her waist. She could feel the coolness of his skin seeping down her body, seemingly giving some relief to how hot & warm she felt. Even after all the intoxication, Avni could clearly make out the amusement & intrigue that he held in his eyes as he looked at her, watching each & every movement.

A small laugh drew its way out of her mouth when she felt his fingers unconsciously moving around her waist with the faintest of touches. Her eyes felt heavy when she grinned at him as she removed his hand from her waist, but before he could pull back, she held his hand, wrapping her palm around his wrist as she led him towards the dance floor with her dwindling steps.

The sensuous music along with the alcohol induced adrenaline gave her enough guts to put the man's lean and long hands on her hips while he just watched her with a flicker of amusement in his eyes. Avni enclosed her arms around his neck as she stepped closer to him so that the toes of her heels kissed that of his shoes. And it was then that she saw the danger that he carried in his eyes. She gulped as she blinked her eyes up at him but her body swayed along with the beats of the music nevertheless.

She figured that she was craning her neck up to look into his eyes yet it felt like he was still towering her when he bowed his head down to look back at her. She bit hard on her lower lip as she tried to ignore the tingles that she felt down her belly when his hold on her hips tightened a bit, even so, Avni never dared to look away from those beautiful eyes.

She took in a harsh breathe before turning around as she put his arms around her lower abdomen, holding them there when she placed her right hand just above her navel where both of his hands met each other around her stomach.

With newfound courage, she pressed herself against him as she swayed her hips with the music. Her left hand rose up to caress the side of his cheek as he stood behind her while she moved her lower body against him. The nails of her right hand dug in his hands wrapped around her when she rested her head against his shoulder as she moved her hips in careless round motions. Her movements became rough and uncalculated when she pressed her ass against his crotch as she very shamelessly rubbed her way up & down against him.

Just when she thought that the guy was either just not interested or was rather interested in men, he moved. Removing his hands from around her belly, he put them at her sides as he tried to hold her steady while he pulled himself a little back. Avni had almost cried at the loss of his firmness when he pulled her back to himself and the tingles in her body transformed to liquid fire in her veins.

"Desperate much, Buttercup!?" - she heard him say as she felt his breathe falling on her neck and if anything, she just felt her thighs tingle at the sensation she felt in the middle of her legs.

Avni could faintly hear him chuckle before he placed his mouth at her shoulder blade. Her body stiffened at the sensation for a second before she finally registered his touch and the fact that it felt so good to her. He left a trail of kisses along her shoulder blade and then up her neck all the while keeping her pressed up against the firmness of his crotch.

It was when he sucked at a particular spot on her neck that proved to be the undoing for Avni. Her hips buckled up as she tried to roll them against him in order to get some relief from the throbbing in her core. His grip was a bit too firm for her to move but she didn't give up. She rubbed herself against him when he was leisurely kissing her neck.

"Someone really is desperate, huh?" - he cursed before grabbing her arm as he turned her around so that she faced him.

Avni did not answer him verbally, she didn't know how to. So just ended up blinking her eyes as she pressed her body up against him as she tried to look for some friction. She noticed how his brown orbs dropped down to her body before he looked back in her eyes. An unspoken threat hanging loose in them as he looked at her, but Avni was beyond rationality at that point.

She ran her fingers through his dark chestnut brown hair while she rolled her hips against him, half ashamed of her clumsy movements and half desperate to get some sort of release.

Cursing under his breathe, the guy then grabbed her ass as he thrusted his crotch against her while his mouth came down to her collar-bone. Incoherent words and moans escaped Avni's mouth when he swirled his tongue around her sensitive skin. She grasped his hair in fists when he sucked and nibbled at the hollow of her collar bone, the action rendering her out of breathe slightly as she tried to draw in a harsh breathe.

Avni felt prickly needle-like tingles throughout her body and when it became too tough to hold on, she guided his mouth towards her chest as her other hand slid his hand up from her waist to the curve of her chest. A moan escaped her mouth just when his mouth came in contact with her chest. The small hair of his stubble rubbing against the soft skin of her cleavage as he put small kisses there. She didn't really know what he heard in her moan but all of a sudden, he pulled back.

However, before Avni could protest, he held her hand as he walked themselves deep inside the club. She carelessly followed his steps and faintly noticed that he had taken a turn before they entered into a lobby where there was no one else apart from them and a set of plush sofa were set against the walls. He left her hand as he watched her looking around and just when she was about to ask him how no one was there, he pulled her towards him as he placed his mouth against hers in a rough kiss. Avni's eyes shut close on their own as she kissed him back with equal fervour. Her hands fisted the fabric of his shirt when her legs started to wobble as she felt weak in her knees. Though, as if understanding her dilemma, he held her by her waist as he took steps forward, making her step backward.

Avni had to press her thighs tight against each other when he sucked on her lower lip. Her legs hit the sofa and it was then that he softly pushed her down as she landed on the velvet fabric with a soft thud. She pulled on his jacket as she tried to kiss him back. However, just when she was about to get a taste of his tongue, the guy took her by surprise when he changed their positions and all Avni knew was that she was now sitting on his lap with her legs wrapped around his waist.

She dragged herself along his thigh till the point she could reach his crotch and her hands held on to his shoulders as she kissed his jaw. Avni moaned against his mouth when his cold hands glided up & down her thighs, massaging them with his strong hands while she kissed on his neck at the same time rubbing herself against him.

Avni could swear that she had heard him groan when she bit on his neck and then sucked the skin. But before she could continue her ministrations, the guy put his mouth on her chest, sucking on one of her breasts through the flimsy material of her dress while he fondled with the other one. She whimpered as his hot mouth sucked and bit on her soft skin while his thumb rolled around the sensitive bud of her other breast. She could feel the wetness and heat of his mouth on her skin from above the fabric of her cloth and she made desperate attempts to find a release as she rolled her hips against his crotch. Thrusting herself against him as she held on his shoulders so that she won't fall down because of their vigorous movements.

Avni felt out of breathe & exhausted but every time she thought she was close, her body would start turning limp, she couldn't chase her orgasm. Frustrated & needy, she put her head in the crook of his neck while he still fondled her chest as she kept thrusting herself against him. However, she pulled back in alarm when his phone rang suddenly, the sharp noise causing a headache to her.

"What?" - he said in a cold tone as he picked the call up, while Avni just blinked her eyes as she watched him.

"Fuck! This better be good, Noah!" - he said before disconnecting the call.

Avni's brows turned into a frown when he looked at her.

"Sorry, Buttercup! I guess, this is how it ends!" - he mumbled with an irritated expression on his face.

"What? You can't leave me hanging like this!" - the words came out before she could even think them through.

"I need to leave!" - his hands stopped her from moving as he held her firmly by her waist.

"Please!" - she hated how embarrassing she was being at the moment, but she just didn't know what else to do.

"Dammit!" - he cursed before he checked his phone once. "Just because I don't deny pleasure to pretty girls!" - he said before he slid his hands down her ass.

Avni just blinked as she tried to register his words when he adjusted her against him before he started moving against her at the same time he guided her against his hardness. Avni's grip on his shoulders tightened as he made some rough yet powerful thrusts against her core while she was nothing more than a moaning mess.

She felt her stomach tightening and core clenching when he made her almost jump on his hard cock. Avni could still hear the way the fabric of their clothes rubbed against each other and she could feel the way his eyes watched her - full of fervour & passion yet making her dizzy with the way he was making her feel at the moment.

Her heels dug into the sofa as her hips bucked up and back arched with the way he was thrusting into her but Avni couldn't get enough. Her lips came crashing down on his when a shot of pleasure tore through her when he gave her one last hard thrust and she came. For him. And she would lie if she said that she didn't enjoy it.

The guy kissed her back as he pushed her hair away from her face before he finally pulled back. The aftereffects of her orgasm could clearly be seen on her face as her whole body felt warm and face had turned completely red. The guy made her sit on the sofa and stood up.

"Be careful, Buttercup! I am sure you would like to fix your look before anyone sees your disoriented sexy-self!" - and he chuckled as he walked out of the lobby with a very much visible hard on down his crotch.

The sexy sound of his husky drawl swirled through Avni's head as she blinked at him, still trying to get her breathe back to normal.

At the moment, a clearing of throat pulled Avni out of her thoughts and she blinked. Hard. As her heart picked up speed when the guy from the club, Mr. Neil Khanna sat opposite to her. In all his glory and prowess. The same whiskey brown eyes staring down at her as she felt herself quivering under his gaze.

CHAPTER 2

There were times when nights were for sleep. All that took place now was chaos. Unhinged & uncalled for!

Neil took a hot shower to provide his body some relief from the cold weather and to take his mind off certain things that unfolded not in a very pleasant way in the span of last twelve hours.

His men had found a mole in their organisation who had been successfully leaking information of their next move to his rival. However, before he could coerce him to provide leads on his rival, he had committed suicide. Also the fact that he just couldn't stop thinking about the woman he collided into at the club last night was beyond his comprehension. Her desperate moans, soft pleas and strikingly captivating black orbs was all that he could think about.

Sighing, he turned the knob of the shower off as he wrapped a towel around him and walked into his closet. Picking up one of his regular pleated dark beige trouser pants and a brown pullover sweater, he dressed himself up before making his way towards his little munchkin's room.

Neil smiled once he entered the room only to find his three years old niece snuggling into the blankets as she was still into a deep slumber.

N - Ishipie! Wake up, baby! Look the sun is up already. - he spoke softly as he massaged her scalp slowly.

I - Sun is running early, N-man! We need to sleep some more. - she mumbled as she tugged upon Neil's hands with her little ones.

N - I thought you'd like to go on a date with N-man today? - he sighed. It's okay if you want to sleep in! - he made a long face to make sure that it would work.

I - Brunch date? - and she was wide awake.

A hearty chuckle escaped Neil's throat as he nodded his head in affirmation. He brushed back her hair as they fell on her tiny face.

I - Will N-man help me get ready for the date? - she jumped up on the bed as she hugged Neil while her arms failed to meet each other around him.

N - Anything for my Ishipie! - he carried her in his arms as he walked to the bathroom.

Brushing her teeth and getting her clean after a warm bath, Neil dressed Isha up in black woollen leggings paired with a light brownish-orange frock. And then came the most dreaded part. It always took Neil almost an hour to get her hair done the way she wanted them to look like. So just like always, Isha chose how she wanted her hair to be done.

I - I want to have braided-piggies, N-man! - she clapped her hands with a big grin on her face.

N - Ishi, how about we settle for a big-girl ponytail. Yeah? - he tried to bargain as he blinked his eyes, hoping that would work.

I - But I want piggies! - she blinked her eyes back and Neil almost groaned at how easily he was sold.

N - Piggies, it is! - he sighed. I guess, I'll just use Youtube! - he mumbled to himself before playing a video on the internet to help him with her hair-do.

After about an hour of tying and untying her hair in braids, Neil was finally able to get done with her braided pigtails as he sighed in relief with a satisfactory look on his face. Though one of the braids was a little crooked, but who cared. His Ishipie just looked cute anyways!

I - You forgot the bow, N-man! - she told him while he nodded.

Getting an off white bow to go with her outfit, Neil completed dressing her as he took her in his arms before walking out of the room. Once they were in the drawing room, he made Isha stand on her feet as he checked the time on his wristwatch. Isha was supposed to start schooling and Neil was paranoid about her safety, so the best option that he could come up with was to homeschool her. He had taken dozens of interviews of the best teachers but just couldn't hire any as they were apparently not good enough as per his giant checklist.

Hoping that the one who was going to appear today would be a good catch, Neil asked Isha to wait for him before he walked towards the lobby once he was informed that the lady had been here.

Neil looked up from his phone screen once he reached the lobby only to find the same strikingly captivating black orbs from last night staring back at him. Shock with a hint of embarrassment was written all over her face and if he was being truly honest, even his stomach did a flip when he saw her sitting there, in front of him, in his house, with those thick glasses as she blinked at him hard, her fingers fiddling with the ends of her coat.

Taking in a deep breathe, he pushed all the swirling thoughts aside as he sat on the sofa opposite to her.

N - Can I have your CV? - he asked, seemingly pulling Avni out of her thoughts.

She nodded to herself a bit awkwardly before fishing the CV out of her bag. With slightly shaking hands, she held them out for him to take and just when he held the file, their fingers brushed. Avni's throat worked on a swallow as her eyes blinked, while Neil's reaction was more intramural and thus Avni couldn't notice it. A sudden flicker of warmth shot through Neil's body when their fingers came in contact and as someone whose body always remained cold for some rare medical reason, he was surprised how warm she felt. His eyes snapped up to hers while she shifted slightly in her seat as she met his gaze. And there was this thing that both of them felt but couldn't name it.

Lust? But it was too intense to be just that! Longing? But how could one long for something one doesn't even know of! Anticipation? But that was just wrong, no matter how right or tempting it felt!

Neil recovered first as he cleared his throat while tugging at the file that Avni was still holding. Blinking her eyes rapidly, she pulled her hand back as she rested them on her thighs while she watched him flipping through the pages of her CV and other documents.

N - Things seem fine with the qualifications and your work-experience. However, I would only confirm the job once we go through a probation period. One month. In the mean time, you too, can get to know about what I expect from you as Isha's teacher. Works?

A - Uh, Okay. I think it works for me, Mr. Khanna. But I'd like to meet the kid first?

N - I'll arrange that. - he nodded. One more thing, I'll need longer hours than the usual. I'm out for work through out the day and Isha needs someone around. So, I guess you'll have to be present from 11 am sharp to 8 pm till night. I'll pay you as per your demands, but the time is non-negotiable. - he finished, eyes held no emotion, tone business-like curt and cold which almost made Avni shiver.

A - I guess I'll have to see to that. We have time till the probation period. I'll let you know if the timing works for me. - she said with a thoughtful expression on her face.

N - Fair enough! - he nodded.

And the discussion went on for a while till the point they had discussed her fees, timings, things that Neil wanted to put forward about his expectation in a teacher for his niece.

N - Miss Mehta, I want you to be a little patient with Isha. She is all excited and goofy but she does get shy whenever she encounters someone new. So, she might take some time to warm up to you! - he told, for the first time his eyes softening as he mentioned his niece and Avni smiled at his thoughtfulness.

A - I'll take care of that, Mr. Khanna! - she said.

N - Well, its settled then. We can start with the probation from tomorrow? - he asked.

A - Sure. - she smiled, her nervousness nowhere to be found now.

N - Would you-

I - N-man, we're getting late! - came Isha's voice as she ran with her little steps towards Neil.

However, her steps took a halt when she looked at Avni. Quietly she walked up to Neil before she settled in his lap, swinging her legs back & forth.

I - Who is she, Mama? - she whispered in Neil's ears while Avni just kept watching the duo.

N - She is going to teach you. Remember, you wanted to count up to hundred? She's going to teach you that! - he told her softly while Avni was just completely mesmerized at how beautiful and comfortable they looked together.

I - Will she teach me how to write my name? - she asked as her big doe eyes moved to Avni.

N - Yes. She is going to teach you all that. You want to go shake hands with her? - he smiled while Isha nodded.

Sliding down Neil's lap, Isha walked up to Avni who was smiling at her warmly. Isha extended her tiny palm in front of Avni as her cheeks turned a faint shade of red.

I - Hi. My name is Isha. - she said, a bit shy as she told her name to Avni.

A - Hi, Isha! I am Avni. Would you like to be my friend? - she asked as she shook her hand. She couldn't unsee how her eyes were exactly like that of her uncle's. The same hazel brown colour with a beautiful sweep of thick lashes.

Isha grinned as she nodded at Avni, and then ran back to Neil, making her laugh at the cuteness. She indeed was curious to

know about her parents and about the fact that why she was staying with her uncle, Mr. Khanna. But going with her better judgement, she kept silent as she resisted to ask about Isha's family.

N - Ishi, could you please go & get your bag-pack? We'll leave for the date, hm? - he asked and Isha nodded in excitement.

Placing a kiss on his cheek, she ran inside to get her bag.

N - Alright then, Miss Mehta, I hope to see you at 11 tomorrow? - he stood up, and Avni followed the action.

A - Uh, about last night! Look, I- -she was cut midsentence & it was only then that Avni realised she was standing only a few steps away from him.

N - Trust me, it's the best for you to forget that last night happened. - he mumbled, voice held the edge of a threat as he took a step towards her, making Avni gulp in anticipation & fear.

A - Yes, I- - she tried.

N - Please come regularly, Buttercup! - he whispered as he brushed back a loose strand of her hair and tucked it behind her ear. Avni could feel a shiver running down her spine as he looked at her with those whiskey eyes, the same danger lurking behind the coldness that he held in them.

Stop! Stop you little menace. He is talking about coming to work regularly & not that coming!

A - Mr. Khanna, I- - she breathed in. I need to leave. See you tomorrow.

Or not? Not so dear Universe! What in the crispy pringles is wrong with you? Was it not embarrassing enough that I was shamelessly jumping his bones last night in a state of complete waste? Now I'm even getting turned on just by his so-hot-that-it-is-stupid voice! And god, that delicious smell! Okay-okay. Sush! Alright, at this point, just stop, Mehta!

Shaking her head in an attempt to clear the fog of her self-derogatory and horny thoughts, she resisted the urge to sprint out of the room while taking each step with precision, not wanting to fall down in front of him. Again!

However, she could swear she heard him chuckle behind her.

Chapter 3

Just the way Big Ben was an integral part of London and winters were incomplete without hot chocolates, similarly, Avni was notoriously famous for being clumsy.

So, stumbling on her own foot and stamping on her own coat more than the number of times she would like to count and nearly breaking her glass frames, she finally made it to the Khanna Mansion at 10:50 am. In proper Avni Mehta fashion, she was ten minutes early for her work and that made a smile appear on her face when she looked down at her wristwatch.

Taking in a deep breathe and hoping that her hormones would keep in check in front of that annoyingly handsome employer of hers, she stepped into the drawing room once she was granted access inside the house.

And in all honesty, Avni was not ready for what she saw when she entered the drawing room. Isha comfortably sat in Neil's lap while he held her little hand in hers and painted them in purple nail-paint. A heart-warming smile found a way to her lips as she watched Isha giggle when Neil poked his tongue out as he focused on the nail art.

N - All done, Ishipie! I think we're good. What do you think? - he said, still analyzing her nails.

I - It's my turn now. I'll paint your nails pink! - she grinned.

Avni almost chuckled when Neil's expression turned to a horrified one and he blinked his eyes in disbelief.

N - Ishi, boys don't wear nail-art. - he said, scratching the back of his neck.

I - No, but you're my best-friend. We have to twin, N-man! - she explained and Avni bit back a laugh.

She cleared her throat to gain the duo's attention and for a moment she could see the warmth in Neil's eyes before they registered her presence.

N - Baby, your teacher is here. We can twin later, okay? - he said as he made her stand and then himself stood up from the sofa.

I - Okay. - she mumbled while holding Neil's hand.

Avni noticed that she was apprehensive of letting him go as she was still shy in front of her. Putting a bright smile on her face, Avni walked up to Isha before she held her hand out for her to shake.

A - Good morning, Isha! How are you this morning.

I - Good morning. I'm good. - she said, slipping her hand into Avni's but the other one still held on to Neil tightly.

A - Shall we start the classes? - she asked softly while Isha just nodded.

Neil bent down to her level as he brushed her little hair back.

N - Ishi, you'll have fun with Teacher. I'll be around, hm? - he smiled while she smiled back.

Isha let go of Neil's hand and looked at Avni with a smile, making her smile brighter at her sweetness.

N - Let me know if you need anything. - he said with a tone void of any emotion to Avni before moving out of the drawing room.

She frowned at how rude and cold he came off as, but then shrugged it off before focusing on Isha.

It had been two hours and Avni had tried almost all the tricks up her sleeve to make Isha open up to her. But the kid, just like her uncle, was a tough nut to crack. She was an intelligent child, no doubts to that, however Avni's modus operandi was a bit different from the others. She couldn't just be mechanical & monotonous with her job, she had to make the work fun to go through it. And, for that she needed Isha to open up to her.

Sighing, she gave her a drawing to colour before making her way towards Neil's office. The mansion was so huge, she was afraid she would end up lost but thankfully a maid her helped her find his home-office.

She knocked the door twice but when there was no answer, she pushed it open slightly before making her way inside. Her eyes roamed around to find him, but all she found was an empty room with a minimalist interior. There were shelves that held numerous files and a huge mahogany table was placed at the centre of the room. There was a wooden coat rack stand besides it and a file was kept at the table.

Deciding to wait for him there, she sat at the chair opposite to his table as she moved around on the wheels out of boredom. When he wasn't there in the next five minutes, she clicked her tongue and sighed before picking up the file that was placed in front of her.

Just when she was about to flick the file open, someone snatched it from her and a gasp escaped her mouth when that someone pulled her up by her wrist. Avni blinked open her eyes to find Neil staring her down with those cold eyes as he put her hand behind her back while still holding on to her wrist tightly.

N - What makes you think that you can roam around & go through my stuff like that? - he gritted the words out and for some reason weird enough to be beyond cognition, all Avni could think was how closely her body was placed against his. Her belly stuck to his woollen sweater while her chest was pressed against his.

A - I...I was just look-looking for you. Had something to talk about Isha. - she managed in a breathless voice. He was so close that her glasses had become slightly foggy when his hot breathe fell on them.

N - What about Isha? Is she alright? - he asked, brows furrowed in worry.

The only time she thought that he was a human and could feel was when there was a mention of Isha. All the other times, he was so in control and devoid of any emotion that it almost felt like he was a cold robot. She looked into his eyes as she blinked, still thinking about the reason for which he was always so distant.

When Avni did not reply him with anything, Neil left her hand as he turned around to go to Isha's room. However, before he could walk out, she held his cold hand with her warm one.

A - Mr. Khanna, she is fine. - he turned to look at her while she still had her hand wrapped around his wrist. She is in her room, colouring in her drawing book. I just came to ask you if we can take her out. I am trying my best but she is still shy. I think an outing would help her get comfortable with me. - she voiced her thoughts out.

N - Uh, okay. - he nodded. Trying his best not to look down at his hand where she was holding it. There was a tingling sensation like his skin was on fire when she touched it. What kind of outing do you have in mind? - he asked, fisting his other hand to control his urge to push her up against a wall and kiss her.

A - May be we can visit an orphanage? Or some charity home? We can donate some of her old toys and clothes, that way we can teach her that it's a good virtue to share things, and can also get her to open up with me? - she explained, clearly unaware of his turmoil.

N - Okay. I'll arrange it. We'll leave after lunch? - he asked.

A - Okay. - she nodded as she adjusted her glasses on her nose.

Not having anything else to talk about, Avni started to step towards the door and it was then that she realised that she was still holding his hand in hers. Her eyes flicked up to his and she looked at him with her warm ones while he just looked back with that same mix of expressions, she just couldn't decipher it no matter how much she tried.

It was all coated with a layer of indifference and aloof coldness, however beneath it was curiosity, intrigue, longing and frustration. Curious to get through each & every layer that she held her heart in, every secret, every promise, every desire, Neil wanted to know it all about her. Intrigued at how she managed to make him feel all these things when he had never had felt them before. He couldn't stop thinking about her, and it was new. Usually, he would just brush people off as some grains of dust, but she was someone who was stuck to his memory, itched in his brain and his heart refused to let go. Longed for how perfect she felt in his arms. He couldn't remember the last time he had felt that warmth with someone apart from Isha. All he wanted to do was to hold her close to his chest as he slipped in & out of her while she enjoyed every bit of it. Frustrated at how he just couldn't do any of it, yet couldn't stop thinking about it. For fucks sake, he was aware that he was not someone who could do forevers or make sweet love, all he was capable of doing was a heart break with his own broken heart. Then why was he not able to control himself, he hated how desperately he wanted her.

Avni swallowed down her saliva as she tried to hold his unwavering gaze, it was too much to take. She felt like he could see through all the layers of her soul. And, probably, with those lifeless eyes, he was searching for something she didn't know of. But somehow, he was searching for it in her, and god knew, if she could give it to him, she would do it in the blink of an eye. She would do anything to see those gorgeous eyes smile.

A - Can I ask you something? - she asked in a whisper.

N - Proceed? - he blinked, eyes moved down to her lips as she spoke before he looked up again.

A - Do you always have these frown lines on your face? - she asked as she blinked her eyes and the spell was broken!

N - Do you always like to be so intruding in people's lives? - his lifeless eyes sparkled with a flicker of amusement.

A - Excuse me? - she blinked in disbelief.

N - Excused. Now, you may leave! - he rolled his eyes.

A - You're insufferable. - she pointed out.

N - And, I'd like to keep it that way. Could you give me some space now so that I could arrange for our visit? - he waved her off with his hands as he sat on his chair while she just watched with a hung mouth in disbelief.

Bro thinks he gets a free pass to be rude just because he is drool-worthy! Fuck that hot body!

Stopping herself from stomping her foot like a kid, she gracefully walked out of the room with a consciously extra sway in her hips.

It was around four in the evening when they finally left for the orphanage. The drive was mostly silent apart from the few questions that Isha asked them about where they were going and Avni let Neil explain her the plan. She was glad that Isha was excited about it all but she very definitely was still mad about Neil's coldness. Crossing her arms across her chest, she refused to look at him as she looked out of the window. However, no matter how hard she tried, she always ended up sneaking a glances of him after every five minutes of the drive.

She sighed in relief when they reached the orphanage and Avni walked ahead with Isha while Neil silently followed them with all the bags of toys and clothes. Usually, he would have his men do all this stuff, but since it was for Isha, he made sure that he was present through it all.

Since Neil had already spoken to the management, the authorities had beforehand set up for them to meet the kids. Avni & Isha together handed over the clothes and toys to the kids as they made small talks with every one of them. Isha was shy at the beginning but Avni could feel her getting relaxed around her.

She was in the middle of picking a toy up from the bag when her eyes fell on Neil who was standing at the corner of the room as he just watched the scene unfolding in front of him. A sigh left her mouth as she tilted her head to the side while looking at him. Apparently, it was not just Isha who needed to open up. He was as tightly wound up as she was! Biting on her lower lip in nervousness, she walked up to him. Neil looked at her with confusion when she was just a step away.

A - Here. - she extended the toy for him to hold. I promise you'll feel better! - she said with a small smile on her face.

N - How does it even matter? I'm already donating this, what difference will it make if I do it with my own hands or not? - he shrugged.

A - No, it won't make a difference. But the smile that those kids will give you will definitely make a difference. - she said as she held his hand and put the soft toy in his hand while he just watched her.

Avni then held his other hand as she led him towards the kids. Turning sideways to look at him, she gestured him to hand it over to them and for once, he simply followed.

And apparently, she had been right, the smile that the kids offered him, was indeed everything that made the difference. He handed over all the other toys and clothes along with Isha while Avni just watched them with a smile on her face.

Once done with the task, he turned around to look at her who was already watching him with a smile. However, Neil couldn't smile back. All this relief and warmth that he felt in his chest had become so foreign to him that he didn't know how to express it. His brows furrowed together as he watched her with that same mix of emotions. It was becoming a bit much to handle for him.

Shaking her head at his stubbornness, Avni walked up to him as she looked him in the eye.

A - Is something wrong with your teeth? - she asked making him frown more.

N - Why?

A - Why are you so adamant on not smiling? I promise I won't laugh even if your smile is funny. Although I doubt that! I think you'll look good! - she grinned.

N - Buttercup. - his eyes dug into hers.

A - Yes? - her breath was a bit heavy than usual.

N - I am not someone whose smile you'd like to think about! - he said before walking out of the building.

May be not! But I am already too invested, Mr. Khanna! - she thought to herself.

Chapter 4

Neil leaned against the bonnet of his car when he exhaled a deep breathe out. His eyes shut themselves close as an acrid taste filled his mouth when the same vision from two years back flashed in front of his eyes.

Blood, cries, shrieks, agony and more blood. All of it was still so fresh in his memory that it felt like he was living the same moment again & again. Stuck like an old cassette! He hated every bit of it.

It was in that very moment that he had decided he would avenge all those who had done him wrong. Blood for blood. Flesh for flesh. And, he had succeeded. He had taken the lives of those who had taken the lives of his family. But he could never succeed to find the relief that he so desperately sought.

However, it was now, after two years of endless agony that he felt relief in his chest. Just by a simple act of service? Was it even possible to feel that way?

Neil had always taken pride in the fact that he did not become the person that he was avenging. Yes, he had killed and destroyed, but he had always done it to the bad. His organisation was involved in tracking people who were involved in human trafficking and child rapes. All they ever did was to blow them up, teach them a lesson before the cops did and handed them over to the system then. But every time he went back home to his little niece and every time she called him N-man, he couldn't help but think if he was doing the right thing? Was he really the good man turned rebel for a cause, or was he just another scumbag who just stunk lesser than the others in the lot. It didn't matter how much he denied, a scumbag was a scumbag, a killer was a killer, and he, for the truth of his life, was one! He did not deserve to be smiled at or to be blessed with something good. He deserved pain, agony and misery, just like he inflicted on the others.

And, then she thought I deserve to smile! - a humourless chuckle left his mouth as his throat clogged and stung.

He was still lost in his thoughts when Avni and Isha walked up to him. Isha's little hand held on to Avni's as she happily marched towards him.

I - N-man! I want up. - she exclaimed as she held her arms out, gesturing Neil to hold her in his arms.

Neil tried to give her a bright smile but that was a failed attempt and Avni definitely did not miss the effort. Nevertheless, he lifted Isha up in his arms as she clung on to him and smiled at him brightly.

I - I had so much fun. - she kissed his cheeks, finally pulling a small smile out of him.

N - Did you thank Miss. Mehta? It was her idea. - he told while Isha shook her head with a frown on her face.

I - Can I do it now? - she asked.

Neil just chuckled and nodded as he turned towards Avni. Walking closer to her, he stood just a step away as Isha leaned forward to place a kiss on her cheek, making her smile.

I - Thankyou, Miss. - she grinned as she clapped her hands.

And Avni could not have been happier that she was being herself around her. She smiled at her brightly before her eyes fell on him, who was already looking at her. His brown eyes sucked the breathe out of her as they gust it back in her lungs simultaneously. She blinked her eyes as she tried to avert them from his and take in a deep breathe.

What in the spicy Mongolian noodles is he doing to me? I can't even think straight when he looks at me like that.

A - You're welcome, Sweetheart. - she uttered, eyes still locked with his.

I - N-man! Can we go to the church, please? - she asked while smiling at him.

N - Uh, okay! - he said. He offered a tight smile to Isha but Avni could see through the effort he was putting in to hold that smile.

It was a fifteen minutes drive from the orphanage which was mostly silent. Parking the car, Neil took Isha in his arms as they started walking into the church with Avni besides them. Isha ran towards the altar of the church as soon as they entered while Avni followed behind with a smile on her face, seeing her excitement. She made Isha sit on her knees as they offered the prayer.

When she couldn't find Neil besides them, Avni turned around to look for him and there he was! Standing near the last bench as he leaned his back against it, scrolling through his phone. A sigh left her mouth as she shook her head. She quickly thanked the greater almighty for everything that she had in her life and then made Isha sit on one of the benches at the front before making her way towards Neil.

A - People come here to pray, just thought to inform you! - she said as she stood opposite to him, crossing her hands behind her back as she looked at him through her glasses.

N - You sure you don't have a disorder that doesn't let you keep quiet for a while? - he spat out rather rudely, however Avni had become immune till now.

A - You sure you don't have a disorder that doesn't let you carry on a decent conversation with humans? - she blinked her eyes with a look of sheer innocence.

However, Neil didn't entertain her little joke as he just rolled his eyes and resumed whatever he was doing on his phone. Clicking on her tongue, Avni took a step ahead, making Neil look up at her with a cold stern face, but there was improvement, his eyes held some sort of emotion, even if it was frustration, Avni could do with that. She just hated the indifference that he treated her with. Anything else would do.

A - Anyways, let me guess! You hold a grudge because something that you wanted to happen, didn't happen? - she asked while looking at him.

N - You think you have me all figured out, don't you? - he narrowed his eyes at her as he slipped his phone into his pocket.

A - Uh, no! Not really. - she shook her head before adjusting her glasses. You're a bit mysterious, so it will take me some time to do that! - she put the fact out making Neil roll his eyes again.

N - Something that I never wanted to happen, happened. - he hadn't decided to tell her, the response was out for her to listen even before he could stop himself from saying it out loud.

His cold rainstorm like eyes bored into hers that only held sunshine and warmth, and she stared back. She gulped as she took a step forward towards him, her eyes held his as she stood just inches away from him, her hands brushing against his in a gentle touch.

A - You know how people talk about the light at the end of the tunnel? - she asked in a whisper and Neil just looked at her, the coldness in his eyes melting due to the warmth she held. Mr. Khanna, in all honesty, there is no light at the end of the tunnel. You, are your own light. And to have it illuminate your surroundings, you'll have to take a conscious leap of faith. Sometimes, things are just blessing in disguise, we don't realise it when they are happening to us, we only understand them in hindsight. - & she didn't realise when her index finger slipped into his and they interlocked as they stood there, so close to each other that they could hear each others' heartbeat because of the silence.

N - Its easy for you to say, Buttercup. - he whispered. But when every moment is a constant struggle to think if you're blessed to be alive or cursed not to die, believing in fate & destiny becomes tough. And it keeps getting tougher! - inadvertently he tightened his hold on her finger as he took an unconscious step towards her.

A - May be it is easy for me to say, but Mr. Khanna, it's never too tough to choose life. Do it for yourself, for Isha. - she urged, not really knowing what change it would make for her. But she needed him to be happy for some non-decipherable reason. If life is giving you chances without any prejudices, why are you so adamant to prove it wrong? Take the hand and don't let go. - she rubbed her thumb at the back of his hand. The rainstorms in his eyes scattering a bit to give way to a tiny ray light.

N - Why do you want me to hold it? - he found himself asking.

A - I don't know. - she shrugged. May be I want to be held. - she whispered as her throat worked on a swallow.

N - Buttercup, I-

A - Mr. Khanna, relax! - she cut him before he could complete the sentence. Taking in a deep breathe, she continued. Just give me your hand and stop thinking for a minute. - she held her hand out.

Neil's eyes flicked from her face to her hand before he travelled them back to her face. Looking into her eyes, he swallowed as he slipped his hand into hers and she smiled. It was not like the other dazzling smiles that she gave him, just a simple curve of her mouth but her eyes shone and Neil could see all the light that he had forgotten existed.

Entwining her hand with his, she walked besides him as they stepped towards the altar. She lit a candle and handed it over to Neil who simply took it from her and put it at the altar. Eyes never leaving hers, neither did she.

Neil didn't really know what he felt in that moment, nor did he have enough energy to comprehend it. But he definitely knew that all that he was searching for while wandering all these years, he could find it all in her. All those resentments, pains, complaints, griefs, bitterness, all of it, led up to her. In that moment, he felt like she could help him go through this hell of his life a bit better, however, he also knew that he couldn't do so without dragging her into his hell with him. And, he refused to do that. She didn't deserve to pay such huge price for the goodness she carried in her heart.

Neil blinked his eyes before he forced them to look away, and just like that, he was cold again. Avni watched him as he picked Isha up in his arms & turned to move out of the church.

N - Let's go! - he said to her, while walking out.

A sigh left her mouth as she shut her eyes close but then followed him out nevertheless.

By the time they started driving out of the church, Isha was already very sleepy and had nearly passed out in her baby seat in the car.

N - I guess I'll just drop you home? Isha is too tired. - he said.

A - Hmm. Okay!

N - Address?

And Avni told him the address before she leaned into the passanger seat comfortably. Exhausted herself, she too closed her eyes as she felt the cool breeze falling on her face through the window.

It was only when Neil cleared his throat that Avni realised that the car had come to a stop.

A - What's wrong? - she asked, rubbing her eyes as she slipped her finger beneath her glasses.

N - We're here! - he said, a hint of amusement lurking in his tone.

A - Oh. - she shut her eyes close in embarrassment. Shaking her head, she opened her eyes to look at Isha and then looked back at Neil. I..I'll see you tomorrow! - she said while Neil gave her a curt nod.

The rest of the day passed rather uneventful for the both of them as Avni just grabbed something to eat and tried to grab some sleep that seemed to have trouble reaching her when she was constantly haunted by whiskey brown cold eyes with that tinge of vulnerability she saw in them. And Neil's day was spent in feeding Isha & making her sleep while he himself struggled to do so.

True to herself, Avni was 10 minutes earlier to work the next day and she found Isha lying on Neil's stomach as they watched some cartoon. Isha smiled and almost ran to her when she noticed her. Smiling, Avni lifted her up in her arms as Isha placed a kiss on her cheek.

Just when she was putting her down, her eyes fell on something placed on the shelf near the TV set, and she was sure it had not been there the day before. Her eyes instantly found Neil's who averted them the moment she looked at him.

N - I, uh, I'll be in my office. Let me know if you need anything. - he spoke in a hurry before placing a kiss on Isha's forehead and leaving the drawing room.

Avni smiled as she looked at his retreating figure. Once he was out of her sight, she blinked her eyes at the Lord Ganesha statue that he had kept at the shelf.

Chapter 5

Now that Isha was comfortable with Avni, the day had been going on quite well & fun. They had learned alphabets and numbers. Avni had told her a story in between and Isha was visibly excited to listen to more of them. However, the excitement was shadowed by exhaustion around five in the evening when she became a bit cranky and sleepy.

Avni put her to sleep for a quick nap and just when she was done with putting her down, a maid brought her coffee.

A - Uh, listen! - she said when the maid was about to leave.

M - Yes, Ma'am?

A - Could you make me an espresso please? - she asked while hiding a smile.

M - Sure. - the maid said as she started preparing the drink.

Handing the mug over to her, the maid left and Avni smiled to herself as she grabbed the mugs of latte & espresso in her hands and walked out of the room after taking a one last glance at Isha.

She bit the corner of her lower lip to hide a smile when she knocked at the door. However, the smile turned to a frown when there was no response. Stubbornly, she knocked again.

She heard him grumbling at the same time she heard footsteps approaching the other end of the door.

Neil opened the door slightly as he stood at the door frame, blocking the inside view for Avni.

A - Hi. - she grinned.

N - What is it? - he spoke in his monotonous cold tone. However, Avni was a bit busy to acknowledge his rude question.

And what kept her busy was his skin fitting, chest hugging and muscle flexing black shirt that he was wearing. It was the first time that Avni was seeing Neil in something other than those sweaters or pullovers that he always wore as a uniform. Don't get her wrong, she did drool over him in them too, but him wearing a casual black shirt and loose blue denim was some another level of a thirst trap.

N - Miss. Mehta? - he called and that made Avni jerk in her place.

A - Uh, oh, I, actually, uh! The coffee! I..I brought you coffee - she finished, blinking her eyes rapidly to clear the haze she was in.

N - I don't drink coffee. You may go now! - he was about to shut the door close but Avni slipped her leg in between to stop him from doing so.

A - May be you should start drinking then. Will help your grumpy mood! - she said.

N - What do you want, Buttercup? - he asked while being visibly annoyed.

A - Coffee. With you. I'll leave then, promise! - she said before she gave him her best smile.

N - Fine. - he sighed. But you won't talk. - he warned.

Smiling, Avni nodded as she entered the room when Neil opened the door fully for her to enter.

Her eyes widened when she looked around while Neil just walked ahead towards the canvas that was placed at the corner of the room.

A - What in the double cheese hamburgers! - she whispered as she turned her head around to look at the various paintings that were placed in the room.

N - Excuse me? The deal was just for a coffee, I don't eat hamburgers! - he grumbled and Avni almost laughed.

A - Oh my god, Mr. Khanna! Are these yours? - she asked, pointing towards the paintings.

N - Oh, no! No. no! All yours! - he said with a sarcastic smile making her roll her eyes.

A - I didn't know the CEO of world's top five real state investment companies is such a great artist. - she appreciated.

N - Drink. The coffee will get cold. - he said as he grabbed the mug of espresso.

A - Who is she, Mr. Khanna? - she asked while pointing to the portrait of an old lady wearing an Indian attire.

N - My grandmother. - he sighed, knowing well that she was not going to shut up until & unless he gave her the answers she demanded.

A - Tell me about her. - she asked as she sipped on her latte, taking the seat next to him.

Neil turned his head around to look at her and so did Avni. She smiled up at him when their eyes met while Neil just blinked.

N - Miss. Mehta, you-

A - Please. - she blinked and he looked away.

N - We used to call her Bebe. She was a renowned artist back in India. Growing up, she used to teach me & my sister how to sketch and paint. It was our favorite activity to do. - a small smile grazed his mouth and Avni found herself smiling.

A - You miss her? - she asked softly.

N - All the time! - he looked at her. I wish she was here to teach Isha. - a sigh left his mouth.

A - You can teach Isha! - she spoke. Their arms grazed against each others' as they sat next to each other. Neil's eyes went to their touching shoulders before he looked back at her.

N - I am not as good as Bebe! - he cleared his throat as he scooted a little away from her.

A - That's okay. - she shrugged. You are you! And, all these painting are masterpieces, Mr. Khanna. - she looked around the numerous landscapes that he had painted, and the abstract paintings, the various portraits, they were all so heartwarming.

N - Do you know how to paint? - he asked, clearly trying to change the topic. However, in all honesty, he did want to know her too. He nodded in understanding when Avni shook her head in negative.

A - Will you teach me? - she perked up.

N - I can't! - he sipped his espresso.

A - C'mon! Please. - she held his hand as she stood up from the chair that was placed adjacent to the wall.

N - Buttercup, I can't. - he said, still sitting while she tugged on his hand.

A - You can try. C'mon! - she tried to convince, finally when he stood up from the chair and she led him towards the blank canvas that he had placed at the corner of the room.

Avni grabbed a random brush and a small glass bottle that contained orange paint. Opening the lid of the bottle, she dipped the brush in it and then made a purposeless stroke on the canvas.

N - What are you doing? - he asked as he stood behind her while watching what she was doing.

A - I am painting! - she grinned while turning her neck to look at him.

All Neil could do was just shake his head as he watched her paint! Avni splashed a few strokes of orange before moving to red and then to ochre. When he thought that she could do with some inputs from him, he held the brush in her hand as he wrapped his fingers around her palm around the brush while he made her paint a wave of ochre through the patches of orange & red that she had painted.

Avni bit on the corner of her lip as she let him lead her hands on the canvas and go with whatever he was doing. Her heart picked up speed when his chest brushed against her back as he swirled the brush around the canvas and then took some yellow to mix with the shade of red. She could smell his perfume of rich spices and countryside air, as she felt herself getting heady. Her body tingled when his breathe fell on her shoulders.

A - Mr. Khanna? - she uttered in a heavy voice.

N - Hm? - he was too involved in the painting now.

A - Why do you paint? - she turned her neck a little to look at him.

Avni swallowed at the fact how close their faces were, if she moved just an inch, their noses would touch. She bit on the corner of her lip as her eyes blinked under the scrutiny of his whiskey brown orbs. Neil's hand around her palm slipped down to her wrist as he looked at her. His eyes moved to her lips when she kept biting on them and he had to force himself to look up at her eyes.

N - When it becomes too heavy to handle, I take it out on paper. These colours are my expressions. - he answered in a husky voice.

A - Why does it become heavy? - she whispered.

N - You won't understand. - he whispered back. And it was lie. He knew that probably she was the only one who would understand, and he was too much of a mess to accept that.

A - I'll try. - she assured as she blinked her eyes.

His hand slipped down her wrist to her hand and travelled up till her elbow. He then placed it at her abdomen as she leaned the side of her back to his arm while their eyes refused to leave each others'. Avni's lips parted on their own and her vision became foggy as her glasses fogged due to their hot breathes. Neil closed his eyes as he leaned in towards her mouth and just when he was about to get a taste, his phone rang.

They jolted apart at the sudden noise and Avni's hand flew to her chest as she tried to calm her racing heart down, while Neil shut his eyes close when he cursed under his breathe. Taking in a deep breathe, he picked the call up and Avni could tell that whoever was on the other end of the call, wasn't speaking about something pleasant as Neil's expressions hardened in a minute while his palm curled into a fist.

N - I'm on my way! - she heard him say before he disconnected the call and her brows furrowed in worry.

A - What-

N - Stay with Isha till I'm back. Okay? - he spoke before she could complete herself.

Avni bit on her lower lip out of nervousness as she nodded at him. He nodded at her back and then turned around to leave but she stopped him as she held his wrist. Neil frowned as he turned to look back at her. He raised his eyebrows at her in question.

A - Will you be okay? - she asked, eyes reflecting fear.

N - I want you to take care of yourself, Buttercup! - he held her cheek in his palm as he looked straight into her eyes. Can you do that? I'll try to come back soon! - he said in whisper and Avni nodded.

Assuring her with a blink of his eye, he turned around and left while Avni exhaled a deep breathe. Her heart thundered against her chest as she watched him leave but she quickly fixed herself before making her way to Isha.

The whole day had passed but there was no sign of Neil. No call, no text, no update and Avni could feel her heart sinking into the pit of her stomach. She had spent the rest of the day with Isha as she taught her numbers and some poems, but there was a constant thought lurking behind every moment. And it was Neil. If he was okay or not! What had happened that he looked so infuriated the time he left.

It was eleven in the night when Avni finally made her way to the drawing room after putting Isha to sleep. She tried to scroll through her social media in order to distract herself and that was when she heard footsteps in the room. Instantly, she looked up and to her relief , it was him, but to her concern, he was bleeding and blood dripped through the deep cut wounds on his body.

A - Are you okay? What is all this? Where had you been? Is everything alright? Why don't you say something? - she rumbled the words out as she walked up to him with shaky feet. For the first time, he looked scary.

N - Ask the driver to drop you home. - he said in a cool distant voice.

A - Excuse me? - she was appalled at his audacity at that point.

N - Miss Mehta, its late. Go home! - he gave her one last glance before walking away.

She gritted her teeth in frustration when he did not let her reply and moved towards his bedroom. Fisting her palms, she followed him behind but before she could reach him, he had shut his door.

She kept knocking at his door and it was only after good fifteen minutes that he opened.

N - Why are you-

A - You asked me to stay here till you were back. So, I stayed. Now, you come back home with so much of blood dripping from your body and scaring the absolute wit out of me and then have the audacity to tell me to leave? I need an explanation, Mr. Khanna! - she exclaimed.

N - There is nothing to explain. I just had a fist fight! - he brushed back his damp hair with his fingers. Avni noticed that he had taken a shower. She gritted her teeth at how easily he was lying to her, cause she wasn't stupid enough to think that it was because of some stupid fight. But knowing that she wouldn't get anything out of him at that moment, she dropped the topic as she tried to calm herself down by taking in a deep breathe.

A - Let me aid your wounds. - she said with a tone of finality and without giving him any notice, she pushed the door open as she entered the room.

Sighing, Neil walked to the drawer near his cupboard as he took the first aid box out and handed it over to her. He sat the edge of the bed while she stood in front of him.

She dabbed the cotton in the antiseptic liquid before starting to clean his wounds. Putting her warm palm on his cold shoulder, she slowly put the cotton on the cut that he had at the side of his chest. Digging her nails in his skin out of fright, she slid the cotton up to clean the skin however, Neil didn't even flinch. He kept watching her as she scrunched her nose up and then pulled her hand back time and again to adjust her glass frames.

Finished with the cleaning, Avni then took out the ointment tube from the first aid box before squeezing out the cream to apply on his wounds. She placed her left hand on his stomach as her other hand applied the ointment on his upper abdomen. She then shifted to the back and cleaned all his wounds before applying the medicine.

It was only when she was done with the task that she noticed he had a tattoo on his neck. Her fingers inadvertently reached out to touch his neck as she slowly moved her fingertips along Isha's name that he had inscribed there in a heartwarming design.

Neil took in a sharp breathe while she kept touching his back as he turned his head to look at her and their eyes met. Avni's eyes wandered down his face, settling on his mouth before she forced them back to his eyes. Neil's gaze dropped down to her lips before his hand stretched out and his thumb rested on her lower lip. His eyes travelled between her eyes and then back to her lips before he leaned forward and kissed her.

Avni's back bent back as she was taken aback by his sudden move. Her eyes closed shut as she kissed him back, slowly pressing her lips against his mouth while he did the same. Her hands wrung around his neck when he bent forward to grab her by her waist and shift her to his lap. Avni gasped as he pulled her closer to him before scooting a little back on the bed to sit comfortably. Neil slid his hand up her thigh while she descended her hand down his arm, feeling each & every muscle as her other arm enveloped his shoulder around itself. His cheek pressed into Avni's arm as she kissed his upper lip while his lower lip opened to suck on her chin.

Neil wrapped her thighs around his stomach before resting his hands at the sides of her waist as he slowly started to move her against his firmness. Avni had to break the kiss to catch some breathe as she pulled back and her thumb massaged his lower lip. Her eyes met Neil's and she could very clearly identify the longing that he held in his, cause it was the same she had in hers. She didn't know when it became so strong that it could tear apart the cold facade that he always covered himself in. But it didn't matter. Cause it just felt so good that she was wanted by someone whom she wanted back. So much. So desperately.

Her hips started to match his rhythm as he rolled his own hips to thrust into her. Their lips again found each others as their abdomens moved in perfect synchronisation. He nibbled on her lower lip as his hands snacked up her back before finally settling in her dense hair. Neil groaned into her mouth before putting his hands upon hers, moving them back to his neck as they had wandered down to his abdomen. And it was then that Avni realised that she had accidently pressed on one of his wounds.

Pulling back, she looked down to see if he was bleeding again, but much to her relief he was not.

A - Are you okay? - she whispered with concern audible in her voice.

Neil did not answer. He was taken aback at her innocence. Or stupidity was it? A humourless chuckle left his mouth as he shook his head while Avni just watched him in confusion.

A - What's wrong? - she asked.

N - Are you not afraid of me? - he found himself asking as he tilted his head to the side.

A - Should I be? - she frowned.

N - It's in your better interest to be, Buttercup! You should stay away from me. - he whispered as he tightened his hold on her waist.

A - What if I don't? - she moved against him as she held her head up.

N - It's late. You should leave. - he said in a tone with an underlying threat.

A - Why do you always try to run away whenever conversations start turning difficult? - she mumbled being utterly frustrated now.

N - Miss Mehta, I said leave. - he gritted his teeth.

A - Not until you finish what you started. Both the conversation and this thing down here! - she was adamant as she refused to leave, aggravating him even more.

N - Fuck it! - he dug his fingers into the skin of her waist. You like making things difficult for me, don't you? - he rhetorically asked.

And he turned them around as Avni's back landed on the soft bed with a thud. Her chest pressed against Neil as he put her hands at the sides of her head, wrapping them with his long hands. He rolled his hips against her core with strong & powerful thrusts and Avni bit on her lower lip to stop the moan that were at the back of her throat. Her stomach clenched as she could feel him edging her, every move driving her insane.

N - Buttercup, neither is my life the fairytale that you think it is, nor am I the brooding hero you've mistaken me to be. So, the next time you see me, run away from me. - he gritted out every word every time he plunged into her. Do you understand? - his palm wrapping around her throat as his thumb pressed her pulse, not to choke her but just to make her slightly breathless.

A - No. - was her simple answer. Her small fist enveloped his wrist as she met each of his thrust with equal fervour and Neil frowned at her stubbornness.

N - Stop being stupid, Buttercup. And escape before I decide to cage you here with me, to me! - he whispered in her ear with one last thrust and she came undone as did he.

Neil slumped down next to her as both of them tried to catch their breathes. When he was sure that she had came back from the high of her orgasm, he sat up and then stood in front of her. Tugging on her hand, he made her stand and led her to the doorstep. Opening the door, he gently moved her out and left her hand while all Avni could do was to watch him. Hurt at his behaviour and disappointed upon herself to keep her hopes so high.

N - Now that I've finished what I started, kindly leave. Miss. Mehta! - he gritted out before slamming the door in front of her face but didn't miss the lone tear that escaped her eye.

Chapter 6

Neil had a throbbing headache through out the night as not even a wink of sleep showed mercy enough to relieve him. Every time he tried to close his eyes, her face flashed in front of them, and that damned hurt look that she had! He hated it. And more so, he hated how much he cared.

But how could he not? The girl had only tried to help him with everything that she could, and true to his reputation, he turned out to be a jerk to her. He shut his eyes close in frustration as a helpless groan left his mouth.

It was tough. Really tough for him to process all those feelings that she was making him feel. The last two years had been so tormenting that he had almost forgotten relief and comfort. And when she tried to offer it, his reflex reaction was to push her away. That was the problem, he couldn't do things in moderation. He had always been the kind who were on the extreme side of the spectrum. And he knew for a fact that that Mehta chic wasn't someone he could let go of once he had her. But at the same time, Neil was well aware that there was nothing for her to gain from him, so it was for her better that he stayed away from her.

The way he had felt at the orphanage and at the church, with her, it was so overwhelming that Neil could actually feel his heart beating for the first time in a long time. The Lord Ganesha idol that he had kept at the shelf in the drawing room yesterday was given to him by his sister, Isha's mother. It was in the church that she made him realise that he had not only been keeping himself away from his sister's blessings but also keeping Isha away from her mother's. And, he wanted her to have faith, he wanted Isha to have all things good. The first thing he did after putting Isha to sleep was to take that idol out of the long forgotten drawer of his cupboard and he couldn't push back the thoughts of Avni when he had kept it in the drawing room.

Earlier that day, when they had attacked Rehaan Qureshi's dungeon, there was a moment or two where he thought he won't make it alive and he was scared how the only two people who came to his mind were Isha & Avni. As much as it was funny, it was really weird & scary at the same time. The woman had literally met him not even a week ago, how could he think about her when he was nearly dying?

But the way she had asked about why he painted and the way she had looked at him, he couldn't unsee the hope & faith that she had shown in him. As if she was some painter who wanted him to be her masterpiece.

But then, of course, he did what he always did, push people away! His heart clenched when he saw that tear falling down her eye, but he was hyper aware of his tendencies. He had to push her away for her own good, for fucks sake!

When he figured that his effort to catch some sleep were vain, he got down from the bed at around six in the morning as he moved to their garden in order to work out & then took a warm shower.

After he had got Isha ready for the day in her Minnie-mouse pullover outfit and a pretty pink bow, he fed her breakfast before eating his own. It was after he had settled Isha in the drawing room as she played with her toys that he made his way towards his office, an obvious attempt to avoid Avni.

However, the resolve was soon abolished when his driver informed him that Miss Mehta had refused to let him drive her home last night and had hailed a cab from outside the Khanna Mansion even after he insisted so much.

Neil clenched his teeth in fury & frustration, and before he could think what he was doing, he was already walking towards Isha's room where he knew he would find Avni.

Knocking at the door, he successfully managed to gain her attention, however as if the woman had oathed to spite his fury in all ways possible, she ignored him as she continued reciting some fucking spellings with his niece.

N - Miss Mehta, come to my office right now! - he spoke while trying his best not to lash out on her.

A - I am busy. - she said in a cool voice, not bothering to look up at him.

N - You don't want to get on my nerves right now, Buttercup! - she spoke in a dangerously low voice and Avni could practically hear the threat in his words. My office. In two minutes. - he spoke slowly, making sure that he put out every word clearly for her to hear while Isha was engrossed in her book.

Neil moved out of the room in swift strides and it was then that Avni released the breathe she was holding. Telling Isha to try to read the words from her book, she quietly followed him behind.

A - What is- - she had started speaking as she entered his office, however before she could complete herself, he had grabbed her by her arm and pulled her so close to himself that it became difficult to breathe.

N - Why did you not go home with my driver last night as I had told you? - he asked through gritted teeth. His face contoured in anger as he held her close in a tight grip.

A - Excuse me? - she forced herself to not notice how his hair looked like a shade of chestnut brown when the sunlight fell on them from the window.

What in the absolute ridiculous walnut cream-cheese dimsums is wrong with me? This stupid stuck up old man is basically manhandling me & I am thinking about the colour of his damned hairs? Just go visit a psychologist at this point, Avni! I should just chop his hair off.

N - You heard me! - his cold expression was uninflected and Avni wanted to bang his head against a wall.

A - I sure did! - she chuckled humourlessly. You very clearly told me to stay away from you, Mr. Khanna. - the frustration gave way to the hurt that she had been feeling throughout the night.

N - It's not about that. - his eyes softened and words fumbled. You're still associated to me. - he pressed.

A - No. I am not! - she stubbornly argued while trying to loosen his grip on her.

N - Fuck Buttercup! - he groaned. Don't you just understand? - he said, pulling her even closer, so much so that her chest pressed against his. There are people out there who are looking for just one single chance to reach to me, and for that they won't think even once before killing those who are around me. - he spoke in desperation.

A - I can protect myself! - she looked away. Why was he even showing all this concern? What did he even care? He could always find another teacher for Isha!

N - I do not doubt that. - he sighed as he closed his eyes for a second. Taking in a deep breathe, he forced them open as he held her chin up to make her look at him. But as long as you're here, you're my responsibility to protect. So from today onwards you're going to go back home with my driver and the same driver will come to pick you up. Do you understand? - & Neil himself was shocked how his command was more of a request out of desperation to make sure that she was safe.

A - Public Transport is safe enough. I can manage on my own! - her chin wobbled as the thought that he would again push her away crossed her mind.

N - Buttercup! - he gritted his teeth as his hold on her chin tightened. If you don't listen to me now, I promise you, you won't like the other ways I'd get you to agree to me. So be a good girl and do what I'm telling you to. Get that? - the command & threat were clearly audible.

A - I hate you! - she childishly stomped her foot.

N - That's not an issue. - he was back to his cold demeanour and Avni wished that someday she'd be able to get past it. Why?

She didn't know! She just wanted to! She needed to! But that was not the time. She knew she'd have to be patient with him.

A - Let me go! - she whispered and he loosened his hold on her.

Neil let out a long breathe as his chest heaved down when he watched her walk away from him.

Avni neither saw nor heard from Neil about anything for the rest of the day. It was around eight in the night and he had not been back home. She had put Isha to sleep once she had eaten her dinner. Afraid that he would again come home with blood all over his body, she decided to wait for him as she sat besides Isha on her bed, caressing her hair gently.

Half an hour had passed and still there was no sign of Neil and that was when she tried to call him. However, before he could pick up, the phone was snatched away from her by someone and thrown away somewhere on the floor.

A scream escaped her mouth as she turned to look at the person and fear clouded her eyes the moment her eyes landed on him. There stood, in front of her, a man with a nasty scar at the side of his cheek that ran down from his upper cheek bone to his jaw and as if that wasn't terrifying enough, he was also carrying a gun that he was pointing at her at that moment.

A - Who-who are you? - she asked, trying to muster up some courage.

"Warming up Khanna's bed huh, girl? How about you come with me?" - the jerk spat.

A - Listen, you jerk faced muppet, I don't know how you got into the house but I'm telling you for your own good to leave! - Avni gritted her teeth as she covered Isha with her body.

"Feisty!" - he laughed evilly. "I see that Khanna is not man enough to get you to learn how to shut your mouth up! Don't worry, I'll teach you well!" - he tried to grasp her chin but Avni pushed him away, making his sick self laugh even more.

A - You can not be even half of the man he is! - she announced.

"You little bitch!" - his eyes flicked with anger as his gloved hands landed at slap at Avni's face, making her fall to her side, thus hitting the side of her head against the headboard.

A sharp pain rippled through her head as she found herself getting dizzy because of the hit, but in an attempt to save herself & Isha, she picked up the vase from the nightstand as she hit the man's head with it. A shriek of pain escaped his mouth as he held his head in his hands and closed his eyes shut. And, Avni took it as her moment as she picked Isha up in her arms and ran out of the room as fast as she could.

The man followed her out of the building as she ran with a still asleep Isha in her arms. Avni hid Isha behind the car as she herself sat besides her, hoping that someone would come before he find them. There were Neil's men around, she was sure someone would find him, the race was against time.

Her heart pounded against her chest as she shivered in fear and prayed to the greater almighty to save them. Yet the peculiar part was that she was again & again thinking about Neil and how would it look if he would smile at her. What had she been thinking? There were chances that she would die, & yet she was thinking about him!

Her trance broke when that scary creature finally found her and stood just in front of her. Grabbing her by her arm, he pulled her up as he slapped her again, her eyes stung with tears as the pain shot through her body all the while she tried to push him away, but all her effort went in vain.

"Fucking Bitch!" - he growled as he was about to throw a punch in her gut, however before his filthy hand could reach her stomach, he fell on the ground with a thud as Avni saw blood oozing from beneath his body.

Avni gulped as she looked up from his dead body to the source of the bullet. And there was he. Standing with a gun in his hand, as he stared at the lifeless man he just killed. A sob escaped Avni's throat as as she picked Isha up in her arms and ran inside the mansion.

Letting his men take over, Neil followed her into the house as he made her way towards Isha's room.

N - Miss Mehta? - he called as he entered the room only to find a shivering Avni as tears flowed down her eyes in an endless shower while she patted Isha gently so that she won't wake up.

A sigh left his mouth as he walked up to them and sat at the edge of the bed, opposite to Avni. His rough hands reached out to his Ishipie as he caressed her head before pressing a kiss on her forehead. Neil's face twisted in pain when he saw Avni purposelessly staring at the floor with her fingers still in Isha's hair.

N - Buttercup? - he whispered gently as he pressed her hand with his and for the first time since he had met her, her body felt cold.

This was what he was afraid of when he tried to push her away every time she took a step towards him. Taking in a deep breathe, he got up from the bed as he poured some water in the glass placed next to them on the nightstand.

N - Drink.- he said but Avni did not respond. Sighing, he brought the glass to her mouth as he made her drink some of it. I am really sorry for what you had to go through. I promise you I'll try my best to let no harm come to you, and I'll make sure of it. - he whispered gently as he held her hand in hers but the stream down her eyes never stopped.

A sob escaped her mouth & Neil could feel the anger & guilt coursing through him. Anger at that bastard step brother of his who had sent his man to his house as a revenge for the attack at his dungeon and guilt at how innocents like Isha & Avni suffer because of monsters like him & his stepbrother!

N - Hey, Buttercup! Please don't cry. - he urged softly as his thumb caressed the back of her hand.

A - I was scared. He...he was scary! - her voice had become raspy & her throat hurt.

Neil's own throat felt soar as it clogged because of the heaviness he felt in his chest. The woman had just met them, yet she chose to stand strong for his niece when the situation called for it. Neil was not aware there were still people like her out there. A part of him was relieved that she & Isha were okay, at least physically, however his heart clenched at how vulnerable & scared she was in that moment.

Before he could get any second thoughts, he got up from the bed as he picked Avni up in his arms and he was surprised how easily she let him, even curled up against his chest as she leaned her face in his chest.

Giving one glance at Isha, he moved out of the room and asked his men to stand in front of Isha's room while he still carried Avni in his arms. Once he was sure that there was enough protection available to Isha, he walked into his room. He slid Avni down his arms till her feet were on the floor and then sat at the edge of the bed while she just stood there.

N - Come here, Buttercup. - he mumbled and Avni followed.

Taking slow steps towards him, she reached him till she was standing in between his legs. He tugged on her wrist softly as he made her sit on his lap. Avni sat sideways on his right thigh as she leaned her body against his chest and wrapped her arms around him.

A - I am afraid of gun shots. I...I was ten when I was shot in my stomach. I still have the mark. I, I hate it. And I hate guns! - she whispered as her eyes stung now that the tears had stopped.

She could feel Neil's body turning stiff as the words left her mouth and his hold around her tightened, providing instant relief to her insides.

N - I am sorry. - he whispered as he ran his hand on her head in a soothing way. He was my rival's man. It has never happened before, I don't know how they breached the security. I'm really sorry, Buttercup! - he mumbled and pressed her close to himself. Do you want to talk about what happened to you? I can listen! - the words were foreign to him too, but he frowned when he heard Avni chuckle lightly.

A - You don't like talking, Mr. Khanna! - she reminded, her voice a little less sad.

N - I can try! - and Avni was shocked how he was really trying hard to make her feel better.

A - I need you. - she looked up at him.

N - I'm here. - he whispered, looking at her.

A - Please hold me tight. - she whispered back and he immediately pressed her closer to him.

Avni's gaze fell on his hands that rested on her thighs. She observed he had cuts on them and she almost flinched at how deep some of them were. She slowly lifted his left hand up from her thigh and brought it towards her face. She put it against her cheek as she leaned her face to his hand.

Neil drew in a harsh breathe when she opened her eyes and look at him. Their eyes met and their chest rose & fell in the same rhythm. Still keeping her eyes locked with his, she moved his palm to her mouth and kissed the inside of his palm. Then moved her lips along the side and kissed there and kept showering kisses until she reached his fingertips. Neil watched her as she peppered light kisses at the tips of his fingers, his eyes holding a storm beneath them as his heart hammered against his chest with all the feelings that were rushing through his veins.

She wrapped her mouth around one of his fingers as she sucked on the blood that was oozing out of a cut on the finger and Neil groaned at the sight. His other hand tightened around her thigh as he tried to stop himself from giving in to his urges. However, Avni had different plans.

A pop sound resonated in the room when she pulled her mouth back from around his finger and before Neil could guess her next move, she was already kissing his neck.

A - I don't know why, but the only person that came to my mind when that man was here and I thought I would die, was you! - she whispered as she kissed his neck, trailing open mouthed kisses down his neck before moving to his throat. The only thought that ran through my mind was that I didn't want to die without seeing you smile. - she kissed his shoulders, running her tongue up at as much skin as his shirt allowed her to. What are you doing to me, Mr. Khanna? - she mumbled as she looked up at him.

N - Exactly what you're doing to me! - he mumbled in a husky rasp before he wrapped his mouth around one of her breasts.

A gasp escaped Avni's mouth as he sucked on her chest while his other hand pulled down the strap of her blouse down her shoulder. He then pulled back as he pushed the other strap down till the point her blouse was bunched around her waist, baring her chest and abdomen to him.

Neil pressed a soft kiss at her cleavage as he kept his eyes on her while her hand flew into his hair as she tugged upon them. His hands palmed both of her breasts from above her innerwear as he massaged them slowly, making her moan in pleasure. Avni had to pull her hand away from his hair as she moved them behind her back to unclasp her only covering and she let it fall from her body.

Neil latched on to her right breast as he sucked on it with his eyes closed. His tongue licked and swirled around her sensitive nub while his other hand massaged her left breast. He sucked on the under part of her breast as he felt her warmth when she pushed herself more into him and he rubbed and tweaked her other nub from his thumb simultaneously, thus, driving her insane with stimulation. Neil then buried his face in her chest as he fondled her breasts around his cheeks. His little stubble tingled Avni's soft skin and a pleasurable moan escaped her mouth as she tried not to slip down his thigh because she was feeling weak in her knees.

Neil lowered his mouth down as he began trailing open-mouthed kisses at her abdomen. His warm mouth sucked on her soft skin gently as he moved from her abs to her stomach, leaving a trail of the wetness of his mouth as he kissed every inch of her skin while Avni had thrown her head backward as she moaned some incoherent words. One of his hands was firmly wrapped around her waist while he was still kissing her belly when his other hand reached for one of her breasts. He pinched her sensitive bud as he kept twisting it sideways, making her gasp in pain & pleasure.

A - Mr. Khanna, I'm too sensitive right now. I..I think I'm going to -ah, I'm going to cum! - she mumbled in between a moan.

N - Ease up, Buttercup! Let it all go. - he encouraged as he wrapped his mouth around one of her breasts and sucked on it animalistically while he kept tormenting her other bud, thus bringing her at the brink of her orgasm.

A loud moan escaped Avni's mouth at his words as she squirted in her undies, while he kept sucking her chest, thus prolonging her orgasm. Her legs shook and body shivered as she rode her orgasm and it took her good five minutes to recover from the high of it.

Neil wiped the sweat beads that had formed on her forehead as he brushed her hair back from her face and it was then that he noticed a bruise at the side of her cheek.

N - What is it, Buttercup? - he asked in a furious tone.

A - Must be some hickey that you gave! - she offered as her body just wanted to collapse in his arms and eyes felt heavy because of the exhaustion.

N - Buttercup! The bruise on your cheek. How did you get it? - he asked again and it was then that Avni understood what he was talking about.

That filthy man had slapped her so hard that it might have left a bruise, and it might have become red now, so it was visibly noticeable to him.

A - Uh, it..actually- - she gulped when she looked into his eyes. He was furious & enraged.

N - Did he hit you? - he gritted.

A - Mr. Khanna, I'm okay. I'm with you. - she whispered as she held his face in her hands.

N - I am really sorry, Buttercup. I- fuck! I couldn't even protec-

Avni sighed as she pressed her lips on his mouth, thus stopping him from both apologizing & cursing anymore. Neil eagerly responded to the kiss as he held her hair in his fist and pulled her closer to him with his other hand. He broke the kiss when he felt her getting out of breathe and then pressed feathery kisses at the side of her cheek where the bruise had formed. His tongue gave it a light lick as he kept kissing it in an attempt to provide some relief. An inadvertent smile found Avni's lips when he kissed her cheek and she closed her eyes to feel his touch.

Though reluctantly, Neil finally pulled back after a while as he helped her get dressed back and Avni let him as she was too tired to do it herself.

N - You sleep here. I'll go sleep with Isha, hm? - he said but she shook her head in negative.

A - I'll sleep with you & Isha! - she answered, making a small smile appear on Neil's lips.

He slid his hands beneath her knees as he lifted her up in his arms and carried her to Isha's room.

Chapter 7

Neil made Avni sit on the bed besides Isha as he put her down his arms. Helping her to lie down on the bed, he adjusted the pillow beneath her head before pulling the blanket over her body. He then walked around the bed and slept at the other side of the bed with Isha in between them.

He watched how Avni held Isha's small hand in hers as she kissed the back of it. He felt a sudden twinge in his heart, the way she was holding his niece close to herself felt too domestic & heartwarming. And these were another emotions that he had forgotten the feeling of. What was this girl even doing to him?

A - She is such a happy child. I love her! - she mumbled as she looked at Neil, still holding her hand close to her own chest.

N - She is a replica of her mother! - a faint smile ghosted his face while Avni listened to him. Same smile, same chubby little cheeks, same tantrums and same sass! - he reminisced as a passive sadness overtook his features.

A - She has your eyes! Same hazel brown orbs. - she pointed and a soft smile played on Neil's lips.

N - She does! - he whispered, voice getting heavy out of exhaustion.

Taking in a deep breathe, Avni held her body up on her arm as she leaned towards Neil while he watched her in confusion. The frown lines on his forehead smoothened when Avni placed a soft kiss on his forehead as her free hand cupped his cheek, her thumb caressing the side of his cheek.

A - Sleep Well, Mr. Khanna! - she whispered as she pulled back and laid down comfortably.

Neil swallowed a lump down his throat as he looked at her. Who was she? Got attacked by a creep, there was bruise on her cheek and she was comforting him? And he killed people for his fucked up sense of morality. They were no match, but then why did it feel so right with her? As if, he could mend it all if he had her besides himself.

Neil didn't realise when sleep took over but he wouldn't lie if he said that it was the best he had slept in the last two years. He woke up to find himself holding Avni's hand as they wrapped their arms around Isha, who was sleeping without any worry in the world.

Neil woke up around seven in the morning and when he looked around while rubbing his eyes, he found Avni awake as she blinked her eyes up at him with a small smile on her face.

A - Good morning! - she chirped and he stifled a yawn.

N - Did you not sleep well last night? - he asked as he sat up, leaning his back against the headrest as his hands stroked Isha's hair gently.

A - I slept good. Just an early riser! - she told and he nodded in acknowledgement.

N - Do you want me to drop you home? - he found himself asking.

A - Would Isha be okay when she wakes up and not finds you around? - she asked in concern.

N - She won't be waking up for another two hours, I'll be back before that. - he explained and she nodded.

Neil took a quick shower while Avni freshened up in the guest bedroom before they left for her place. Needless to point out, Neil made sure that Isha was completely safe before stepping a foot outside the mansion.

The ride was quite as Avni leaned her head against the passenger seat. He was a good driver, the smooth ride helped her relax as she looked outside the wintery London morning, while stealing glances of him every now & then.

She looked at Neil when he stopped the car in front of her house.

A - Uh, do you think you'd like to come up? Coffee, may be? It's so cold. - she suggested and before he could rethink it, he nodded.

Avni gave him a bright smile as she led him up the stairs to her cozy little home while he followed silently.

A - Welcome to my humble abode! - she smiled nervously as she let him in.

Neil bit back a smile as he followed her. He didn't know if it was a big deal for her or not, but he definitely felt special when she invited him inside her home. It was stupid, but he had always thought that one's home was one's own sanctuary, a place where we can be our most natural selves, and the fact that she trusted him enough to let him in her personal space warmed his insides.

Though he had given up the hope to find himself a home apart from Isha, he definitely wanted Avni to have one.

On the other hand, Avni felt like a high-school girl who had invited her crush over to her home for the first time. She was relieved that her mother had not been here at the moment as she would have showered a frenzy of questions & teases her way. She hoped that Neil wouldn't notice the slight reddening of her cheeks as she tried her best not to blush.

N - Do you have a twin, Miss Mehta? -he asked as he looked at the photo frames hanging on the wall.

A - No! Why would you ask that? - she was confused when he asked that while she was midway opening the window in the drawing room.

N - So, you mean to say that this chubby girl with two pigtails is you! -he asked with tease audible in his voice and Avni jumped in absolute horror.

A - Mr. Khanna! You're not supposed to see that! Back off! -she exclaimed as she stood in front of the frames, blocking him from looking at them. You sit in the drawing room, I'll prepare coffee. - it was an obvious attempt to distract him.

N- But let me see them! - he teased, the glint in his eyes a clear give-away and for a moment, Avni thought how would it feel to have him laugh with her.

Would the sound of his laughter be boisterous or husky-deep, would it crinkle the corner of his eyes, or would it make his nose scrunch a little? Dear universe, Kindly show some mercy and let me focus! Why in the soggy manchurians can't I stop thinking about him?

N - Buttercup? - he snapped his fingers in front of her when she had zoned out in her thoughts.

A - Uh, Yeah! Come sit. - she held his hand & almost dragged him towards the dining table.

Neil stifled a laugh as she pulled out the chair for him & bowed down in front of him dramatically, gesturing him to sit.

A - I'll just get your coffee ready, Sir! - she said before moving to the kitchen.

Avni came back in some time as she carried two coffee mugs in her hand. She gave Neil a house tour as she took him around the house, telling him about each & every minute detail that every corner held while he listened to her as if she was telling him the most important thing in the whole world.

A - And this, Mr. Khanna, is my favourite spot of the house! -she pointed towards the balcony.

N - Why so? - he asked as he sipped his coffee.

A - Come here! -she held his hand as they sat at the window sofa. Because, this is the corner of the house where sunlight falls directly. You know, whenever I feel gloomy or anxious, I leave all my tasks, take a break, come & sit here. The sunlight serves as a free therapy. -she told, making Neil smile a little as he felt some warmth inside him, was it the sun, or was it about her still holding his hand, he didn't know. Do you see that piano over there, Mr. Khanna? -she asked as she pointed towards their opposite direction while Neil nodded. That's my father's. He used to teach me how to play piano when I was a kid. - she smiled in nostalgia while Neil looked at her with an intensity he himself was unaware of. Mrs. Davies lives next door, you know she plays this old radio in the evenings, it creates such an irritating hissing & Mr. Parker's pet dog Wiskey, starts barking whenever she plays the radio. And, you know, it rains a little more on this side of the house, so we just can not leave it open. Once, when I was small, Dad had left the window open & all the rain water came inside. Mom was so angry, we had to clean it up all by ourselves. -she laughed while narrating the story.

Neil did not laugh. He felt a tug at his heart as the melodious sound of her laughter filled his senses and his insides felt warm. His eyes stared at her beautiful face as the sunlight radiated her skin in a golden cast. He took in a rough breathe when his eyes wandered to the side of her right cheek and he noticed that the bruise was still very much there. His hand rose on its own as he touched her cheek gently while brushing his knuckles along her skin and Avni's laugh died down. Her eyes snapped to his which were still in a trance as he kept brushing his knuckles along her cheek.

A - Mr. Khanna? - she whispered as she frowned while looking at him.

N - Hm? - his thumb moved along her jaw.

A - Why do you always look at me like that? - she finally put the thought out that had been going on in her mind since the time they had met.

N - Like what? - he asked, knowing exactly how he looked at her.

Like some crow watches its prey, and like some fire burns an innocent, like some icy frost cuts through someone's skin, and like a thief fascinates an antique, like some misfortune waiting to happen, and like some beast about destroy the beauty!

A - I don't know. Like you want to drag me in the darks and have your way with me? - her voice mere above a whisper.

N - That's exactly what I do, Buttercup! I ruin pretty girls like you. I'll feed off your light and then leave for good once I'm done. - his breathe fell on her face as her glasses slipped down the bridge of her nose a little.

A - I don't think that's true. - she objected, making him frown.

N - Did you not see enough last night? - he reminded her of the dreading moment.

A - Mr. Khanna, I do have my questions regarding whatever happened last night and also about Isha's Mom and everything. But if there is one thing I can put my life on, its the fact that you're not the monster that you claim yourself to be. Yes, you might have committed things that aren't fairly correct or moral, but I'm sure that you must have had better intentions than the rest. I trust you, Mr. Khanna. - she looked into his eyes and they were the same again, that same expression of intrigue, curiosity, longing and frustration. Why could this man just not let it all out?

Sighing, she raised her hand up as she moved her fingers along his forehead, easing the frown lines on his forehead. She then gently dragged her hand down his face as she left feathery touches all over from his forehead to his nose, his lips & then to his chin. Cupping his cheek in her hand, she slowly stroked his cheek to ease him up a bit and she could see his eyes dilating.

A - You'll get wrinkles if you keep frowning so much. - she said with a cheeky smile. Don't you think you're a bit too pretty to have wrinkles, Mr. Khanna? - & he finally graced her with a lopsided smile.

Neil bowed his head as he tucked his lower lip inside his mouth while biting on it, shaking his head in light laughter, he looked up at her as he found her already smiling at him.

N - Do you have any idea how badly I want to bend you over and fuck that little body of yours on this very sofa? - he said in a husky drawl & Avni could already feel the wetness in between her legs. She took in a deep breathe as she shook her head.

A - May be you should tell me! - her voice had become breathy.

N - You're too good for me, Buttercup. - he told.

A - Then ruin me! - she blinked her eyes up at him and it took everything in him not to bend her over and ruin her just the way she wanted him to.

N - I guess, I'll just better myself! - & there was a promise in his eyes, Avni held on to the hope.

Inadvertently, their eyes dropped down to each other's mouth as their faces inched closer, but before they could touch, Neil pulled back, making Avni blink her eyes in confusion.

N - You don't have to come to work today. I'll look around the security of the mansion and then let you know, okay? - he said in a cool tone and it took Avni a moment to realise that he had gone back to his usual cold self.

She nodded in affirmative at what he said as she felt a tiny ball of disappointment building up inside her.

N - I, I'll leave! - he nodded to himself and started walking out of the door while Avni just watched him go as a sigh left her mouth.

Neil couldn't brush back her thoughts through out the drive back to the mansion. No matter what he tried to focus on, the essence of her lingered behind every thought. Sighing, he finally parked the car and made his way toward his little bundle of joy who was cuddled up in her blankets due to the chilly morning air.

N - Ishipie, wake up, Baby! - he spoke softly as he shifted her in his lap.

I - It's cold. - she mumbled while cuddling in his arms.

N - Mama could make you hot chocolate, would you like that? - he asked and her eyes shot up in delight.

I - Yes! - she squealed as she hugged him tight.

N - But for that Ishi needs to wake up, right? - he stifled a laugh while caressing her head.

I - I am up! - she exclaimed as she jumped on him and he caught her with ease, laughing at the excitement.

N - C'mon, let's get my little princess ready for the day, shall we? - he rhetorically asked and she nodded.

Neil bathed Isha in a warm bubble bath before getting her ready in her favourite ninja turtle pajamas. He was lucky that the little sassy princess agreed on a big girl ponytail for her hair and Neil happily obliged. Though the pony was a little loose and crooked, Isha rewarded him with a kiss for the effort. He added some sparkles in her hair before he carried her to the dining room for breakfast.

Isha wore her little chef's cap as she insisted on helping Neil to prepare the breakfast. Knowing that there was no way out, he made her sit on the kitchen slab as she helped him mix the pancake batter. Neil then poured the batter in the hot pan in small round pancakes as Isha watched.

N - Baby, you need to stay a little back. It's hot. - he spoke as he kept her in check while flipping the pancakes over.

I - But I want to do it all by myself, N-man! - she chirped as she stuck her lower lip out to make a puppy face.

N - Okay. Could you get N-man a banana, please? - he asked politely.

The little girl obliged as Neil helped her get down the platform and she grabbed a banana from the refrigerator. Neil placed the pancakes in their dishes as he spread some maple syrup on hers and then chopped the banana in little pieces.

He grabbed the plates and placed them on the dining table while Isha followed him behind. He ate his own breakfast only once he was done feeding her. He then made her sit on the couch in the living room as he played her favourite Peppa Pig on the TV while he himself moved to the kitchen to prepare her hot chocolate.

Neil then made her drink the hot beverage before she settled in his lap as she watched the cartoon.

When she was engrossed in the show, Neil's mind wandered back to the issue at hand. The security of the mansion. His right hand assistant & friend, Noah Williams had provided him with a complete report on how Rehaan Qureshi's men had breached his security system and he had to get it rebuilt now. It would take nearly a week to get it all done and till then, they had to move to another place.

Neil dropped a quick text to Noah to book a cab to Hambledon, a small village near London, where Neil owned a house. It was one of their family homes and he had spent a lot of good times there. It could definitely work as a stress buster & as a safe haven.

He made Isha sit on the couch once as he got up & dialed Avni's number.

N - I want you to pack your stuff for a five days trip. We're going to Hambledon. - he told, his voice cold and authoritative.

A - What? I mean, why all of a sudden? - she was confused.

N - I've a house there. We'll stay there till the security of the mansion is resecured. I've given holiday to the staff, you're the only person who was present in the house that day apart from the staff & Isha. So, you'll have to come with us so that I can insure your safety. - he explained and Avni nodded to herself in understanding.

A - Okay. When do we leave? - she asked.

N - Tonight. Not to leave any trace, we'll book a taxi. I'll pick you up around four in the evening. Is that fine? - it was more of a command rather than a question.

A - Uh, okay! I'll be ready. - she replied.

N - Good. See you in the evening then. - he said before disconnecting the call and Avni felt a shiver run down her spine as it was the first time that he was so commanding in front of her, as if he controlled her. The funny part being she liked how easily he managed to channelize her submissive energy and agree to him without any resistance.

CHAPTER 8

In the past two years, all Neil had done was running. Constantly planning and thinking and rushing from one thing to another, fighting mindlessly to get things done. Their family business, Isha's upbringing and his night-time business. He had deliberately kept himself so busy that he never had time to stop and feel. Not even a single moment probably.

It had always been some award that he received as the CEO of his construction company, or Isha's first steps, her first words, her hair-styles and her happiness, and whatever time was left was spent in rescuing victims of trafficking and rapes. He couldn't say that he was some saint, no! He was as tainted as the people he had killed, the only thing that differentiated them both was the intention behind the kills. However, in a very long time, Neil had forgotten how it felt like to have a heart that could actually feel. Contentment, satisfaction, peace, happiness? Any of it, actually!

Isha was the only breathe of air that he had to keep himself sane. But then, she came along and it felt like his whole life was spiraling upside down. She made him feel. It was in moments like these when she made him do things that he had thought he would never do again. Just one blink of her eyes and he agreed to play fucking snow fight on their way to Hambledon.

For fucks sake, he killed people for pleasure! Not stop his car on random highways to watch sunsets and make snowmen!

But here he was, trying his best to gather as much snow as he could to make the biggest snowman that his niece had ever seen while the said niece and her teacher flocked around in snow like penguins.

Neil blew air on his cold hands that he had almost stopped feeling due to being in ice for so long, as he was almost done with his creation.

N - Ishi! Baby Look, its done! - he called as he put a swig on the top of the ice to make the supposed eyes of the snowman.

He was about to turn around to call them, however, before he could do so, a strong force collided with his back making him stumble on his steps and since the ground was slippery due to the snow, he fell with his face buried into the snowman he had just made.

Soft sounds of Isha's laughter accompanied by Avni's constricted one filled his ears as he tried to pull his face out of the chilly ice. Neil felt the cold ice prickling on his skin as he sat back up on his knees, dusting the snow out of his clothes while his eyes threw a murderous glint at Avni who could only stop her laughing fits this much.

A - I am really - she couldn't control a snicker that escaped her mouth. Sorry, Mr. Khanna! I..I was just running around with Isha &... - she bit on her lips to stop herself from laughing anymore.

However, it was too late. Neil grabbed a handful of snow as he hit Avni with it, making her gasp in equal parts shock & surprise.

A - Mr. Khanna! You're calling for a fight now! - she bent down to make a ball of snow in her small palms.

N - Oh yeah? Bring it on! - he challenged as he got up on his feet and easily dodged the hit she threw his way.

Isha clapped her hands in between fits of laughter as she watched the two adults running after each other, throwing snowballs at each other. To Neil's surprise, Avni's stamina was really quite good. The woman ran like a trained athlete and efficiently dodged all his attacks.

Neil bent over in an attempt to duck the throw she just made, but then ran towards her when she stumbled across a bump on the ground. Avni lost her balance as she was walking backwards while laughing at him and landed with her ass on the cold snow covered ground as a groan escaped her mouth.

N - Hey! Are you okay, Buttercup? - he asked once he reached her and crouched next to her.

A - Yeah-yeah! I am okay. - she laughed. Just slipped! - she gave him a bright smile to him and then to Isha who had come running to her.

N - Show me, did you sprain your heel or something? Is there any pain? - he asked as he examined her face for any trace of inconvenience.

A - Mr. Khanna! - she held his hand in hers. Relax! I am okay. - she blinked her eyes, making a subtle warmth spread across his chest. Could you please help me up? - she asked and he nodded.

Neil held her arms as he pulled her up on her feet and Avni put both her hands on his shoulder to balance herself.

A - You're cute when you're worried! - she whispered as she gave him a small smile.

N - I'm anything but cute, Buttercup! - he whispered back in a husky ramble, hands trailing down her arms until he rested them on her waist. You, out of all the people, should know it by now! - and he gave her waist a firm squeeze before pulling back and turning around to carry Isha in his arms.

Isha giggled when Neil spun her around in the air while holding her firmly in his arms. And then she witnessed it! Him laughing his heart out. The boisterous rumble of his laughter settled deep in the pits of her stomach, creating a warm fuzz inside of her chest as she breathed in the sight of his hazel brown orbs shining with delight. He laughed more as Isha clung on to him while he continued to move her up in the air.

Avni noticed how the corner of his eyes crinkled as he kissed the top of her head before pressing her up against his chest while she wrapped her little hands around his neck. A small smile spread on her own lips as she followed them behind and Neil settled Isha in her baby seat.

They stopped by the Starbucks as Isha threw a fit about wanting to eat bacon gouda sandwich. Grabbing the sandwich and a vanilla drink for her, spiced pumpkin latte for Avni and a double espresso for himself, Neil quickly made his way out while they waited for him outside. Settling on a nearby bench, Neil made Isha sit on his lap as he fed her the sandwich while reminding her to chew well.

The warm fuzzy buzz that Avni always felt around him intensified at the sight of him being all gentle and domestic. His cold demeanor was almost non-existent at that point as he wiped the sandwich crumbs away from Isha's face. She couldn't unsee how both of their beautiful hazel eyes had turned a shade of brown under the setting sun. Their ears and cheeks were flushed due to the cold and Neil had to promise Isha a date at the park to make her wear a beanie.

She had zoned out while mindlessly twirling her straw around in her tumbler and was taken aback when Neil leaned forward as he took a small swig of her latte. His freshly trimmed stubble brushed against the back of her hand and Avni could do nothing to control the tingles she felt all over her skin.

N - How do you even drink this? Its too sweet! - he grimaced once he sat back straight.

A - I like one little sweet & little spice! - & she so very definitely was not talking about the drink.

However, Neil couldn't guess. He just nodded his head in acknowledgement and Avni shook her head as a silly smile threatened to appear on her face.

N - Shall we go? It's getting dark! - he looked around and Avni nodded in agreement.

As much as she didn't want to reach where they were off to because she just couldn't get enough of this happy, at peace & warm man. She wanted more & more of it, and she wanted to store it all for herself so that his warmth could keep her from cold whenever it became too much to handle. But at the same time, she wanted to get to the place he was taking her. He had told her that it was one of their family homes and she would lie if she said that she wasn't excited. The possibility that she might come across some part of him, his childhood excited her to no bounds.

Isha had knocked out on their way to Hambledon after the stop at the Starbucks and the car ride was mostly silent with a few stolen glances every here & there. Avni looked around when Neil stopped the car and a whitewashed duplex came into view. The guard let them in & Neil parked the car at the end of the driveway.

Wordlessly, he got down the car and carried Isha in his arms. Just when Avni was about to get down, Neil opened the door for her and gestured her to come out by nodding his head forward.

For some reason unknown to herself, she felt nervousness creeping up in her veins as she bit on her lower lip while following him inside. The house wasn't huge like the mansion they had in London, but it was beautiful and radiated coziness. Avni took in a deep breathe as she looked around the living room. The light coloured walls had intricate designs on them and the mahogany furniture emitted absolute elegance.

A - Your house is so beautiful! - she told truthfully as Neil laid Isha down on the couch.

He looked up at her as a sigh left his mouth and then a soft smile spread across his mouth.

N - My father was an interior designer. - he told and Avni couldn't unsee the way his eyes shone in that very moment. He always used to tell me how in the wake of glorifying minimalist interior, people have forgotten & let go of the beauty of minute intricacies! - he told and Avni gave him a small smile, afraid that one wrong move & he might just wrap himself up in his coldness again. She wanted in! This was the first property my Dad built on his own after shifting to UK from India. We used to spend our vacations here. - he told as he stroked Isha's head in lazy thrums.

A - Show me around? - she asked in a trance, deciding that the sight of his happy face was the most beautiful sight she had ever seen.

N - Come! - he simply said without any second thought.

The guards that had gathered around dispersed once Neil asked them to and commanded them to be vigilant through out the night. He asked the house-help to keep the luggage in their respective rooms before turning his full attention to Avni.

They walked besides each other as Neil walked her through the corridor.

N - Me & my sister used to run through the corridors all the time. Dad could never get us to stop! - he said and she found herself smiling.

A - Growing up with a sibling must be fun, right? I always used to ask Mom to get me a sister so that I can doll her up! - she laughed, making him smile.

N - My case was quite the opposite. I still remember my sister used to make me wear her frocks and tie bows on my head! - an adorable frown itched on his forehead and Avni couldn't stop the laughter that escaped her mouth.

A - Can I see a picture? - she asked in between fits of laugh.

N - It's not funny, Buttercup! - he warned in a fake stern voice.

A - But it is! - she continued laughing, making him shake his head in disbelief.

Neil showed her around the house, giving all the details and some memories associated with every place and Avni couldn't help but smile.

N - Our old cook Mrs. Brown makes the best pancakes in the world. We'll go visit her tomorrow! - he told as they exited the kitchen and walked towards the house-library.

A - So many books! Are these yours? - she asked in amazement as she looked around the large shelves of books around the enclosed room. Strangely enough, that room smelt like him. Sugar & spice mixed with countryside air.

N - No! - he chuckled. These are my sister's. She was a reading freak. But this library used to be my favourite spot to hang out. I used to paint here, near the window. Over there! - he pointed towards the window and Avni followed his direction as she smiled inadvertently.

With amazement clearly visible in her eyes, she looked around, walked up till the window and pushed it open only to welcome the chilly air against her face. Still smiling like a fool, she turned around as she brushed her fingers against the various books that were placed on the shelves until her eyes fell on the portrait that hung on the wall in front of her.

It was a family portrait. A man looking like an older version of Neil sat on the sofa as he smiled brightly at the camera while he had his arm wrapped around a young woman. She was beautiful, her eyes exact copy of Neil's and her smile like that of an angel. Behind her, stood a young man with striking black eyes and a warm smile. And next to him was Neil! Without any stress lines on his forehead or a cold shield in his eyes as he carried a baby Isha on his shoulders. Isha had fisted his hair in her small fists as her little legs dangled down the side of Neil's neck while he was captured laughing in the picture. Avni figured that it was probably an old portrait as he looked a bit younger.

Oh, Not even in the crispy chilly roasted chestnuts get me wrong! The man still looked like Adonis, but just an angry one. While in the picture, he looked like a sweet little lad who would bring you flowers on a date. Dear Universe, how did this cute chocolate boy transitioned into a hot-shot Daddy!?

N - What are you looking at so attentively? - he husked behind her ear, making Avni jolt in her feet as she was taken back from her state of zoning out.

A - Uh, I was just...thinking! - she blinked her eyes as she turned her neck a little to look at him. This is such a beautiful picture. - she smiled but it faded when the shine in his eyes dampened a little.

N - Thankyou! - he managed a smile but Avni could see the effort behind it.

A sigh left her mouth as she turned around completely to face him and then slowly wrapped her arms around his neck as she rose on her feet to hug him closely. Neil closed his eyes shut as his hands wound around her petite waist and his face buried in the crook of her neck. He breathed in her scent, which provided some relief but the hollowness that he felt in his chest was still there. He didn't know what to put there to fill it. He hated how he simply couldn't escape this hollow feeling.

N - I hate this portrait. - he confessed, voice just above a whisper but she was all ears anyway! Reminds me of what I've lost & will never have again! - a sigh left his mouth and she gave his back a gentle caress. Sometimes when I look at it, I just feel like throwing it away. But then, I know I'd choose burning in fire if I had to rescue this from it. Cause it is also the only thing that reminds me that I was a human too, may be even a good one! - his voice was thick with emotion and his throat felt clogged.

A - Mr. Khanna, wherever they are, I'm sure that they're proud of you. - she whispered as her fingers ran along the nape of his neck.

N - I don't know! - he released a long breathe from his mouth while he subconsciously pulled her closer to him.

They stood there in silence while holding each other close. No words were exchanged and Neil was grateful for it. Anyone who could see them in that moment, could clearly see that the both of them were simultaneously giving & taking comfort from each other. Obviously, Neil was getting his cluttered emotions together in her embrace but Avni too, was seeking the comfort of his closeness that strangely worked to heal her wounds that she had hidden from the whole world.

A - Mr. Khanna? - she finally spoke after a long stretch of silence.

N - Yes, Buttercup? - he asked and that made Avni's chain of thoughts stop as her focus shifted on a more important issue at hand.

A - Why do you call me that? - she asked as she pulled a little back from the hug.

She placed her hands on his shoulders while still standing on her toes as she looked at him. Neil's hands held her waist tightly as he pressed her close against his chest.

N - You don't like it? - a frown marred his forehead as his hands unconsciously caressed her waist.

A - Oh, no! - she laughed at the way he had become so worried. I, of course, I lov-like it! - and she was suddenly shy. It was so out of character even she only realised that she was being shy when she fumbled with her words. I just..wanted to know why? - she blinked her eyes and he relaxed a bit.

N - Let's just say I & Buttercups go a long way back! - he shrugged.

A - And do I wanna know it? - it was a rhetoric question, he knew it.

N - Bebe loved them. Pretty little yellow flowers. They resembled sunshine for me. And, they were the first flowers I had ever painted. I still have that painting! - he smiled. In our teen years when we had grown a liking for gardening, Buttercups were the first flowers that I & my sister had planted. - he told and a small smile grazed Avni's lips. That day, in the club, when we had first met, I was having a really bad day and then you came along! Stumbling and falling, looking at me with these bright eyes, I found you the closest thing to sunshine I could ever get my hands on. In that moment, I wanted you to be my last first kiss, Buttercup! That way, Buttercups will be all my firsts. - he said and Avni's heart picked up speed.

A - Buttercups are poisonous! - she whispered, her hands fisting his sweater now.

N - I am aware! - he whispered back as their eyes locked with each others'.

They couldn't tell who started first, but both of them found themselves leaning towards each other as their mouth parted slightly. Neil's eyes dropped down to her luscious lips while she had shut her eyes close in anticipation. Just when his lips brushed against hers, they jolted apart in surprise as they heard a knock at the door.

"Sir, the dinner is ready!" - came a timid voice and Avni could feel her cheeks brightening with blush due to the embarrassment while Neil just sighed in half annoyance and half frustration.

Chapter 9

The dinner was a silent affair and mostly revolved around Isha telling Neil & Avni about how Peppa Pig had gone to her friend's house with Mumma-pig & Papa-pig! Though they had been allocated different rooms, all of them ended up sleeping in the same room when Isha insisted on doing so.

Avni didn't know what was the reason behind, but she felt these unnerving maternal instincts towards this particular child. She was so fiercely protective of Isha and she could do anything & everything to make her happy. Initially she might have regarded it as sympathy due to the absence of her parents but very soon she realised that what she felt for her was pure love and care, and nothing of it germinated out of sympathy. Why would she? Isha had the best guardian as his uncle one could ever get and she knew that Neil would rather die than let any scratch on her.

Exhaling a deep breath out, Avni kissed Isha's forehead as she wished her night and was rewarded by a bright smile from the little girl. Her eyes then drifted to similar hazel brown eyes she had come to adore so much. She doubted he must have noticed how her eyes twinkled when she found him already looking at her. Caressing Isha's head in an attempt to put her to sleep, Avni kept her eyes on him who was looking at her back while holding Isha closely to himself.

A - Hi! - she whispered once Isha had dozed off.

N - Hi. - his husky low voice made Avni feel tingles in her skin.

She felt her skin getting warm under his gaze as heat crawled up her insides. But as much as it unsettled her, it provided her a comfort and sense of being protected like nothing or nobody could have provided. Her eyes felt heavy as her eyelids drooped down due to exhaustion. Avni didn't realise when sleep took over, all she remembered was that she had fallen asleep while watching him.

Rays of the morning sun filtered into the room through the glass windows and Neil watched Avni snuggle more into the blankets, with a fascination he himself was unaware of. He watched as she squinted and blinked her eyes open, rubbing the sleep off them. Fully awake, she turned to look at him and her eyes widened in surprise for a moment.

A - Did you not sleep? - her voice came out hoarse.

N - Not even a wink! - he replied, brushing a strand of hair away from her face.

Neil brought his hand back as he put his face on his hand, never taking his eyes off her.

A - Stressed? - she asked, leaning forward as she traced his under eyes with her thumb.

N - Strangely not! - he clicked his tongue and her eyes met his.

It was unsaid, but Neil hoped that she would know it was because of her. Avni's throat worked on a swallow as she felt her stomach flip in her insides, her thumb rested on his upper cheek as she held his face in her hand.

A - Tell me something! - she heard herself asking and Neil contemplated for a moment before a sigh left his mouth.

N - You snore really loudly. - he spoke with a serious expression and it took Avni a minute to understand what he was saying! Every time I tried to sleep, it just went a volume higher than before. - he frowned as he blinked his eyes.

A - Mr. Khanna! - she sat up. Eyes wide with disbelief evident in them and hair a beautiful mess. Stop lying, I do not snore! - she established the fact as she put both of her hands at the sides of her waist and looked down at him.

Neil had to bite the side of his lower lip to stop the laugh that was bubbling up inside him. He followed her action and sat at the foot of the bed as a chuckle escaped his mouth when she was staring at him, clearly offended at his claim.

A - Stop laughing! - she tried hard to keep her voice low as Isha was still slumbering.

Embarrassed, she got down from the bed and was midway marching out of the room but he stopped her by holding her wrist. Losing balance, she stumbled back and landed on his lap as her hand grabbed his shoulders for support. Neil held her firmly as he wrapped his arms around her waist and his chest vibrated with another chuckle while she had her eyes shut close.

A - Could-could you just stop manhandling me, please? - she whispered as she blinked her eyes open. Her arms firmed their grip on his shoulder as she sat comfortably on his lap. Neil wanted to laugh at how her words were a complete contradiction to her reactions.

N - Why? Turns you on or what? - he asked in a husky drawl, his hand trailing up her thigh.

A - You're delusional! - her throat worked on a swallow as she took in a sharp breath.

N - Am I, Buttercup? - he dragged his palm up her thigh in a deliberate slow motion.

A - Mr. Khanna? - she placed her hand on his and put it around her waist. She noticed how his eyes concerned at her serious face.

N - Yes? - he asked sincerely.

A - I needed to ask you something! I just can't stop thinking. - she bit on her lip nervously, her hands fiddling with the fabric of his T-shirt.

N - Ask me! - he said, tucking her hair behind her ear & somehow that made some of the uneasiness settle for her.

A - The attack. - she started and there was a sudden shift in Neil's mood. Who-who was it? - she asked as she swallowed the lump down her throat. He would be mad, wouldn't he be?

N - A business rival. - came his short answer.

A - Just a business rival? - she pressed and he sighed in response.

N - He is my step-brother. - he finally spoke after a while.

Neil hadn't planned on letting the information on, but she deserved to know. Especially after she saved Isha from the attack. And now that he was unfolding the truth in front of her, he thought to go all the way out.

N - Rehaan Qureshi. My mother's son with her second husband. - Neil felt her stiffen at the mention of the name. In an attempt to ease her up, he stroked her hair gently while he held her firmly on his lap. It was funny how he himself was feeling a flux of bile in his stomach as he prepared himself to let her in on the most dreaded part of his life, but he was trying to comfort her. A few days ago, he would have laughed at the idea, but here they were!

A - I, I'm sorry, Mr. Khanna! I didn't mean to cross a line. It's okay if you don't want to talk about it. - she bit on her lip as she averted his eyes.

N - You didn't. - he stopped her from biting her lip as he traced his thumb on her lower lip.

Slowly, he held her chin up to make her look up at him, Neil was surprised at the glistening in her eyes.

A - Is it why your mother wasn't there in the portrait? - she asked and he simply nodded.

N - I was five! - he took in a deep breath, his hands tightening around her waist.

Sensing his discomfort, Avni wrapped her arms around his back as she put her head against his chest, listening to his beating heart. The top of her head pressed against the base of his face and she pressed a small kiss on his chest against the fabric of his clothes.

N - My mother ran away leaving us behind. My sister & I were just kids then. And, you know what the worst part was, my father loved that woman till the last breath he took! - he gritted his teeth as he felt his eyes stinging. I had decided back then, I would never marry anyone because I was afraid I'd turn into my mother. As a kid, the worst thing that one can go through is to see your parent cry to sleep. I & my sister witnessed it everyday. Dad never showed it to us. He was the best father one could ever get, and he raised us both as a father & a mother, but we could see the way his eyes used to turn distant & void of any happiness whenever he was alone. Growing up, I hated my mother. I still hate her. Every thing I do, every word I utter, there is this constant fear that I might just end up becoming her. - his breathing had turned ragged and in that moment, all Avni wanted to do was to hold him close and kiss all his pain away.

A - You're nothing like anybody, Mr. Khanna. You're you! Loyal, respectful, kind and caring. - she reassured him and Neil felt his heart skip a beat at the audible conviction in her voice.

N - You're a bad judge, Buttercup! - a humourless chuckle escaped his mouth and Avni frowned. However, before she could protest, he continued. You saw me put a bullet through a man's body and you think I'm kind? You don't have to lie. I know I'm a monster and- -she put her hand on his mouth as she pulled back from the hug and looked at him with a deep frown on her face.

A - You're not going to talk like that about yourself from now on. Is that okay? - she asked in a stern tone and Neil was surprised to say the least but he listened to her nonetheless. When I say that you're kind & caring, I mean it in every sense of it, Mr. Khanna! Yes, I saw you putting a bullet through someone's flesh and you killed him, but that man posed a threat to you, to Isha and consequently to me. You just saved me from him. I don't know what you do with all those brick-like men around you, neither do I know why you possess a gun, nor do I have an idea why you come home with blood dripping down your body, and I have no clue why your step brother is after you & Isha, but I can bet anything to prove that you have the best of hearts out there and the best of intentions one could ever have. - she held his cheek in her palm and Neil felt the warmth of it spreading through him. Mr. Khanna, you asked me to come with you to some village I had never stepped my foot in just after the day I almost got killed at your premises. But I came here without any second thoughts. Why? - she pressed her thumb pad against his cheek bone as she looked into his eyes as both of their hearts thrummed in sync. Because I trust you. I know that you'd do anything in your capacity to keep the innocents safe. Don't ask me why & how, because I have no explanation for this strong sense of trust, faith & pride I feel for you. I simply do! - and it was that exact moment, when he found hope. May be, there was still some of it left for him too.

N - Buttercup, I-

A - No! - he was taken aback at the protest. Do you understand, Mr. Khanna? - she asked sternly.

N - Fuck! You're feisty, Buttercup. - he couldn't stop the chuckle that escaped his mouth. Yes, I understand, Little-Miss-Sunshine!

A - You better do! - she tried hard to hide the effect his deep voice had on her.

N - Would you like sandwiches or waffles for breakfast? - he asked.

A - Whatever you like! - came her simple answer and she frowned when a smirk spread across his lips.

N - Oh, I'd like something entirely different but can't starve Isha, right? - whispered in her ear before biting on her earlobe. Avni pressed her lips together to stop the moan that was about to leave her mouth when he tugged on her earlobe before putting a feathery kiss beneath her ear.

A - I, uh. Need to- Isha like waffles! - she managed, making his smug smirk reappear on his face. She wasn't even embarrassed anymore. It was a lost battle. She was like clay in his hands, he could do anything he wanted and she was sure she would enjoy every bit of it.

N - Okay, waffles it is! - he said as he made her stand on her feet and himself stood up from the bed.

Just when he was about to walk out of the room, she held his wrist and then walked around to stand in front of him.

A - Please forgive your Mom, Mr. Khanna! Not for her, or for anybody else, but for your own self. Set yourself free of this hatred towards her and the fear of becoming her. People don't think rationally when in love. By no means I am saying that what she did was correct, it was not & no child deserves to be treated like that. But having said that, she might have had her reasons, Mr. Khanna. Don't let your past clutch your present into disdain. I promise you the future will be a better place! - she raised herself on her toes before placing a kiss on his cheek.

Pressing her lips against his light stubble, she kissed the hollow of his cheeks before pulling back and running out of the room. Neil watched her run as he inhaled a deep breathe in.

What was this girl doing to him?

Neil had asked the maids to come late that morning as he himself wanted to prepare the breakfast for Isha. He was almost done with the batter and was setting the waffle maker when Avni entered the kitchen.

A - Want help with something? - she asked as she smiled at him.

N - I'm done with chia pudding & the coffee is about to be ready. Waffles will be ready in a minute, could you help me with the fruits? - he asked as he stirred the brewing coffee in the pot.

A - Uh, okay! - she said as she took the fruits out from the refrigerator.

Both of them fell in a comfortable silence as they prepared the breakfast. Avni was midway cutting the fruits when her phone rang. A bright smile plastered her face when she saw the caller id. It was her mother - Neela. Having both of her hands busy, she put the phone on speaker as she picked the call up.

A - Hii Maa! How are you? - she chirped and a small smile grazed Neil's mouth inadvertently as he slightly turned to his side to look at her.

Neela - I am good, Avni. How are you, Baby? Are you wearing your beanies or not? You catch cold very easily! - she enquired & Avni nearly groaned in embarrassment.

A - Mom! - she groaned when she heard Neil chuckle. I am a big girl now!

Neela - Okay! Okay! Big girl! - she laughed at her daughter's expense. How are things with that hot boss of yours? - she teased, clearly unaware of that fact that the mentioned hot boss was right there to hear her.

A - Mom! - her eyes widened in shock while Neil looked at her as he raised his eyebrows in amusement. Wh-what are you talking about? - she shook her head at him while he smirked.

Neela - Baby, you don't think you can hide things from your mother, right? So, tell me, are you two a thing now? - Avni closed her eyes shut as she mumbled a prayer, simultaneously cursing the papaya that was spread in her hand that made her put the phone on speaker in the first place.

A - I...Your voice is cracking. - she wiped her hands as she quickly grabbed a tissue and held her phone to her ear. There might be some network issue, Maa. I'll call you back. Bye. Love you! - she spoke hurriedly.

Neela - Avni, listen-

A - Byee Maa! - & she disconnected the call to save herself from further embarrassment.

N - Hot, huh? - he asked after a minute and she shut her eyes close as she bit on her lip hard.

A - I..I had said, uh, Old? Yes, I had said old, she might have misheard! - she let out a vague chuckle like noise as she blinked her eyes.

N - Are you implying that I'm old, Buttercup? - and he was just a step away now. When did he come so close? Avni took in a deep breath. Wrong move. All she breathed in was his smell.

A - Are you offended? - her voice was breathy as she bit the inside of her mouth.

N - No. - he tucked her hair behind her ear. But what if I say yes? - his fingers intwined in her damp hair.

A - Then I'd say I like someone older, preferable if that someone has hazel eyes! - she whispered, gathering as much confidence as she could in his proximity.

N - Are not you being too brave these days? - his eyes flickered with something in between a challenge and a threat.

A - You're too good a catch to be subtle about it! - she took a step forward, towards him. And I'm just a girl, trying my chance at forever. - she looked him in the eye and he blinked. The smugness on his face being replaced by something on the lines of anger.

N - I don't do forevers, Miss. Meh-

A - Buttercup! - she was quick to correct, making him close his eyes shut as a sigh left his mouth.

N - Buttercup! - he said it as a prayer. I've seen enough life to not believe in something as stupid as a forever. As much as I want you, I can't ruin you! - and his voice was cold again, like it had been initially when they had met.

A - You won't ruin me! - she didn't lose hope.

N - No, not intentionally. - he shook his head. But my life is too much of a mess and its going to follow wherever I go! - he put his forehead against hers as he took in a deep breath.

A - Everyone has their mess. I've mine! - she whispered as she closed her eyes, rubbing her nose against his.

N - Fuck, Buttercup! - he grabbed her waist in his large hands and pulled her close to himself. Why don't you understand? - his fingers dug into her skin and a gasp escaped her throat. People like me simply don't deserve people like you! And this is no fiction. There will be no character development or redemption arc. The things I've done, the people I've killed, the mistakes I've made will always be mine. That is my forever, Buttercup! This sick monster inside of me that I see every time I look into the mirror, he is not going to go away. Do you get that? - he pulled back as he looked at her. Voice merely a whisper and Avni could feel her eyes tearing up. I don't know if there is any chance for your sunshine to overpower my gloominess, but my darkness will surely consume you.

A - Then why don't you try & work on the redemption arc, Mr. Khanna? Am I not worthy enough? - she blinked her tears back.

N - That's not- -he was explaining but she turned around to leave. Fuck, Listen! - he called.

However, Avni didn't listen. The roar of blood in her eardrums was too much and her eyes felt stung as she tried her best not to cry. Why in the stupid cheese sandwiches was he even affecting her so much? Why did she care so much? And why did he not? Angry at her own self, she marched out of the kitchen.

N - You're worthy of so much more, Buttercup! - he whispered to himself as a sigh left his mouth.

Chapter 10

Avni wiped the tears away and put on a brave smile on her face before making her way towards Isha. Inhaling a few deep breaths, she sat next to her as she slowly stroked her hair in an attempt to wake her up.

A - Good morning, Ishi! Wake up, Baby! - she cooed as she massaged her scalp gently.

I - Good morning, Buttercup! - she mumbled and Avni's eyes widened in surprise.

A - What? - she was sure she had misheard her.

I - Buttercup! - the little girl giggled as she rubbed her eyes.

A - Where did that come from? - she asked, ignoring the ripple of pain that she felt spreading through her chest.

I - N-man call you that. Can I call you Buttercup too? Pwease? - she mumbled in her groggy morning voice and Avni's heart melted at the cuteness.

A - Yes, you can! - she smiled at her as she kissed her cheek and Isha smiled back.

I - Where is N-man? - she asked once the sleep had wavered off.

A - Uh, Baby, he is preparing breakfast. How about we get you ready in your princess outfit & give him a surprise, hm? - she asked. As much as she wanted to spend time with Isha, it was also an excuse to buy herself some time to avoid Neil and all these strong emotions that she was feeling these days.

Unaware of her dilemma, Isha happily agreed and Avni carried her to the washroom to get her ready for the day. Once done, they made their way downstairs where Neil was already waiting for them.

Isha ran towards him to show him her new princess outfit as she twirled around and he gave her a hearty smile.

I - Do I look like a little princess, N-man? - she asked as she looked at him with her big bright eyes.

N - You're my little princess, Ishi! You look so beautiful. - he carried her in his arms as he pressed a kiss on her forehead making her giggle.

I - Look, Buttercup did my piggies so well! - she exclaimed in glee and Neil's eyes wandered off to Avni's.

Their eyes met and both of them sucked in a sharp breath almost at the same moment. Whatever they had going on in between them was getting a bit too much to handle, and the fact that their reflexes about dealing with it were entirely opposite to each others' didn't really help much. Avni wanted to give in to this constant pull of desire that she felt towards him while Neil wanted to escape the pulsing want he felt for her.

Neil was the first to avert eyes as he brought his attention back to Isha. Inhaling deeply, he put on a small smile on his face as he made her sit on the dining table.

N - Look Ishipie, N-man has made your favourite waffles! - he told and Isha clapped her hands. Come! - he said to Avni as he looked at her with hesitant eyes and she wordlessly followed.

Both of them did not talk to each other through out the breakfast as neither knew what would the course of their relationship be henceforth. It was after breakfast when an old acquaintance of Neil's father had visited them that Avni felt anger coursing through her veins as liquid fire.

She was an old lady who had come to see Neil, but that wasn't what bothered her. What bothered her was the lady's daughter that refused to take her eyes off Neil. And surprisingly, he too showed interest enough to entertain her stupid attempts at making a conversation.

"Now that you've joined business, you don't come back here at all. Don't you miss us?" - the young lady said in a sugary sweet voice and Avni wanted to gag at the sweetness.

N - It's nothing like that, Sophia. Of course, I miss you guys! - & that was when Avni thought it would be alright to grab the nearby vase and hit him with it. The stupid old cheese loaded sausage had told her that he didn't do forevers and was always wearing this cold shield around his heart! But now he was missing this little chic all of a sudden! What even in the poached bananas!

She knew that look very well. The one that the young woman was eyeing Neil up with. The kind of gaze with which you look at someone you'd want to fool around with and go all hanky-panky. The sultry eyes, pitched voice and that twirl of hair. She knew all too well!

Anger & frustration coursed through her veins in equal measures as she fisted her hands in tight balls and convinced herself to sit through the conversation for Isha's sake. The little kid deserved each & every bit of love that people showered on her and she wasn't going to refrain her from any of it.

Neil sighed at the way she blatantly ignored him and walked out of the living room once their guests had left. Thinking & hoping that giving themselves some space might help their situation, he busied himself with work as he threw instructions to his employees over call.

The next few hours passed in a blur for both of them as Neil was busy with his office and Avni was busy doing her job, they had decided to work on spellings that day. Avni felt so proud of the little girl that she herself was surprised at the intensity of it.

This uncle-niece duo was definitely messing with her head & heart!

It was around noon that Neil made his presence in Isha's room and she almost threw herself in his arms while Avni just watched the two interact as an inadvertent smile spread across her lips. She couldn't help it, they were too cute to handle.

N - Ishipie, we're going to Mrs. Brown's place for lunch. You remember she sent you cupcakes last month? - he asked as he cleaned the corner of her mouth that had some cookie crumbs spread on it.

I - Yes! - she nodded.

N - Are you going to be nice and thank her for that? - he asked politely and Avni nearly swooned at how gentle he was with her.

I - Yes! - she exclaimed excitedly and Neil gave her a big smile.

N - That's a good girl! - he kissed her forehead. And, you know Mama has got a surprise for you! - he said and Isha's eyes glimmered with excitement.

I - Can I know it? Pwease! - she blinked her eyes as she clapped her hands.

N - But then it won't be a surprise anymore, Baby! - he chuckled and she pouted.

I - Can I take my Minnie plushie along? - she settled for it.

N - Yes, you can! Go, get it fast. - he said as he made her stand on her feet.

Once Isha was out of earshot, Neil turned to Avni who was just standing there as she fiddled with her fingers and bit on her lips. A sigh left his mouth as he walked up to her.

N - Get ready! I'll be waiting for you in the car. - he said softly.

A - I, I think I'd like to skip, Mr. Khanna! Enjoy yourselves! - she refused to meet his eyes and started walking out. However, it was a failed attempt. Neil grabbed her arm as he pulled her to his chest as a gasp escaped her mouth.

N - Can you just stop with the temper tantrum? - he gritted his teeth. And, do not ignore me, Buttercup! - he raised her chin up to make her look at him.

A - Both of them are your forte! - she wasn't going to back down either.

N - Get ready in five minutes, or else I'll take you in whatever state you're! - and that was the last thing he said before storming out of the room.

Avni gritted her teeth as she stopped herself from stomping her foot on the ground out of frustration. For a good minute, she contemplated defying him just to get on his nerves and see what would he do in order to get his way with her, but not wanting to spoil Isha's fun, she quickly got ready in a beige coloured short sweater dress as she tied her hair up in a messy bun.

It was a test of his patience to not touch her and bend her over to see just how aroused she was for him in that stupid tiny piece of fabric, but Neil did surprisingly well. The afternoon was spent chatting and catching up with Mrs. Brown and her husband, an old married couple who Neil had grown up watching. He was glad that Isha had clicked with them instantly and was comfortable at their place. They watched a movie in the late afternoon, however Neil couldn't tell what was going on in the film. His sole focus was on that one woman who was turning his life upside down and was seemingly unaware of it too! It irked him how she was deliberately ignoring him as if she had made it a point not to look at him at any cost. In that moment, all he wanted to do was to shove her into the nearest corner and punish her hard for being so!

His self-control floated on a thin line when the urge to kiss her hard overpowered all his thoughts while she bonded with Ashton, Mrs. Brown's son. He was probably her age, blue eyes, blonde hair and a body girls would swoon over. And, Neil hated how good they looked together. After a point, he had to physically keep himself in check so that he didn't end up punching something in his wake.

His anger had reached its peak by the time evening rolled by but he had no escape. He had promised Isha about the surprise and he didn't want to break it. They were supposed to go to the winter carnival that was organised in their neighbourhood every winter. And, the Brown Family was supposed to join them.

Neil made it a point to focus on Isha and not put too much of a thought on who her teacher spent her time with but failed miserably. Every time they laughed together, the urge to kiss her grew stronger and it wasn't even about possessiveness anymore. It was fueled by a deeper wound. Insecurity. No matter how cold he acted or how unbothered he showed himself, the woman made him feel things. And, he hated how he felt afraid that she'd just move on from him one day. That he'd just be a long lost memory, just like the rest of his life has been. A memory. That's it! He despised how ugly his insecurities were. Constantly churning inside of him and making his heart bleed with pain & agony.

Neil was relieved Isha was enjoying herself with Mrs. Brown as she took it upon herself to show her the different rides. And for a moment, he watched. His steps stuck to the ground as he watched Avni dancing with Ashton on some slow song that the indie artist band was playing. She looked beautiful under the moonlight, he noticed. His eyes burned with jealousy and hands curled into a fist when Ashton put her hands around her waist and she laughed at something he said. A dry chuckle escaped his lips as he watched them dancing and it was in that moment he was reminded of the fact that he really was miserable and alone. Lonely! The grief soon converted into anger when she looked at him and their eyes locked. The smile she had on her face vanished and Neil's heart dropped at the predicament.

Avni bit on her lips as she watched him and she figured he was in pain. Her heart clenched in her chest to see his beautiful eyes full of agony and before she knew it, her feet were taking her towards him.

Her thumb traced his cheek bone as she held his face in her hand, her other hand brushing against his in gentle touches.

A - Are you okay? - she whispered and the primal monster in Neil took over the moment her innocent eyes blinked up at him.

Without a second thought, he held her hand in his as he led her towards what he had in mind. Avni followed him without any questions but was confused when he stopped in front of a Ferris Wheel. Her frown deepened when he walked ahead to talk to the operator and within a minute, all the capsules of the wheel were vacated.

Neil held her hand as he walked her to the wheel before making her sit comfortably in the narrow seat and then he himself joined her. The operator locked their capsule bar and went back to start the wheel and soon, it came to life.

The chilly wind cut through her as she looked beneath them, at the ground while rubbing her palms along her arms in an attempt to provide some warmth. The air became colder as the wheel turned around slowly and in no time, they were on the top.

The night was colder than usual, Avni could see her breath coming out in puffs. She was still mad at him for the little argument that they had had in the morning & also at the fact that he was being so sweet with everyone else apart from her, but the anger dissipated as fear took over when the wheel stopped and they were still at the top. Her throat worked on a swallow as she looked at Neil while they literally hung feets above the ground in a small iron case. Her frown deepened when Neil was still sitting there perfectly composed like some God. His long leg crossed against another as he watched her with a cool expression.

Freaking out, she got up from the narrow seat of the open capsule as she tried to call for help, however her throat refused to let a word out. Her hands wrapped around the ledge of the capsule as she looked down, her eyes immediately shut down close in fear. Her body tensed in fear & anxiety as she felt her knees getting weak and just when she thought she would fall, he wrapped his arms around her stomach. His cold body somehow made a warmth spread through her body.

N - Breathe, Buttercup! - Neil whispered in her ear and her body relaxed once his smell hit her nostrils and she immediately felt her body loosening under his touch.

A - Mr. Khanna! - she breathed. We're stuck. - her chest heaved as her breathing had turned heavy, body leaning on to him nevertheless.

N - Was he good? - his deep voice settled in the pits of her stomach, leaving tingles along its way.

A - What? - his hands tightened around her small figure as his rested his chin on the top of her head.

N - I don't like someone touching what's mine, Buttercup! - he whispered, voice dangerously low and Avni's heart hammered against her chest. I know I can't have you, I shouldn't! But I ain't saint enough to see you in someone else's arms in front of me. Do you understand? - his hands wandered around her chest as he cupped both her breasts in his hands, fondling & squeezing them in his palms, making her gasp for air.

A - I, he...I am. Mr. Kha-

N - Do you understand, Buttercup? - he gave her a firm squeeze, earning a delicious moan from her.

A - Ye-yes! - she shivered. I understand, Mr. Khanna! - she had thrown her body against his chest by then.

N - That's a good girl! - he whispered as he kissed the top of her head.

Her messy bun loosened as a few strands of hair escaped it and brushed against her face, tickling her burning skin under his touch. Neil kept showering kisses on the top of her head as he fondled with her breasts, tweaking and pinching her pebbled buds in between.

A - Some-someone might see! - the thought thrilled her as her hands fumbled behind to hold him in an attempt to steady her shivering body. Her body was starting to draw pleasure from his perfect movements as soon as she realised that it was him who had made the wheel stop.

And before she could process what was happening, she was in his arms with her legs wrapped around his waist while he held on her waist tightly. A gasp escaped her throat as Neil took a step forward and made her sit on the ledge of the capsule as he stood in between her legs. She wound her thighs tight around him as she held on to him feverishly close.

Avni's throat felt dry when her eyes fell on the ground. She wasn't afraid of the fact that she was sitting on a thin ledge feets high above the ground, because she was sure that Neil wouldn't even let a scratch on her. However, the fact that anyone who looked above would definitely be able to watch them put her to an edge and as crazy as it sounded, she could feel her body heating up from arousal.

Her mind shut down the ability to think when Neil trailed a hand up her thigh, higher and higher, beneath her small sweater dress. The heat of his mouth set her on fire when he licked her earlobe, leaving feathery kisses behind her ear and then moving down to her neck. One of his hands was firmly wrapped around her waist while the other kept her thigh in position as his mouth kept sucking & biting her neck. Her left leg slipped down his waist as she felt tingles down her core, her eyes fluttered close when he sucked on her weak spot leisurely as she moaned in absolute pleasure.

Avni rested her forehead against his shoulder as she craned her neck to provide him easy access, and Neil feasted on her delicate skin, painting it with his marks.

N - Who is it that you crave to be touched by, Buttercup? - he asked against her skin.

A - Hm. - she mindlessly moaned in response as he tormented her with his lingering touch.

The back of his fingers brushed against her wet undies that were soaking in her arousal by then, and Avni visibly shivered at the contact.

N - Answer, I said. - his voice was a low yet deep growl as he slid his hand inside her undies and brushed his knuckles across her swollen clit.

A - You! - she whimpered. It's your touch that I crave. - she moaned the answer out.

N - That's right. It's me! - and a smack landed on her clit, making her gasp as she jumped in her place out of pleasure. Tell it to the world, Buttercup! Tell it to the moon. Tell the stars! - he whispered in her ear as he gave her sensitive clit another whack of pleasure and Avni was afraid she would come right then and there.

A - M-Mr. Mr. Khanna, P-please! - she moaned when he rubbed his thumb across her clit, flicking her hardened bud while his fingers slid along the slit of her entrance.

N - I said, tell it to the world, Buttercup! - he gritted as his other hand wrapped around her throat and his lips descended down hers in a fierce kiss.

Avni rocked her body forward towards his hand at the same time she tried to match the movements of his tongue as they fought for dominance, a fight that Avni lost miserably. She gasped for air when he finally let go of her mouth and began thrusting his fingers in & out of her together with mercilessly flicking her clit at a maddening speed.

A - To the moon & to the stars, I, Avni Mehta, belong to Neil Khanna. - she whispered in between a moan and Neil's heart swelled in pride as did his cock when she squeezed his fingers inside her. And, so does he! Neil Khanna belongs to Avni Mehta! - her insides clenched around his thick fingers and Neil almost thought that she'd end up breaking them with her tightness.

Avni's hand tightened around the ledge as her other hand grasped his hair in a tight fist when she captured his mouth in a slow kiss that was completely contradictory to the torment he was carrying out on her down there. The insides of her stomach tightened and body tensed up as she felt her orgasm building up. Neil's fingers pounded in & out of her heat as he kept stimulating her clit with the fervent movements of his thumb.

She moaned into his mouth when a gust of cold wind brushed across her hot flesh and Neil gave her a hard thrust of his fingers at the same time he pinched her clit. With a sharp cry, she came all over his hand as he kept sliding in & out of her, prolonging the pleasure. Her soft moans mixed with the sound of the night air and Neil had never heard a better melody.

Her thick juices dripped down her thighs and just when she felt the effect of her orgasm wavering off, Neil got down on his knees as he hiked her dress up & ended up groaning when her sweet scent hit his nostrils. Her knees wobbled when he took her undies down and brushed his stubble against her sensitive flesh, his hands trailing up & down as he massaged her thighs.

Avni clutched the edge of the capsule tightly in her palms as she raised her hips on the bar so that he could reach her needy core. Still massaging her inner thighs with his large hands, Neil placed a soft kiss at her entrance and Avni's whole body shook at the impact. Her clit throbbed and insides tingled when he licked the lips of her slit before sucking on them as he placed deep smooches there.

Avni tightened her hold on the bar of the capsule as she felt her hips slipping down the ledge due to the shivering of her body and her other hand wandered down to grasp his soft hair. She bent her neck down only to find his head disappearing down her dress as he continued showering her with boundless kisses down her core.

Neil flattened his tongue against her clit and gave her a rough lick before he started picking up speed and thrusted inside her wetness, making her whimper in pleasure. His tongue hit all the right spots inside of her and he tugged on to her flesh with his mouth as he sucked on her delicate bundle of nerves. Avni's thighs clenched around his face as she desperately grinded against his mouth while tightly holding on to the ledge. Her moans growing louder to the point they overpowered the sound of the clanking of metals of the capsule as it shook along with the movements of their bodies.

She was basically sitting on his face by then, and Neil held on to her hips tightly to keep her in position while he sucked and nibbled and devoured the scorching heat of her arousal for him. Once he had found her spot, Neil's tongue flicked and his mouth wrapped around her nerve as he sucked on it as if it was the sweetest thing he had ever tasted. A loud gasp escaped Avni's mouth as her upper body jolted in pleasure and she could hardly feel her legs anymore. The pleasure that was coursing through her veins was maddening and Neil knew exactly how to heighten it even more. There was a point when she was shamelessly riding his face as he swirled his tongue on her clit, simultaneously darting his fingers inside her heat until the point he was knuckles deep.

A symphony of moans and some incoherent words left her mouth as she begged him for more at the same time she pleaded him to show some mercy.

A - Mr-Mr. Khanna, please! I want to- I want you to kiss me! - she told and that made him look up at her, her dress now bunched up at her waist in the front.

Wordlessly, he followed her request and rose up to his feet while still keeping his fingers inside of her. His hand now cupped her sensitive sex as he had three fingers inside her hot flesh and his thumb pressed against her swollen clit.

Avni's mouth desperately found his as she pressed ardent kisses on his lips. Her hands ran up & down his arms and chest before they held on to his face as she kissed every inch of it. His fingers stretched her in pleasure while she placed passionate kisses on the side of his forehead, cheeks, jaw, nose and mouth.

N - If I could change one thing in life, Buttercup! I wish I had met you earlier. - he whispered before latching his mouth on to one of her breasts from above her sweater dress and Avni threw her head backwards when his fingers gave her relentlessly powerful thrusts.

A - You have me now! - she whispered and her hands flew into his hair as she brushed them back from his forehead while he kept sucking on her chest. The saliva of his mouth damping her dress and leading to form a wet patch on the fabric.

N - This is wrong. - he whispered against her mouth as he buried his fingers deep inside her.

A - Nothing has ever felt so right. - she moaned, clutching on to his shoulders as she dug her nails in his neck.

N - Fuck! - he groaned at the mess she had become. Come for me, Buttercup! - and his hand landed on her sensitive entrance in a hard smack, making her squirt in his hands.

She bit on his neck to drown out the sharp cry of pleasure as her entire body trembled with pleasure while Neil tightly held her close. He stroked her hair in a gentle caress as she came so strongly that her body slumped onto him as a heap of lightening pleasure.

He made her sit on the narrow seat of the capsule as he took his kerchief out to wipe her clean from her slick juices that dripped down her thighs. He slid her undies off her legs and put them in his pocket as she couldn't wear them anymore. Fixing her dress around her legs, he brushed her hair back and wiped the sweat that glistened her skin in beautiful pearls even in chilly minus degrees.

Once done, Neil took a final look at her and it was so sudden, the realisation hit him like a thundering bolt. She looked like a mess. Kohl smudged beneath her eyes, lip gloss halfway gone, hair tangled in a beautiful mess, dress had a wet patch on her chest and the woman gave him a dazzling smile of delight. The primal monster in him felt proud of how beautifully he had corrupted her. The rational part though, felt guilty of giving her hope when he knew what the end would be.

The shambles of his sanity were torn in between wanting her & pushing her way. The larger part however, screamed at him to hold her close to himself and never let her go, but was it the right thing to do?

CHAPTER 11

Neil sat opposite to her as the Ferris wheel descended down once he had instructed someone on call to do so. Avni's heart hammered against her chest as he watched her with an intensity that made her tremble under the ferocity of it. She noticed his eyes weren't shielded by the coldness that he always used to carry around him, instead she could see a plethora of raw emotions running through those gorgeous hazel twinkles like livewires.

All Avni wanted to do in that moment was to hold him tightly and never let go but she also knew that she would only get her heart broken in the process. She was well aware that she was not supposed to feel all these soul-stirring emotions for him, but she just couldn't help it. It felt like he had etched himself in her system and she couldn't stop thinking about him.

Growing up, she had always struggled with trusting people, she did have a lot of friends credit to her outgoing personality but if one puts a genuine thought to it, all of them were just acquaintances. She wouldn't trust them with her secrets or even anything minutely personal. Hazel was the only friend with whom she had passed the test of time and the two had been friends since school.

However, with Neil, it was different. She trusted him with everything that she could. She trusted him with her secrets, with her life, with her body and with her heart. Somehow, she had this feeling in her gut which told her that this particular man, no matter how stubborn he could get at times, was definitely becoming the person she would want to spend the rest of her life with.

Her train of thoughts came to a halt when the Ferris Wheel came to a halt and Neil cleared his throat to gain her attention.

Who would tell the guy he already had it all?

Neil stepped out of the capsule as he held his hand out for her to hold. Avni looked up at him before slipping her hand in his, a shiver ran down her body at how cold they were. Nevertheless, she wrapped her palm around his as he led her down the stair-case of the wheel. The pad of his thumb roamed around her inner-wrist before it finally found her pulse and Neil firmly placed his thumb over there. Avni's pulse fluttered under his touch as she turned her neck sideways to look at him.

N - Keeps reminding me that you're okay. With me! - he muttered as his eyes found hers and her pulse picked up speed. He could feel it.

Avni's throat clogged with emotions she wasn't very well-versed with, so for lack of having enough courage to identify them and name them, she simply let them takeover as they rushed through every vein of her body. On its own, her body turned to him fully as her arms wrapped around his neck and she nestled her face in the crook of his neck, raising herself on her toes to hold him close. Their chests pressed against each others' and Neil's hands snaked around her lower back as he put his chin on her shoulder.

Avni's lungs were robbed of their breath and she was filled in with his rich masculine scent when he roamed his hands around her back, pulling her up close to his chest, making her stand on the tip of her toes in the process. She tightened her arms around his neck as she pressed a warm kiss on his neck.

A - It's going to be alright. - she whispered as she inhaled more of his rich spice perfume mixed with his own odour.

N - Isn't that something I should assure you with? - he asked as a pained smile stretched across his lips.

Avni's eyes closed as she took in a deep breath. He was probably regretting what just went through between them up in the air. And the thought hurt. More than it should have. More than she had thought it would. Ignoring the dull ache that spread through her chest as she bit on her lip to stop herself from crying out loud, she pressed herself against him, basking all the closeness that she could in that very moment.

A - I'm cold. Hold tight! - it was a silent plea.

Neil obliged. Not wanting to hike her little dress up even more by pulling her up, he bent down as he nudged his nose in the crook of her neck and rested his face in the warmth of her body. They stood there in each other's embrace for a while, seeking comfort and warmth that the both of them had been craving for so desperately.

It was when a gust of chilly wind blew & Avni could feel it passing through the fabric of her clothes that she pulled back as she put a strand of hair behind her ear that had escaped her bun.

A - We need to go home. - she bit her lips nervously as she blinked her eyes. I, need to, - she looked down at her feet, hoping that he'd understand. you know!

It didn't need Neil to think much in order to figure that she needed a change of clothes. Acknowledging her concern with a nod of his head, he pulled his hands back from her waist as he cleared his throat.

N - Let's go find everybody else! - he said before turning around as he started to look for Isha & Mrs. Brown.

A sigh left Avni's mouth at the loss of contact from him, but she brushed it back as she followed him with small steps.

They offered their greetings to the Brown Family before Neil carried a very tired Isha in his arms and they started walking towards the car.

The drive was silent as Isha dozed off soon after they hit the road and both Avni & Neil were silent as they dealt with the rush of emotions that they were going through. Reaching home, he carried Isha to her room while Avni moved to her room in order to get a warm shower.

Once done with the shower, she walked up to Isha's room only to find Neil standing in the corridor as he leaned on the railing of the balcony while looking up at the moon.

Tell it to the moon, tell the stars! - the words echoed in Avni's ears as warmth spread in the pit of her stomach.

A - Hi! - she said as she stood besides him, making him turn sideways to acknowledge her presence.

N - Isha, uh, slept! - he said as he looked away.

A - Are you- Is everything okay? - she couldn't help but ask. A pang of disappointment rippled in her chest as his cold eyes.

N - Hm! - he didn't bother to look at her.

A - Selenophile, Mr. Khanna? - she put up a smile as she asked after a minute of silence. Desperate to strike a conversation. To know what was going on in his head. To know what they were. Where they stood in their relationship, if they had any in the first place.

N - No! - came his simple answer and Avni could feel her disappointment turning into frustration and anger.

A - Is this how you deal with things? By pretending that they don't exist? - she gritted her teeth at his adamancy.

N - What do you want, Buttercup? - he ran his hands across his face as he exhaled through his mouth.

A - Exactly what you want! - she took a courageous step forward as she looked straight into his eyes.

N - I want you to go away. - he muttered, voice holding a threat and demeanour as cold as Antarctica's coldest territory.

A - You sure? - her voice was a mockery as a humourless chuckle escaped her mouth. What made you so bothered when I was with someone else then? Stop making claims you can't stand by, Mr. Khanna! - her eyes blazed with anger at the same time they glistened with hot tears that stinged her.

N - You don't want to go further than that, Buttercup! Stop for your own fucking good, alright? - he gritted as his calloused hand wrapped around her elbow, holding her in a firm grip.

A - It's not me who's confused about what I want! - she didn't know where was she getting all that bravery from, but she was done being pushed & pulled like a rag doll. What do you even want, Mr. Khanna? Just clear it out. Because I'm not sure how long I can handle your dual personalities anymore. One moment you kill a man for me & then you tell me to run away from you? One moment you tend to a little bruise on my cheek as if it pains you more than it does me and then you yourself carve a deeper wound in my heart. One moment you pleasure me the best I've ever been in my entire life, ask me to tell the damned moon & stars about you, and then you claim that you want me gone? Why do you look at me like that when you don't want me? - she was just a decibel below yelling as a string of hot tears flew down her face.

N - You think I'm confused about wanting you? - his fingers dug into her skin as he firmed his grip around her elbow. No, Buttercup! I am definitely not. - he gritted his teeth. Every bone in my body, every beat of my heart wants you. With an intensity that burns me and also puts me to rest. - he stepped closer, making Avni gulp as she felt goosebumps rising on her skin. I don't know what have you done to me that I feel all these overwhelming emotions and can't seem to contain them even after my best effort. Neither do I have any explanation for this burning rage and intent to kill that I possess for anyone who so much as even looks at you. I don't know why I feel all this when I've never felt it ever before. I hate the way I feel so drawn to your fairy like drizzle that you seem to carry everywhere you go. It should annoy me, should make me feel appalled and repulsed, but the irony is, - his adam's apple bobbed down as his throat worked on a swallow. All I feel is an attraction that threatens to consume me whole. Like a moth attracted to fire!

A - Why do you not give in then? - her voice merely a whisper as she tried to hold herself from shattering at the inevitable rejection he was going to throw her way.

N - Because I am not someone you should want! - he mumbled as his chest felt tightened with all those emotions that he was witnessing going through him.

A - That's for me to decide. - she dared.

N - Damn it, Buttercup! - Avni shivered at the way his voice pitched higher in frustration. Don't you just get it? We- I can't

A - Let me go! - she was afraid he wouldn't even hear her in such a low voice.

N - What? - he frowned at the demand.

A - Let go. - she repeated, a bit firmly this time. I am sorry for pestering you. I still have a probation of around 25 days to serve. You can choose not to hire me after that. And lets just keep it professional between the two of us. - she tried her best to keep her voice cool & distant but Neil could hear the pain in it.

N - Buttercup, listen! - he didn't know what he was going to say but the desperation to have her close in that moment was too much to ignore.

A - Good night, Mr. Khanna. I shall see you at breakfast tomorrow. - she jerked herself out from his hold as she turned around to walk away.

The moment she locked the door of her room, tears streamed down her eyes like a waterfall as her back slid against the wall & she sat on the cold floor while hugging her knees. It was inevitable, she knew it. But for once, she had hoped that her stars wouldn't snatch away from her the people that she desired. Avni felt like someone was tying her chest up with ropes as it became difficult to breathe with every passing moment. The more she tried to draw some air in, the more she was reminded how every space she walked in smelt of him. She smelt of him.

Avni didn't remember when had sleep taken over and she succumbed to the peaceful darkness involuntarily. On the other hand, Neil couldn't get even an ounce of sleep. He knew she had been crying. He could tell by the way her shoulders shook when she had walked away from him.

Everyone thought of him as a rude jerk with no feelings. But that wasn't true. As much as he acted all cold & tough, he really wasn't. His already tainted heart shattered even more every time he brought her pain. Every time he brought her tears. Agreed he had hardly known her for days, but the woman had made such an imprint in his heart & mind that Neil had to question almost every thought & every belief that he had ever had. Was it only love when it was announced out for the world to listen? And was it only pain when it was let out through tears? Unfortunately, Neil didn't find himself strong enough to pour his pain out through tears, rather it slowly consumed his insides in its vicious fire and he could see himself ablaze. For her.

It was around seven in the morning that he left the warmth of his bed to take a hot shower before making his way to Isha's room. Waking his little bundle of happiness up, he got her ready for the day in one of her many woollen dresses as he made two ponytails and accessorized the little princess with matching bows.

It was almost nine in the morning when Neil descended down the stairs to the kitchen only to find Avni helping Mrs. Brown out as they prepared breakfast together. A sharp pain shot through his chest as he watched her dull eyes. They had always been so bright & vibrant. He hated himself a bit more in that moment.

Isha ran to Avni as she hugged her legs and Neil was surprised how she gave the little girl a bright smile even though she was anything but in the mood to smile. Or may be, she had learnt the fact that he wasn't worthy enough! The thought worked like a punch in the gut.

A sigh left his mouth when Avni averted his eyes as she carried Isha out of the kitchen in her arms while holding her breakfast. He watched as she sat on the sofa with Isha in her lap as she started feeding her the oats that she had prepared.

N - Need help, Mrs. Brown? - it was a desperate attempt to distract himself from her thoughts.

Mrs. Brown - How many times do I've to tell you that its Aunty for you, Neil? - she schooled as she narrowed her eyes and Neil just nodded in an answer.

He helped her with putting the coffee pot for a brew as the older lady chopped the fruits.

Mrs. Brown - She is a lovely girl. - she said, grabbing Neil's attention, more like catching him red-handed while staring at Avni. When do you plan to tell her?

N - Huh? Tell her what? - a frown marred his face.

Mrs. Brown - Don't tell me you still haven't realised it yet? - she chuckled, seemingly unaware of his dilemma.

N - I ain't sure what you're talking about? - he averted her experienced eyes, but Neil had never been good at lying.

Mrs. Brown - You like her, don't you? - she chose not to beat around the bush knowing well how thick-headed Neil could be in the matters of heart.

His eyes watched how a small smile spread across Avni's mouth and her eyes got some of their twinkle back as Isha giggled in her lap. A thick lump formed at the back of his throat as he watched the two of them interact.

N - Anybody could like her! - he shrugged as he blinked his eyes, the pressure behind his eyes increasing with every passing moment. Could he just cry? For once?

Mrs. Brown - Yes! But you're the guy she likes back, Neil. - she offered a genuine smile but Neil couldn't return the gesture.

N - There is no point, Aunty. - his shoulders slumped. You know it! - he looked her way with a pained smile on his face.

Mrs. Brown - How long, Neil? Just how long are you going to punish yourself for something you had no control over? - her eyes filled with worry and concern.

N - She deserves better! - he argued.

Mrs. Brown - Then be better! - she refused to let the topic go.

N - You don't understand. I.. - a sigh left his mouth as his chest heaved down and he shut his eyes close. I'm my mother's son, Aunty. What if I turn out like her? What if I...what if I just hurt her like Dad was hurt? I can not. She wants a forever, and I don't think I'm capable of that. - the pressure behind his eyes and ears increased ten folds as he felt it difficult to draw in enough breath.

Mrs. Brown - But you're also Mr. Prakash's son, Neil. - her voice had become soft as she put a hand on his shoulder. He raised you. And he never taught you to treat someone lesser than what they deserve. You've grown in front of me, Neil. And I know for a fact that you'll be the best partner one can ever get. - she assured the disheartened man who will always be a little boy for her. Someone like her son. And tell me one thing, would you be okay when she finds someone for herself? Would you be able to live happily knowing that she isn't going to come back to you? - she tried to make him understand the consequences.

N - Happily & I don't really fit well, Aunty! I've given up on that long ago. - he shook his head lightly as he clicked his tongue to stop himself from feeling the acrid taste that spread in his mouth and his eyes started stinging. Moreover, I've Isha. Even if we do get together, I don't think I can promise her all of me. She might want to have a family of her own, children & everything. I can't compromise, Isha! - he voiced his concerns out.

Mrs. Brown - Look at them. - she gestured towards the two ladies who happily occupied the space in each other's presence. Does she look like she would ever ask you to do that?

N - I don't know, Aunty! I honestly don't. - he quickly rubbed his face with the heel of his palm as a tear slipped down his eye.

Mrs. Brown - Good Lord! - her heart pained to see him in pain. You're one stubborn kid, Neil. You know what? Give me your hand.

N - What? - he frowned. Why?

She sighed at the stubbornness. That was something that he had always had. Shaking her head at him, she took his hand in hers while Neil looked at her with a deep frown on his face.

Mrs. Brown - Promise me that you're going to try. It's okay if it doesn't turn out well. But at least try to give yourself a chance. Will you? For me? - she urged and Neil knew there was no way out. Mrs. Brown had always been the mother figure that he had lacked.

N - You don't- - he failed at the attempt.

Mrs. Brown - It's a simple 'Yes' or 'No', Neil. Will you? - she was literally schooling him now and Neil resisted the urge to groan out loud.

N - Fine! - he sighed. Yes! I'll try.

Mrs. Brown - Promise? - she didn't want to take any chance.

N - Promise! - he committed, more to himself than to her. You can be a handful sometimes! I wonder how does Mr. Brown handle you? - he shook his head, earning himself a light smack at the back of his head as a small laugh escaped his throat.

He was gonna try. To be better. For her!

CHAPTER 12

Avni had spent the whole day in Isha's company and hadn't really seen much of Neil as he remained locked up in his room. She had seen him last at the breakfast and he had even attempted to pass her a smile and her heart had wrenched when she ignored the effort. It was too tough. To know that he was there and to act like she didn't care. Cause every cell in her body knew that she did. A lot.

She was aware that there were things about him that were not morally white per se, but neither were they black in their entirety. He had his shades of grey and she struggled to explain to him that it didn't matter to her. From a very young age, Avni had known that no one was perfect, perfection was just one theory that people fed to themselves to save themselves from the uncertainty of taking a step into the unknown. But love! She had always believed that love was worthy enough to a step into the oblivion, knowing that you might end up all alone & miserable, yet, merely the possibility of finding someone who you don't just want to live with, but can't live without was reason enough to take that leap of faith. She was not in love with Neil yet.

But she was certain that she had come a long way on the road, and there was not much that she could do to stop herself from falling. Love, to her, as she had watched her parents, meant to stay together, no matter how different or opposite you're to each other. She didn't know how to show Neil how perfectly they fit together. The guy was apprehensive that the jagged pieces of his broken heart would pierce her. But that was far from the truth. The reality was, that the cracks in his heart were to make some space for her, to give her solace in his company. Somehow, she knew that the pieces of his broken heart would fit with her own broken one. How could they not? There was some force greater than themselves that was working to bring them together. Cause she definitely did not go around straddling strangers in a club, neither did she so desperately prayed for man's happiness, also the fact that the said man got her wobbly in the knees with just some lazy smile and half smirk was getting too tough to ignore.

Her heart sank to the pits of her stomach when he didn't step out to the dining room even for lunch and called for the food in his room itself. The better part of the day had been spent in teaching Isha colours and shapes which she quickly caught up with. Evening passed in a blur with Avni sipping her coffee as Isha played with her favourite play-dough clay. Once done with dinner, Avni put her to sleep before she came out to stand in the open balcony. The cold wind made her teeth clatter as she wrapped her hands around her arms, rubbing them over as she looked up to watch the moon.

It didn't matter how much she try, she would never be able to look at the moon the same as she used to before last night. An inadvertent sigh left her as she closed her eyes and let the chilly wind brush against her face, seeking some relief for the sting she felt in her eyes.

N - Selenophile, Buttercup? - she finally heard the voice she had been aching to hear.

A - No. - her throat hurt as a acrid taste filled her mouth and the pressure behind her eyes increased.

She heard him sigh as he stepped towards her and kept his hands at the ledge of the balcony, his cold hands brushed against hers and she immediately pulled back. Taking in a ragged breath, she swiftly turned on her feet as she attempted to walk away but he stopped her as he held her wrist.

Neil took in a deep breath as he pulled her towards himself and her back hit his chest as he wrapped his arms around her stomach and rested his chin on her shoulder. Avni's chest heaved up as she sucked in a breath at the same time as she blinked her eyes rapidly to make sure that she didn't end up crying in front of him.

A - Let go. - her voice came out thick & hoarse.

N - I didn't mean to hurt you. - he whispered as he breathed her scent in, feeling an instant relief in his chest. Somehow, it became a bit easy to breathe.

A - Doesn't matter. Let me go, Mr. Khanna! - she tried to take his hands off her but his grip only firmed.

N - Stop fighting, Miss Mehta. - he steadied her with one hand making her slump her shoulders in defeat.

A - What do you want me to do then? - she gritted her teeth in frustration.

N - There are things I...I want you to know. About me. If you still think that you'd like to give this...whatever we have, a chance then I'm willing to better myself, Buttercup! - he said and Avni could feel the outrageous rise in her pulse.

A - What-what things? - she mumbled, afraid that she would turn some wrong switch & he would be distant again.

N - Five is a young age to realise that your mother is never going to get back home, Miss Mehta. I had, - he had to click his tongue to get the words out of him as his throat felt choked. I had waited for her initially, I had thought that she might have just forgotten her way back home, or you know, may be she was tired and stopped somewhere to rest and that she would be back in sometime. But she never did. - he paused to suck a breath in. Didi was eight back then and I used to keep asking her about our mother's whereabouts but how could she answer my relentless questions when she herself was as clueless as I was. - his arms around her tightened unconsciously as Avni felt his chest stiffen against her back. All we knew was that Dad wasn't happy. He used to put on the brightest smile on in front of us but we knew he cried himself to sleep every single night. Mrs. Brown was like a sister to my Dad, she was the one who took care of our family during that time. - his chest heaved up as he drew in a long breath. Slowly, with time, I & Didi accepted the fate, Dad did too, the only difference being he still had hope that our mother would miraculously return someday. - he chuckled humourlessly as he finished the sentence and Avni felt a sharp pain shoot through her heart. Only if she could hold that scared & scarred five years old kid who couldn't understand why his mother disappeared from his sight!

A - Can I see you? - she whispered and Neil immediately loosened his hold around her so that she could turn around to look at him.

Avni ran a smooth finger along his brows to soothe the crease that had formed on his forehead before she gently rubbed the creases of his eyes. Raising herself on the tip of her toes, she pressed her mouth against the centre of his forehead in a deep kiss. She then kissed both of his eyes before descending down to his cheeks, successfully pulling out a small smile from him.

N - You know, even when I believed that forevers weren't for me, I wasn't bitter to the notion of it. In fact, I was so happy when Didi had found Jiju. They were so beautiful together. - by then Avni had wrapped her arms around his back as she put her chin against his chest and craned her neck up to keep looking at him while listening to him with all her attention. Then Isha happened and I thought, life wasn't that bad either. - his eyes lightened up for a moment before they were melancholic again. I was too early to judge, I guess! - a sigh left him. Life was just as cruel as it had always been, I was just delusional about the world being a nice place. - he said, making Avni frown. Zain Qureshi, my mother's second husband was a renowned white-collar businessman for the world but it was all a lie. The truth was, the business was built on the blood of the weak & the poor. - and Neil could swear he saw something close to fury pass through Avni's eyes at the mention of his step-father.

A - What went wrong? - she asked as she rubbed her thumb across his cheeks, an attempt to ease him and Neil had to take in another harsh breath before letting the most dreaded part out.

N - He was responsible for my family death. Blew up the jet they were travelling in. - and Avni was compelled to think just how much he had gone through to tell her this without breaking into fits of sobs. Fortunately or unfortunately, I was back in London with Isha as she had fever because she was teething at that time. Otherwise, we'd have been dead too. - even the thought didn't set well with her.

A - Don't say that! - she put her hand on his mouth in reflex and Neil found himself relieved at the worry & care she held in her eyes for him.

He held her wrist of the hand that she had kept on his mouth, kissing it in gentle brushes, he put it on his chest as she blinked her tears away.

N - It was a blood bath, Miss Mehta! - she watched how his throat worked on a swallow. When I got to the terminal, the bodies were burnt and there was blood all around. - she rubbed her hands along his arms as he closed his eyes shut as if he could still see the scene unfolding in front of him and a lone tear escaped his eye. That day, - he opened his eyes and Avni was terrified at how cold they had become, devoid of any emotion or life. I had sworn that I'd avenge the people who did this to my family. It was not a tough quest to figure that it was the Qureshi's behind all this. Zain Qureshi had always envied my father's empire of business. He wanted to be on the top and for him to achieve that, he had to remove NK Constructions from the market, my father's company. Buttercup, trust me when I say this, I had worked day in and day out to make sure that NK Constructions not only captures whole of the UK Markets but takes the entire world's real state markets by storm. And it did!

That was the legal & law-abiding revenge that I had taken from him, but the beast inside me wasn't satisfied. It felt unjust & unfair to have him live a life when all I did was to count my breathes till I wait for death. I didn't sleep nights at a stretch to find at least some sort of evidence to prove that it was him who was behind the crash of the jet. But no matter how much I tried, I couldn't find any. Zain had bought the entire circle & there was no scope to get justice legally. That fucking lady of justice really is blind! So I started this Mafia association, we started off as an underdog, only defensing in the beginning to firm our footings around the business. And then, after making sure that the Qureshi's were still trusting of me, I attacked. In the last two years, I've blown up and reported six human trafficking rackets that he ran and rescued not less than a hundred girls from his clenches. That was only the start of his doom, once he was weakened financially & tainted in the inner social circles, I attacked his business. Worked day & night without a wink of sleep to collect evidences of the frauds that he had been making through out the years. I landed my hands on it after good one & a half year, and the moment I did, I turned them in to the cops. Zain died of an heart attack when he was arrested and the shares of his company crashed, the company was at the verge of bankruptcy. And it was then that Rehaan, Zain & my mother's son took over. I had not planned to have any animosity or vile intentions towards him but he started it all. Attacked my factories, stole my business plans & threatened the life of those who were even remotely related to me. You know what the sad part was, in all this, I never heard anything from my mother. And that broke me, you know! Somewhere deep inside, I had wished

& hoped that she would reach out to me, at least when I was creating havoc in her perfectly crafted life. But she never did. I guess, I was never a son to her. - another tear fell from his eye as he bit on his lower lip to stop himself from crying out loud.

Avni's throat felt choked as she saw him crying, she had never thought the man who always used to carry this ice persona around him would break down in tears in front of her. She wasn't ready to witness it and her chest felt tightened to see his agony. In that moment, she really hated each & every person that had been the reason of his tears.

A - Mr. Khanna, have you ever tried to find out if she is okay? Your mother! - she timidly asked as the thought struck her.

N - No. - he shook his head. And honestly, I do not even intend to, Buttercup. I..I can't. - he blinked his eyes as he looked up at the night sky. This ambiguity is fine with me, but the thought that she might not even be alive, or the probability of ever coming across her, it scares the shit out of me. I won't know how to feel. And I hate how mixed and unsure I feel whenever it comes to her. I..after Dad & Didi, I thrive on control, Buttercup! I can't let my guards slip, cause those are the only things I'm left with. - he confessed and Avni's eyes brimmed with fresh tears.

A - It's okay! - she couldn't help but kiss the tears that fell from his eyes until they stopped.

There was a stretch of silence between them, Neil simply healed himself in the comfort of her embrace while she held him tight in a desperate attempt to put him to ease. She needed to have him alright to make sure that she herself was at peace.

N - That day, when you took us to the orphanage, it was that day that I finally had a proper sleep after two long years, without guilt gnawing my insides with every passing second. Remember you told me that the smile that they would offer me will make all the difference? Guess, you were right! They...I, I couldn't take the thought out of my mind that those kids were probably orphans because of people like us, who killed without putting a thought to the family that awaits them home. Sure, I have never killed someone innocent, and have only taken lives which were better off not present in the world, but that day at the orphanage, I realised that, it was not my job. I was no God to decide who gets to live & who gets to die! All I can do in my capacity is to be a better person. - Avni gave him an encouraging smile as she put a kiss on his chest. That day, when you made me offer a candle in the church, I clearly remember that it was in that particular moment, I realised that all this while of trying to defeat Zain Qureshi, I had probably become another Zain Qureshi. This was not what I had wanted. This was not how my father raised me, or my sister wanted to see me! This wasn't what I wanted to teach Isha. You remember I put the Ganesha idol in the living room? - he asked and she nodded with a small smile on her face. That was not the only change that you brought in my life that day, Buttercup! That day, I had decided that I'd stop this mafia work. In fact, I planned to open a different wing of business for the Khanna Group of Industries. We would provide intellectual services and also train and supply private detectives to work on high-profile crime cases like these with the minimal charges possible. Today, I was locked up in my room because I was getting in touch with some government delegates and officials to get the initial business set-up formalities fulfilled. This way, I'd be able to save those little children from the filthy hands of the likes of Rehaan Qureshis and would even save myself from getting any more blood on my hands. I promise you, Buttercup, I'd try my best to be the man that you deserve. At least I'll put in all my efforts. - he said and Avni's heart swelled with pride at the man in front of her.

Some would say that it was the bare minimum that he could do for her, but for him, it wasn't! Avni understood that after the death of his family, it had become a way of life for him. Violence had become his escape, all the fights and wounds worked to numb him to the point that he couldn't feel the pain that ripped his heart in the first place. And he was willing to change that for her. He was willing to change his way of living and to better himself because he thought that she deserved better. It was no small thing and the fact that he was trying meant a lot to her.

Giving him a bright smile, she kissed his forehead while he closed his eyes as he hugged her tight, the hollowness in chest finally getting filled bit by bit.

CHAPTER 13

Neither of them could recall how long they had stood there in the corridor while holding each other in their arms but it was Avni who pulled back first, only to hold his face in her warm hands.

A - I am so proud of you, - she smiled. and also of the fact that you chose to do the right thing. I can understand that it has been tough for you, Mr. Khanna. Twenty-five years old, left with a one year old child to take care of and having to deal with the loss of your family all at the same time is tough. But you refused to be brought on your knees. You refused to wallow in your own pain and took such good care of Isha, just as her own parents would have. And now, you could have easily avoided telling me the truth, I wouldn't have guessed anything about you being involved with violence & murders. But you chose to tell me the truth. That says a lot about the way you treat others. And it only affirms my claim about you being loyal & respectful to the people around you. - she offered him a smile, a simple small curve of her mouth but Neil could see the genuineness of it in her eyes.

A bit too overwhelmed with all the emotions that he felt in that moment, he simply responded with a small smile as he held her hand and led her to his room. Avni simply followed.

Turning the knob of the door, he pushed the door open as they stepped inside and the censor lights illuminated the room. Neil walked them to the balcony as he sat on the swing chair and then pulled Avni towards him so that she landed on his lap sideways.

A - You can stop with the manhandling, you know! I'll simply oblige. - she whispered as she wrapped her hands around his neck.

N - That much of a good lil' girl huh, Buttercup? - she loved the teasing glint in his eyes.

A - Whatever that means! - she rolled her eyes as she looked away from him to hide her smile.

She put her head against his chest as she heard the rhythmic thumping of his heart while his fingers traced light patterns on her back. Neil could feel an overwhelming sense of calm washing over him as he held her in his arms, he was astonished how simply holding her close to himself could melt away all the stress of the day, probably of the entire lifetime he had lived so far. He was respected and feared by many, but she was one of those very few people who understood him, the list so small he could count it on his fingers.

Avni's heart throbbed in her chest as he kept watching her with his gorgeous eyes that looked nothing less than sin & heaven mixed. She could feel herself getting all hot & bothered under his intense gaze as she drew in a rough breath when he tucked some of her hair behind her ears.

A - Stop staring, Mr. Khanna! - she mumbled while biting the corner of her lower lip, feeling uncharacteristically shy.

N - Remember you asked me if I'm a selenophile? - he asked and she nodded, slightly chuckling at his question. Guess, I am. It just so happens that my moon lives on earth! - he said as if it was something casual and Avni could hear the roar of blood in her eardrums.

A - I never knew you could flirt so well! - she said, biting her lips as she felt them twitching to spread into a dazzling smile.

N - Well, there is a lot more that I can do. Only if you allow me to! - he whispered as he traced the tip of his nose down the side of her cheek as his hand gently massaged her thigh.

A - Stop being so pompous! - she slapped his hand away as she laughed.

Neil looked back at her in surprise as she laughed her heart out with her eyes shining in mirth while he pretended to be offended at her remark.

N - Talking a bit too much, aren't we? - he said as he traced his thumb along her lower lip.

Avni's laughter died down when his other hand stroked her waist in slow motions and her throat worked on a swallow when his lips pressed a sloppy kiss on her slender neck. His tongue swept around her skin as he bit on her flesh before sucking on it, Avni had to stop herself from moaning out loud in pleasure. Placing another kiss on her neck, he looked up at her, finding her looking back at him with her bright eyes hooded with desire.

N - I love your eyes. Boundless black seas. Just can't get enough! - he brushed his lips against hers and Avni's mouth parted just an inch as she sucked in a shallow breath.

Neil encased her mouth around his as he sucked on her lips while his hands roamed around her back and Avni found herself eagerly responding to the kiss as her tongue swirled along with his. She wondered how the cold night had suddenly started to feel so warm & comforting when his soft lips kissed hers, as if massaging them in slow gentle rubs, licks, & swirls. It was a slow kiss, they were not fighting for dominance, nor were they rushing into the next step. Just a loving caress from a long lost lover, someone who they had been finding from so long and now that they had found them, they couldn't let go of each other even for a fleeting second.

Neil pulled back when he felt her running out of breath. Caressing her cheek with his long fingers, he smiled at her, under the moonlight and she suddenly felt an overwhelming sweep of emotions washing over her.

A - You smile at me more than I deserve! - she said as she looked into his eyes. A certain kind of fear settling in the pits of her gut.

N - You deserve so much more than that. - his lips curved up in a lop-sided smile. You deserve sunshine & roses, moonlight & orchids. You deserve someone who will laugh & cry with you, oppose you & fight with you, but will also assure you & stand by you, someone who will mourn with you in times of loss & celebrate with you in happiness. Someone who will love you, with all those things that he has got! - and this time, he couldn't smile. Instead, he felt himself at war with his own-self. The part of him who was scared to let his heart open, who was scared of getting it broken, who was scared of being left alone, once again.

Avni's skin laced with prickly goosebumps all over her body at the sheer intensity he held in his eyes. Taking in a deep breath, she held his cheek in her hand as she pressed a long kiss on his mouth.

A - You know, if someone present me with the power to rewrite my life, I'd definitely make sure I meet you & choose you every time I get a chance. I'd find you in this life, and in the next. - she said and all Neil wanted to do was to hold her close to himself till the point he was swarmed with all things her.

Avni had a fair picture of the fact that it was difficult for him to open up, but he still did. Literally unfolded all his life in front of her, and she doubted he felt exhausted with all the brain-storming, both for his business, and emotionally. Giving him a small smile, she stood up from his lap as she held her hand out for him to hold. Wordlessly, he obliged and followed her inside the room.

Avni gestured him to lie down on the bed and then herself laid down opposite to him. Putting the lights off, she settled her head comfortably on the pillow as she watched him while he watched back.

On their own, her hand reached out to him as she ran her fingers through his hair before tracing them down his face. She gently massaged his eyeballs as he closed his eyes and a smile pulled on her lips when he was finally into deep slumber.

How in the flamboyant black sesame mochi can this man sleep like a baby. Look at those annoyingly gorgeous eye-lashes. Certainly not very pleased Universe, couldn't you grant me such beautiful eyes? Why does he have to be so beautiful? I almost love him anyways!

She didn't realise when sleep took over but she was well aware of the fact that she hadn't slept so good in a while. The weight of his delicious arms around her waist cocooned her in their comfort and protection as she slept with all her worries melting away.

Being an early bird, Avni woke up around seven when sunlight filtered in through the balcony. The masculine smell of rich spices was the first thing that she registered when her slumberous state sobered up. A smile of content pulled out on her mouth when she found him asleep while he had his leg wrapped around hers and his cheek was pressed against his hand on the pillow as he had his mouth agape in not a very sophisticated fashion that he always carried himself with. A soft chortle left her throat when he rubbed his eyes before squinting them open.

A - Hi! - she whispered while Neil was still struggling to open his eyes fully.

N - Hi! - he mumbled.

A - How are you this morning, Princess Aurora? - she stifled a laugh at the use of the movie reference, clearly referring to him as Sleeping Beauty.

N - Who's her? - he frowned in confusion.

A - Nobody! - she chuckled as she raised herself on her arm and bent down to press a kiss on his cheek. C'mon, get up! We need to go check on Isha. - she said and Neil nodded.

Sitting up, he sighed as he rubbed his eyes while she watched him with a fascination that was evident in her eyes.

N - You're not wearing glasses? Weren't wearing them yesterday also, right? - he asked as his brows joined into a frown.

A - Uh, I..wear lens. Sometimes. - she fiddled with the blanket as she passed him a small smile while he simply nodded.

N - You know, your eyes! - he tilted his head in thoughtfulness. I don't know what it exactly is. May be I'm seeing too much into it, but beneath all the sparkles and stars that you carry in them, they speak about lost endings to me. You know what I mean? It's like...there is something that keeps a part of you hidden from me. I don't know if that even makes sense! - he dismissed the thought with a shake of his head when Avni took in a sharp breath. I'm sorry, Buttercup! I didn't mean to hurt you. I-

A - Relax, Mr. Khanna! You don't hurt me. - she smiled as she scooted closer to him.

A sigh left her as her chest heaved down when she wrapped her arms around his neck and he immediately reciprocated.

A - Let's just say that I'm too afraid to lose you! - she whispered.

N - You won't lose me. Not until you actually want me gone! - he assured as he stroked her hair, making her smile a little.

A - I don't think I'm ever going to want that! - she mumbled as she pulled back from the hug.

She blinked her eyes in an attempt to brush away her saddening thoughts before she gave him a full smile, making him smile back.

A - It's my Mom's birthday today. - she whispered & Neil guessed that was the reason she was a bit sad.

N - Let's pray for her wellbeing & wish her many happy returns of the day, shall we? - he spoke softly and successfully managed to get himself rewarded with a smile from her.

A - Once upon a time you would have never said that! - she mumbled, still smiling.

N - Once upon a time I wasn't aware you existed! - and he wasn't loitering around. It was strange how the girl had managed to reaffirm his faith in God in such a short span of time.

A - Let's go & see Isha! - she mumbled as she got up from the bed, as she tried to hide the blush that adorned her face by his words.

Both of them went to Isha's room and the three of them had some good time together. By the time Avni herself got ready after getting Isha ready, Neil had already prepared the breakfast. They ate the food together after which Avni excused herself to make a phone call to her Mom.

N - Ishi, it's Miss Mehta's Mom's birthday today. Do you think you'd like to bake a cake for her? - he asked as he made the little girl sit on his lap.

I - Yes, N-man! I'll bake the cake all by myself! We'll put blue sprinkles on it! - she exclaimed, making Neil smile.

N - Alright! Come, let's bake the cake. - he said as he stood up while carrying her in his arms.

I - No! I'll do it! - she was adamant.

N - Ishipie, won't you let N-man help you? - he blinked his eyes innocently.

I - Uh, okay! But I will mix it, okay? - she bargained.

N - Whatever my princess says! - he smiled, kissing her cheeks.

Neil made Isha sit on the kitchen platform as he quickly gathered all the ingredients they needed to prepare the cake. Isha took the requisite ingredients out in the measuring spoons as Neil politely asked her to and once they were sure that they had put all the things in the mix, Isha took the whisk in her hand to mix the batter.

I - This is too thick! I need help, Mama! - she mumbled while a small smile graced Neil's face.

N - Here, Princess! Always at your service! - he said as he took the whisk from her and mixed the batter till there were no lumps remaining.

Isha watched how Neil pre-heated the oven and then poured the batter into the mould.

N - Do you want to help N-man put it into the oven? - he asked while Isha nodded excitedly. But be careful, okay? - he warned as he held her in his arms and she put the mould into the oven.

I - How long will it take?

N - Um, around 45 minutes, I guess! Let's go watch Peppa Pig till then? - he asked.

I - I want to watch Frozen! - she told and Neil simply had to give in.

N - Frozen it is! - he said as Isha placed a sweet kiss on his cheek.

Avni made her presence felt just when he had started playing the movie, smiling at the duo, she settled next to Isha as she watched the film with them.

Neil gestured Avni to take care of Isha as he went to look after some work and she assured him with the blink of her eyes.

I - Can we put sprinkles on the cake now? - she asked after sometime and Avni frowned in response.

A - What cake, Baby? - she asked.

I - It's your Mom's birthday so Mama & I baked cake. - she clapped her hands and Avni's heart melted.

Completely awed and touched by the gesture from her & her uncle, she smiled a bright smile at Isha while the said Uncle was busy with work. She kissed her on the cheeks as Isha giggled.

A - Come, let's see if we can ice the cake yet! - she said.

She carried Isha in her arm as she walked into the kitchen. Avni turned the microwave off as she took the cake out and checked if it was baked fully by poking it with a toothpick. Once assured that it was good, she put it out for sometime so that it could cool down while she, obviously with Isha's help prepared the frosting for the cake. She noticed that Neil had already put all the required stuff at the slab.

Unknown to her, he stood at the threshold of the kitchen as he watched them lovingly while leaning at the side of the door-frame. He was correct when he thought that spending some time with Isha would definitely help with her mood. She was probably missing her mother, who would not? Even when he hated his mother, he too missed her in times of misery.

Not to let his thoughts wander back to those old wounds, he quickly put up a smile on his face as he walked inside the kitchen.

N - Hey! You guys are frosting the cake without me? - he said with dramatic disappointed look on his face.

I - N-man, Look this is blue sprinkles. - she grinned while pointing to the sprinkles that Neil had got for the cake.

Kissing her cheek, Avni iced the cake as she helped Isha to put the frosting on the cake. Isha then drizzled the sparkles on it while grinning ear to ear, Neil watched them all the while.

A deep breath left her when she turned to look at Neil and an effortless smile graced her face.

A - Thankyou! Really means a lot, Mr. Khanna! - she smiled.

N - Thankyou, Buttercup! - he placed a quick kiss on her cheek while Isha was still busy with the cake.

Avni's eyes widened in equal parts shock & surprise as she pointed to Isha with her eyes, only to get him laugh silently at her bewilderment.

N - Okay Ishi, who wants to go to the park to cut the cake? - he asked as he carried her.

I - Me! - she clapped her hands. We'll go to the park! - she exclaimed making both of them smile.

Packing the cake in a box, Neil drove themselves to the nearby park as he and Avni spread out the picnic cloth on the grass and put the cake out so that they could cut it while Isha had gone playing with the new friends she had made.

I - N-man look, I got a boyfriend! - came her excited voice much to Neil's horror. Avni laughed hard at how his eyes widened more than the sockets of his eyes could probably take.

N - Boyfriend!? Little miss, you're not allowed to have a boyfriend! - he marched upto the swing where she was playing with another kid, her supposed boyfriend.

I - But I wike him! We are out on a date. - she mumbled, holding her ground strong.

N - Ishi! Baby, the only date you'll go on is a date with N-man! - he said softly, not even liking the idea of his little niece going on a date with someone. And you, little man, kindly go back home, its quite late. - he gave the little kid a pointed look making him blink his eyes.

A - Mr. Khanna! They're kids. What are you doing? - she had to interrupt before he could go all the way out to scare the kid away.

N - Ishipie, we'll go straight home after cutting the cake & you'll sign a deal with me. You're not getting yourself a boyfriend till you turn 30, may be not even after that! But we can always renew a contract. Do you understand? - he spoke as if he was going to crack a life-defining deal and millions were at stack while Isha just shook her head.

I - 30 is old, N-man! - she spoke matter of factly and Avni laughed out loud at the little sassy princess.

N - Then stop growing up, Ishi! - he said and the kid laughed as did Avni.

Why in the cheese margherita basil pizza were these two so cute? She could never get enough!

They cut the cake while singing happy birthday for Avni's mom and then Neil helped Isha with the slides and swings around the park, all the while making sure that no boy eyes his little princess as Avni laughed at his antics.

By the time they reached back home, Isha had already dozed off into a deep slumber. Putting her in her bed comfortably, Neil stroked her head for a while till he was sure she was fast asleep. He then went to his room to collect the gift that he had prepared during the time he had excused himself from the movie.

N - Can I come in? - he asked as he knocked on Avni's door.

A - Hi! - she smiled as she opened the door for him.

N - Hi! - he smiled back. Brought you something! - he said, and Avni could make out he was a bit flustered.

A - Show me? - she simply comforted him with a smile.

Visibly flustered, he chuckled a bit awkwardly in an attempt to ease himself as he forwarded her a roll of canvas with slightly fidgety hands. A look of confusion crossed Avni's face when she took the paper from him but it was soon replaced by a mix of awe and surprise when she unfolded the canvas.

A - This is so... - her throat felt chocked. Mr. Khanna! This is so beautiful. - she whispered while her fingers ran across the painting of her with her mother, smiling without a care in the world.

N - I didn't know anything else, so-

He couldn't complete the sentence when Avni literally threw herself in his arms and a chuckle vibrated in his chest.

A - Thankyou so much. This is so precious! - she mumbled as she pressed her face in the crook of her neck while he simply smiled.

Chapter 14

Neil smiled at the giddy feeling inside of him when Avni hugged him tightly as she dug her face in the crook of his neck. It felt so good to hold her close to himself. It felt home. She felt home. He slowly brushed her hair as she hung on to him but had to pull himself back when he heard her sniffing.

N - What's wrong, Buttercup? Why are you crying? - he asked softly as he wiped the little tears away from her face. Is everything okay? - he asked.

A - Yeah! Just a little...emotional. - she chuckled as she wiped her face with the back of her hand. I'm good. - she smiled making Neil sigh in relief.

N - Would you like to watch something? A show or a film, may be? - he offered, trying to lighten her mood.

A - Let's go! - she smiled as she held his hand.

They walked to the drawing room as Neil turned the TV on and played some murder mystery that Avni insisted on watching. She had a weird liking for all that freaky stuff.

However, at that moment, if you asked her what was going on in the film, she couldn't tell as all her attention was on the man sitting besides her. Avni adjusted her frames on her face as she chuckled at how engrossed he looked while watching the movie.

A - Mr. Khanna? - she called as she turned towards him.

N - Yes? - he looked at her.

A - If you had a colour for everyone, what would I be? - she asked making him chuckle in confusion at her question.

N - Blue. - he answered nevertheless. You are the colour I would paint my sky with. Blue. - he smiled fondly while Avni just watched him.

For someone who only scowled and frowned at people other than Isha & Noah, Neil had been smiling a lot lately in Avni's presence. Was it just Hambledon or was it the company, he wasn't sure. Okay, that was a lie. He did know but wasn't sure enough if he should answer that question just yet. He didn't want to haste into things.

Every time he smiled at her, Avni felt like an imposter. Like she wasn't deserving enough. He was so beautiful and his eyes were so mesmerizing, she couldn't decide if she wanted to escape them or let him consume her.

N - What would you paint me with? - he asked.

A - Red. - she answered in a heartbeat. The colour with the longest wavelength. No matter whatever else scatters, you'll always be clear and imprinted on me, Neil! - Neil's smile faltered at the intensity she held in her eyes. He had asked her just randomly, not expecting any meaning attached to her answer. But the way she was looking at him in that moment and the way her words carried raw honesty in them had his heart tumbling over.

In the last two years, Neil had convinced himself that the pursuit of happiness was a vain concept. That happiness was just another emotion and there was no use in dwelling too much into the euphoric high when it was only for a few moments. What prevailed, at least in the lives of people like him, was gloom and grief. Grief that would burn your insides, render it all in shambles and one wouldn't know how or where to start putting the pieces back from. Spending time with Isha was his euphoric high. And that was the only time he let his emotions take over. But then she came along, leaving behind a trail of sunshine & roses everywhere she stepped, and Neil was scared. Happiness was scary & hearts were slippery. But in this particular moment, he realised that Avni was probably all his what ifs and could have beens that he had ever thought about. The salvation that he prayed for and the life that he wished for. In this particular moment, the pursuit of happiness seemed a lesser vain concept and may be, just may be, he could have some for himself too. May be it was just him who was scared and not happiness that was scary. What if he just tries once. What if he just allow his heart to slip away this time? He knew it meant giving Avni the control to twist and butcher his heart. But he believed she wouldn't. He believed she would keep his heart tender & soft. May be he could give in to his desires once?

What could go wrong?

Well, everything!

But he was doing it anyway! He was giving his heart away to her. He was going to be what she deserved and he was going to be a happy man.

A - Mr. Khanna, you're staring again! - she pulled him out of his head, making him shake his head at his thoughts.

N - Aren't you what my daydreams look like? - he teased as he pulled her on his lap.

A - I don't know! You tell me, what do your dreams look like? - she asked as she smiled at him.

N - Oh, they sure look a lot like you, Buttercup! - he nuzzled his nose in the crook of her neck and his stubble brushed against her skin, making her laugh at the tingles.

They laughed their hearts out for a while, while the movie played in the background. Avni comfortably lounged in his lap while he held her close to his chest as he kissed the top of her head. Their hands were intwined as Avni played with his fingers.

N - We'll be leaving for London tomorrow. - he told after sometime, making her look up at him.

A - So soon? You said it would take five days. - she had a frown on her face.

N - Yeah, we thought so. Noah called this evening & told me that the security had been renewed and we can move back. - he told as he rubbed his knuckles across her jaw.

A - Okay. - she said before putting her head against his chest.

N - We can come back, you know! - he said, trying to cheer her mood up.

A - I like here. - she mumbled and Neil simply caressed her hair.

They didn't realise when sleep took over but it was only in the morning that both of them woke up. Avni gave him a morning kiss on his insistence and it was then that he moved to Isha's room to wake his princess up.

Once Avni was ready for the day, she moved to Isha's room to see if the uncle & niece were ready to go or not.

Apparently, not! She heard a loud cry from Isha when she entered the room. She noticed that Neil had taken a shower and had even packed his & Isha's stuff but the kid wasn't ready yet.

A - What's wrong? Why are you crying, Baby? - she asked Isha who was weeping loudly now.

N - She doesn't want to leave. Have been throwing a fit since I told her. - he sighed and Avni frowned at the predicament. Same, Isha same! She took a breath in.

A - Baby, but you've all your toys there. And even your friends are there, right? - she tried as she crouched next to her.

I - No, I want to stay here! - she cried as she refused to let Neil do her hair.

N - Baby, we can come back. I promise. - he spoke slowly as he took her in his lap.

I - But I wike here. - both Neil & Avni's heart pinched at the tears falling down the little kid's eyes.

A - Baby, hear me out! - she wiped her tears away as she still sat on Neil's lap. Mama & I have some work back in London. How about we go there, get the work done & then we can come back, hm? Do you think we can do that?

I - But here is good. - she was adamant.

A - Yes, Baby. I know! But we need to take care of the work, right? And Mama & I might need your help back there. So, would you please come & help us? You might come back here on vacations? - she cooed the words out as she matted her untangled hair. The cries had stopped now & Isha looked visibly calmer.

I - Can we come back after work? - she looked up at Neil with her big brown eyes and he simply smiled.

N - Yes, Baby! Of course we can! - he kissed her forehead.

I - Okay! - she smiled a little and Neil's heart was at peace.

Once Avni ensured that Isha was all better and was willing to go back, she ushered her to head down for breakfast as she & Neil followed her.

N - Uh, Thankyou! - he said as he walked besides Avni while keeping an eye on Isha so that she steps down the stairs carefully. She is a good child. Doesn't fuss much about anything but sometimes-

A - Mr. Khanna, relax! Why are you thanking me & giving explanations? She is at that age. Toddlers do get cranky sometimes and honestly, I love her! It's alright. - she blinked her eyes and Neil was at ease.

N - Thanks for understanding! - he smiled as he put a haste kiss on her cheek and followed Isha behind. Careful, Princess! Mama is gonna get you! - he growled, making the little girl giggle as she stepped down running from him. While Avni just watched the adorable duo. She loved them!

Once done with the breakfast, they hit the road after saying their greeting to the staff and a promise to return back soon. And this time, Neil was going to fulfil that promise. Neil listened as Isha & Avni talked animatedly about Disney movies and cartoons, they stopped by Starbucks to get something for lunch. The distance between Hambledon & London wasn't much but they had to drive slow because of the snow.

They were about forty minutes away from Khanna Mansion when Neil felt that they were being followed by someone. He increased his speed as he tried to lose them but the car followed behind.

N - Fuck! I can't let Isha & Avni get into this mess. Not again! - he cursed under his breathe as he tried to move as fast as the slippery snow-laden roads allowed.

A - That car is following us. Do you know them? - she asked slowly as he tucked a sleeping Isha in her baby seat.

N - I can't see the driver's face. The glass is shielded. But I think they are Rehan's! - he gritted his teeth.

A - Can't we change the route? They might not follow us if we're are in some place crowded? - she suggested as she looked behind to see how far the car was.

N - The other route has been shut because of the snow. This is the only-

A - Neil, watch out! - Neil was cut short when Avni shrieked at the same time another car overtook them and stopped across them on the road.

N - Dammit! - he muttered under his breathe as he quickly sent his location to Noah. Stay in the car, Buttercup. Don't step out. - he glanced back at both the ladies.

A - Don't worry, she'll be alright. - she assured with the blink of her eyes.

N - I need both of you alright, Avni! - he said before getting out of the car and despite everything, Avni couldn't stop the little flutter in her heart. This man was going to be the death of her.

Avni gulped and a rough breath left her when she watched Neil walking out of the car. The car was bullet proof and shielded, so she knew that no one from outside could see them. Her heart raced as a fear of something happening to Neil gripped her heart. She didn't think she was strong enough to deal with it, let alone witness it. Her eyes fell on Isha's sleeping figure and those maternal instincts took over. As much as she dreaded the possibility of something happening to Neil, she couldn't let anything happen to Isha either. The little girl had become a part of her in the last few days.

Taking in a deep breath, she took Isha out of her baby seat and made her lie down on floor of the car, beneath the seat as she covered her with her blanket. She made sure that even if the men outside happen to see her, they couldn't find Isha if they hopefully didn't look vigilantly enough. She sighed and tried to calm her racing heart once she had hidden Isha from the potential onlookers. Noah was going to reach here anyway, god forbidden, if anything happened to her, at least Isha would be safe.

Her hands grabbed the leather covers of the car as she watched Neil fighting with the men that were in the car. Her body itched to go out & do something to save him. But she doubted that would end up bringing more trouble to him.

Her mind flooded with the memories of the night when Neil had confessed to her that he would give up the means of violence. She couldn't think of any form of love that was higher than that. Someone trying to be calm & trying to deal with their inner battles and mess because they want their beloved to be alright. Avni well understood how tough it is to manage the chaos one feels inside of them, and how agonizing it is to pick up all those clutters to make space for something as tender & fragile as love when all you've known is hurt & pain. She knew it because she had her own mess to deal with. Every moment was a struggle on its own and there had been times when she was just one step away from giving it all up. But, she wasn't sure if she could give up on Neil & Isha. That would be a torment that would shatter her sanity and render her burning into the flames of grief and regret.

In her twenty four years of life, she had never believed in the concept of destiny, but meeting Neil had changed that. It is said that one ends up where one is destined to be. And probably that was why she was at the club that night. She was destined with him. Cause if not, there was no other explanation of the stupidest decision she ever took in her life.

Avni stepped out of the car when she heard the gun-shot that came from somewhere around Neil. Her mind had stopped working for a moment but the next moment, it screamed at her to go out and do everything that she can to save that man who had successfully made her whole life revolve around his orbit.

She walked up to where the bloodied men were. Neil was dodging the attacks that the masked men made on him. The snow on the road was now reddening because of the blood that they had shed and the chilly wind seemed a bit too harsh on their cuts.

"Aah, the girlfriend, huh?" - one of the masked men eyed her down as a sick smirk spread across his face and Neil's heart stopped at his words. His worst fear coming alive. "Khanna, quite a nice catch you have there!" - he walked towards Avni however before he could reach her, Neil threw a punch in his gut and he howled back in pain.

N - Avni, I asked you not to step out! - he gritted his teeth as another man punched him on his face and Neil fell on the ground at the impact as his whole focus was on Avni.

A cry of helplessness and pain escaped her when she noticed the blood dripping down the side of his face. And without thinking, she sprinted towards him as she crouched besides him and took him in her arms.

A - Hey, keep your eyes open, please! - she tapped his cheek gently as she caressed his hair. Tears falling down her face in a never-ending cascade.

N - Go back in the car & lock the door, Buttercup! I told you I need you alright. - he gathered all his might & strength to whisper the words out.

A - I am not leaving you! - she finalised.

"Tsk, tsk! so much love! Who would have thought Khanna was capable of love, for all we knew, your emotions only ranged from anger to anger, nah?" - the man laughed as he pointed the gun at Neil and Avni's heart threatened to leap out of her throat.

Avni failed to notice, but Noah's car stopped at a little distance from them as an army of men stepped out of it and walked towards them. She covered Neil's body with hers when the masked man pulled the trigger of the gun in panic when he noticed Neil's men rushing to them, led by Noah. However, before he could stop Rehan's puppet, he had already fired the bullet.

CHAPTER 15

There was a mayhem. From the corner of his eyes, Neil could watch how his men overpowered Rehaan's men and on Noah's order, they shoved them in the car and drove off to their dungeon.

But none of it mattered.

Noah's commands rang through his ears like sirens, piercing through him but he couldn't make out the words that he was uttering. A constant beep of his heart beat echoed in his ears as he sat there in the middle of the road. Holding Avni in his arms. She laid there with her body lying on the snow while her head was in Neil's lap and he was too shocked to even react to any of it. A tear fell from his eye as he watched the blood oozing out of the side of her lower back but she didn't utter a cry. She was still, calm as she always had been. And Neil hated himself. He hated how he wasn't even near to anything that she deserved. He had failed her just like he had failed everybody else who were not even around anymore.

Noah - Neil, are you okay? - he asked as he crouched next to them.

Neil did not answer. Noah had to shake him by his arm to make him look up at him and the look on his face was of such drastic pain and distraught that Noah was suddenly unsure of what to do.

Noah - Neil, she has fainted. We need to get her to the hospital. Please, don't hang on me right now! She needs you, Neil. - he said and the words somehow made sense to Neil once he registered and processed them.

That wasn't the moment to wallow and cry to God why he was being so unfair, it was the time to fight for her.

Neil wiped his tears from the back of his hand as he & Noah carried Avni to Noah's car.

N - Isha is in the car. Please take care of her till I get her to the hospital. - he spoke desperately as he looked at Noah. He knew he could rely on him.

Noah - Don't worry, I'll be with Isha! - he assured and Neil nodded as he started the car.

By the time the engine took off speed, Neil was functioning like a robot. He didn't allow himself to think about what had just happened because he knew that he wouldn't be able to stop himself from breaking down and Avni needed him in that moment. The least he could do for her was to get her to be treated on time.

So swallowing his raging emotions down, he drove to the hospital as fast as he could and made sure that she got treated by the best of doctors. He had signed as family member on the consent form and had posed as her 'boyfriend' though he wasn't sure if he held any authority to do so. He was aware he wasn't entitled to the privilege but he had do what had to be done! To save her. He couldn't compromise that.

Once Avni was taken to the emergency room, it was then that he let the dam break. It felt like standing in a queue and waiting for death to come & knock you down. Cause losing Avni wouldn't be anything less than being dead for all he knew. It felt unjust and unfair how he was left alone to suffer, to pick up the pieces of himself scattered on the ground only to find out that most of them had gone along with the person he just lost.

A chuckle escaped his mouth when a thought surfaced. He could clearly picture Avni in his head, telling him that its going to be okay. That things do get broken in life but they also repair. And then she would tell him that life always rearranges or realigns itself to compensate for the loss.

But in this moment Neil found it impossible to believe any of it. It was impossible to live if he lost her. He dreaded the consequences. He felt exhausted and tired to deal with all those ugly emotions that coursed through every cell of his body.

When the shaking of feet and tapping of fingers and biting of lips did not seem to help much, he resorted to what had now become his new coping mechanism. Neil found himself walking to the prayer room that they had in the hospital and took a corner seat as he prayed for Avni's well-being.

After a hour & a half, he did feel some calm in his heart and made his way to the ER as the operation was supposed to be over by sometime now. He waited for a while before the doctors walked out of the ER and he looked at them expectantly.

Doc - We have taken the bullet out. The patient is out of danger now. Her body is weak because of the blood lost but she'll recover soon! - he assured and Neil could feel himself breathing right.

N - Thankyou so much, Doctor! I shall forever be grateful. - he nodded his head while the doctor patted his shoulder once before leaving the lobby.

It was right that moment when Noah made a presence.

Noah - Hey, is she okay? What did the doctors say? - he asked as he looked at Neil.

N - She is fine. Weak but they say she'll recover soon. - he told while the other man nodded. How is Isha? Did she cry? - he asked, frowning.

Noah - Relax, Neil. She is fine. I took her home. She did ask about you & some Buttercup a few times but calmed down when I told her that you've some urgent work to attend to. We ate dinner and to distract her I put a movie on. She slept halfway through it & Bryer is at home with her now. She'll be alright. - he told and Neil visibly relaxed.

Noah had always been a brother since they were kids. And after the death of Neil's family, he & his wife, Bryer had always been there for him & Isha. There were times when Neil didn't know how to go around with things and it was in those times of need that they were with him. True friends indeed.

Noah - Bro, at least get your wounds treated. And go home, take a shower and some rest. I'll be here till then. You come back after sometime when we can get her discharged? - he suggested.

Neil was about to deny but then gave up. Noah was correct anyway, he needed energy to take care of Avni once they took her home, so with that thought in mind, he simply obliged and headed home to freshen up.

By the next afternoon, Neil had arranged a room completely ready for Avni and a 24x7 nurse to cater to her along with all the other equipments that were needed. She was still unconscious as the doctors had put her on sedatives but the progress was commendable. They got her discharged by early evening and Noah and Bryer brought Isha to Khanna Mansion as Neil had asked them to.

They had dinner together and Neil asked Bryer to stay back with Isha as he & Noah took care of work. Bryer was aware of what work it was supposed to be and thus she didn't ask much questions in front of Isha.

Once he was sure that everything was settled back at home, he & Noah drove to the dungeon where they had kept the men who had attacked them. The anger & tension dissipating off Neil was quite obvious and evident and he made no efforts to hide it.

The inner beast who Neil thought he had learned how to tame reared its head back the moment he entered the dungeon. The dark underground walls made him sick to the stomach but the ugly monster inside of him fed on it. He needed to take it out. Noah was well aware that there was no point holding him back at that moment because he wouldn't listen. So, he quietly followed Neil inside when he grabbed the man who had shot Avni by his collar and threw him to the ground with a punch on his face. The sick man groaned in pain but laughed the next moment.

Neil held him up as he landed a punch in his gut and he collided with the wall behind. In that moment, anyone who saw Neil couldn't identify him, the fury in his eyes promised ruin and that rage was the only emotion that his eyes reflected in that particular moment.

Noah knew that it was a result of the fear that he had felt for Avni & Isha in the last few days but reason told him to stop his friend before he did something he'd regret. Neil went on a frenzy when he pounded punches on punches on the man's face while he bled non-stop. Neil welcomed the pain that greeted him when he hit him initially but eventually, his hand had become numb and he had stopped feeling the pain there. The only one he felt was the one in his heart. The pain of seeing Avni in pain. The pain of being so weak that he had to hide his own niece at his friend's place.

The sick monster inside Neil felt cathartic on seeing the man at his mercy. The blood that trickled down his face soothed his insides, and the knowledge that he could take his life by just one twist of his wrist, or by just pulling the trigger of the gun lying besides him felt godly.

Prakash's son Neil, and his sister's little brother Neil felt horrible at who he had become, but he couldn't seem to care when it came to Isha & Avni. He was minutes away from killing the man with his own hands when Noah walked up to him and attempted to stop him.

Noah - Neil, that's enough! Stop it now. - he mumbled as he tried to snatch him off the man's throat.

N - Don't get in between, Noah! I'm going to kill him today! - Neil was beyond reason at that point.

Noah - No, you're not. You're not going to do any of it. We're going to turn him in to the cops and they're going to take care of it. Stop now! - he pulled Neil back while the shooter slid down the wall as blood sputtered out his mouth in between some coughs.

N - You think cops would give him a death this surreal! - his eyes held the same rage as they did a while ago. Noah had to think of something to calm him down. They didn't need any more blood on them.

Noah - Bryer called, Avni has regained consciousness. We need to head home. - he said and Neil turned his head from the man to him and his eyes softened. Noah wanted to laugh at how whacked he was in love. But what did he hold? He himself was as whipped for his wife.

N - You're lucky she woke up! - Neil gave one last kick to the man, making him cough more blood out before he walked out of the dungeon.

Noah heaved in a deep breathe as he instructed their men to take care of Rehaan's men before he followed Neil out.

Neil slid into the passenger seat as he took his blazer off and folded his sleeves up till his elbow. He leaned against the seat and his eyes closed in exhaustion while Noah drove quietly.

Noah - Bryer didn't call, I lied to you about her regaining consciousness! - he told after some time of silence. He was aware Neil was going to throw a fit now.

N - Fucktard, stop getting on my nerves! - he groaned in annoyance as he turned to look at him.

Noah - Oh yeah? Then stop being a bitch, Khanna! - he argued back lamely. You promised her that you won't do any of it again, didn't you? So, if anything, stop being an asshole and thank me for saving your dumb ass! - Neil simply rolled his eyes at his best-friend's smug glory.

N - Thank you, my ass! Stupid birdshit! - he mumbled as he closed his eyes again.

Noah - At least better than you, stinking horseshit! - he was just trying to take Neil's mind off things now. This was their way of lightening each others' mood.

N - I'm gonna ask Bryer to divorce you!

Noah - I'm gonna ask Avni to dump you!

N - We're not even together, bitch!

Noah - That's because you're such a pus- Hang on! Bryer is calling. - he put his bluetooth on as he answered the call.

Neil watched him while Noah listened to his wife like a dutiful husband. If you asked him a few days ago, Neil would have laughed at how whipped he was for Bryer, but now, he was jealous of it. He wanted something like that too. A sigh escaped him.

N - What did she say? - he asked once Noah disconnected the call.

Noah - Well, Bitch! My wife tells me that your girl has woken up! She is asking for you! - he told, clearly emphasizing the wife part and as much as Neil wanted to throw a punch at him, he was too relieved to hear that Avni was getting better. And that's why, ladies & gentlemen, yours truly let his very annoying bestfriend go without a scratch on his face.

Reaching home, Neil walked to his room as he took a quick shower because he very well knew that Avni would ask a thousand lot questions if she saw him splashed with blood like that.

Bryer gave him a small smile as he entered the room where Avni was and Isha was sleeping besides her.

B - You're just a tad-bit late. She slept out of drowsiness. But I think she'll wake up soon. You wanna be beside her when she wakes up? - she asked while Neil simply nodded.

N - Bry, thankyou so much! - he gave a small smile.

B - Save it, buddy! I'm gonna go see my husband and you take care of your girls, okay? - she grinned then and Neil felt his ears turning red.

N - Good night, Bry! - he ushered her out while she laughed.

Now that he was sure that Avni was okay and was responding to the treatment well and that Isha was safe and here, with him, he could think clearly. Agreed the session of beating the shit out of that man helped him take some anguish out but he was thankful that Noah stopped him when he did.

It was in the heat of the moment that he knocked his sense of right & wrong off the window and behaved so animalistic, but now that the fog had cleared, he never wanted to do that again. Sitting in his house, in front of his two girls, as Bryer put it, he couldn't help but feel that this was what he wanted. A normal life. Basic. Get up in the morning, argue over coffee with Avni, help her do laundry to make up for the fight, run after Isha as he chased her around the house, take her out for park-dates, go to dinners with Avni, take Isha out for ice-creams. This was what he wanted. So much.

And he was going to work for it. Whatever it took. He had already started working on his new business project and now the only hurdle was Rehaan Qureshi, who he knew wouldn't stop budging him at every step he took. But for now, he'll have to settle at playing defensive at his attacks and that was how he was going to go around things.

He didn't realise but it was almost midnight and he was still sitting besides Avni on the bed while waiting for her to wake up so that he could hear her voice. He leaned forward as he placed a kiss on Isha's forehead and then one on Avni's.

Neil intwined their hands as he kissed the back of her hand and brushed some of her hair back. He had been on edge at every moment the last two days and now, with her, all the emotions were flowing back & forth at an intensity that scared him. Neil felt his eyes stinging as they teared up when he watched her.

Avni's eye lids squinted as she fluttered them open and looked around. The warmth that she felt in her hand told her that Neil was around and a small smile graced her face when she found him sitting right besides her.

A - Hi! - she said.

Chapter 16

A - Hi! - she said as she smiled a little despite the pain.

N - Hey! - his throat clogged as an acrid taste filled his mouth and saltiness filled his eyes.

Neil bit on his mouth as he tried to blink back the tears that threatened to fall out of her eyes.

A - It wasn't your fault, Neil. - she said as she tried to sit up.

However, Neil didn't let her as he shook his head and gestured her to rest. Avni sighed when she noticed the bags underneath his eyes and the cuts he had on his hands and at the side of his face.

N - Wasn't it really? - he chuckled humourlessly as a tear slipped down his cheek. You must think of me as such a pathetic jerk and good for nothing. Couldn't even save you in a fight. - he laughed as more tears oozed out of his eyes. You'd be right in thinking so. I really am such - he swirled his tongue around his dry lips as his throat clogged and it became difficult to speak. such a good for nothing fool who claims himself as dangerous and all! You must laugh at me. - he looked away. Couldn't keep any of my promises! - he mumbled as his eyes reflected the pain he felt inside of him. They looked lifeless.

A - Neither do I think that you're a coward, nor am I going to let you torment yourself like this. It wasn't even your fault to begin with. It was me who stepped out of the car when you clearly asked me not to. They wouldn't have even known that I or Isha were there by the time your men arrived. So, it was just a bit of bad luck & none of it was because of you, Neil! - she spoke as she leaned her back against the pillow to look at him.

N - I'm so sorry you had to go through all this! - he whispered as he met her eyes but she had a small smile on her face.

A - You don't have to be sorry, you know! Just give me a smile and it will be alright. - she said making him chuckle with his glassy eyes.

N - You know, when you were in the ER, I had some time to myself. Everything that happened was an indication to let you go. That you deserve better. - he said and Avni felt her heart beat in fear. And Avni, if I had been slightly nicer, I would have let you go. But I am not, and I can't let you go. Not after what you did for me. I'll spend the whole of my life serving you, but I can't watch you leave, Buttercup! - he said, kissing the back of her hand as his tears fell on her hand and Avni smiled through her glassy eyes.

A - You don't have to, Mr. Khanna! I plan to stay. - she chuckled as she wiped his tears.

N - I'm sorry I got your frames broken, we can go get you new ones once you are well! - he said as he noticed that she wasn't wearing her glasses.

A - That's okay! - she said as she gave him a small smile.

N - Try & get some rest. Your body needs it. - he said as he helped her lie down properly on the bed and adjusted her pillows.

A - So do you! The bed has enough space, why don't you sleep in here? - she asked and he found himself smiling.

After covering her up with the blanket, Neil walked around the bed as he lied besides Isha and let sleep take over. His heart felt at peace.

So it really wasn't about the place, but the person! Hambledon, or London, Neil's peace was where Isha & Avni were.

A week passed with Neil taking care of Avni & Isha, and Khanna Mansion felt like any other domestic household after two long years. In the mornings, Neil would bring breakfast in bed for Avni and feed her with his own hands while she adored him doing so, then he would go wake Isha up, get her ready for the day and feed her breakfast. By the time he would be done eating his own, Avni & Isha would start with their lessons. In the meantime, he would supervise the staff to prepare lunch for Avni as per the chart advised by the doctors and he & Isha would eat whatever Isha felt like eating. The girls used to nap in the afternoon and that was the time Neil got to work in his home office. By the time evening rolled by, they spent some time together, mostly in the garden as Avni went for a walk and Isha used to play around. That had become Neil's favourite part of the day. Dinner used to be fun with Isha reciting her poems and Neil & Avni cheering up for her. Then Neil used to put Isha to sleep and move back to Avni's. Sometimes they talked, sometimes things got steamy, and sometimes they just used to lounge in each others' presence in silence.

Neil had even handed Rehaan's men over to the cops to take over. So far now, they had not mentioned Rehaan and the cops were still gathering evidence, but Neil had stopped putting too much thought into it.

Avni's wound had healed and there was no chronic pain as such that she felt around the injury but Neil was being extra cautious about everything. Avni was appalled at how he had outrightly denied touching her as they always ended up getting down to do dirty and he didn't want to strain her back.

But amongst it all, the last week had been pure bliss to the both of them. And it felt natural and right, neither of them questioned it anymore, they were going with the flow. Taking each day as it came.

It was Monday night, reminding Avni that a whole week had passed since she had been discharged. She was scrolling on her phone when Neil stepped in and she found herself smiling at him.

Why in the caramel mocha cupcakes was he so gorgeous? The guy personified charisma!

Avni wanted to swoon when he walked up to her and placed a soft kiss on her forehead, making her smile in delight.

A - Did Isha sleep? - she asked as she looked up at him.

N - Hm! - he answered as he settled on the bed, definitely exhausted after a long day.

A - Tired? - she chuckled.

N - Yeah, a bit! - she smiled back as he turned to look at her while leaning against the headboard. Come here, Buttercup! - his voice was soft but Avni knew it was a command.

Biting on the insides of her mouth, she scooted close to him as she settled in between his legs, her back pressing against his chest.

N - You look so beautiful today! - he nuzzled his nose in the crook of her neck and his stubble tickled her making her hum in pleasure. Avni? - he called.

A - Yeah? - she answered as she leaned on his chest.

N - Can I ask you something? - she didn't fail notice the audible hesitation in his voice.

A - Yes, Neil! What is it? - she encouraged and felt him taking in a deep breathe as he contemplated how to frame the question he wanted to ask.

N - Remember you told me that you had been shot when you were a kid. Can I- I mean, only if you're comfortable, can I ask how & why that happened? - he spoke finally, cautious and careful, not wanting to hurt her.

A - It was in the past Neil! How does it matter! - she chuckled in an attempt to lighten the sudden shift in the air.

N - I wouldn't have asked if it didn't matter, Avni. You said that you are afraid of gunshots and that was why I just wanted to ask, may be speaking about it would help you let it out. But, its okay if you don't want to talk about it. How about we watch a movie? - he then said, trying to comfort her and Avni sighed.

Of course, it mattered. It definitely mattered when she still used to get nightmares about that particular day till recently. And it was only fair that he knew about it because the nightmares had stopped since she met him. Now all she dreamed about was him!

N - I'm sorry. I didn't mean to upset you. I was just- - he was saying when she was silent for a minute but she didn't let him complete.

A - Neil, relax! It's alright. - she wrapped his arms around her stomach as she put her head on his shoulder. There was a stretch of silence between them before Avni finally spoke and Neil listened to her with all his attention. My parents married against their families' will. My father was a Hindu & my mother was a Muslim. They had met in college and fallen in love during that time. Both of their families were quite orthodox and didn't allow the marriage, - she sighed. so they ran away. After getting married they came to London. Life was good for them here & then I happened. We were a happy little family. - she said as she bit on her lips to stop herself from crying. Neil tightened his hold around her as he rubbed her arms in gentle motions. I remember Papa used to get me candy-floss everyday when he returned from work. Maa used to get mad and scold Papa that he would end up spoiling me. - an inadvertent smile spread on her lips. But I & Papa used to laugh at that secretly. Everything was really good you know, we used to go on picnics, vacations and I remember I loved going to school & everything. But then, one day Papa didn't come back home from office. - she gulped, a tear fell from her eye and Neil had this urge to take all her pain away. Maa was very scared and called up all his friends & colleagues but we couldn't find him. I remember, I didn't sleep that night at all. I was sitting in Maa's lap the whole time, asking her when Papa would come back. - she closed her eyes, that dark night still haunting her. The next day, it was around six in the morning that we heard some noises from the balcony and before I could understand what was happening, Maa was already carrying me and running out of the house from the back door. We ran a lot, Maa had not even put on any slippers. She was running barefeet on the cold deserted roads as she carried me in her arms but we couldn't make it far. - she choked on her words as her throat clogged. Maa was pregnant at that time. They caught on to us and grabbed her by her hair. - her nails dug into Neil's hands as she held them. Neil, she was crying and yelling in pain but those men didn't show any mercy. They dragged my Maa in a car and when I ran after her they - they shot me. In my stomach. - she was weeping now. Couldn't stop the tears anymore. The ten years old girl couldn't make sense of what was happening, but the twenty four years old Avni knew that that day, her life was snatched away from her. I thought it was my time to go back to God. But unfortunately, I survived. A kind lady picked me up from there and admitted to the hospital. Mrs. Neela Parekh. - she wiped her tears as Neil held her close. When I regained consciousness, I requested her to get to my house. I was around ten at that time, so I knew about addresses and everything. Papa worked at a software developing company. I gave her all those details. When we reached my house, the whole house was a clutter and the dead bodies of my parents were lying there. Rotten and - and disfigured. - she closed her eyes shut when the pain became unbearable and Neil's own heart hurt at her agony.

However, he did not say anything, he wasn't sure if she wanted him to talk or to give her some space. So, he just held her close in his arms as he turned her around and she willingly sat in his lap, wrapping her arms around his torso.

N - How did you manage everything? - he stroked her hair gently.

A - The lady who saved me, she adopted me. - she sniffed but was much calmer now. She is the mother whose birthday you celebrated in Hambledon. My Neela Maa! The only family I was left with. - she looked up at him and Neil kissed her forehead, she closed her eyes to feel him.

N - Was it your grandparents? They killed your parents? - he then asked, unable to stop himself. He wanted to put those people in their place who made her go through so much pain.

A - I don't know! - she whispered as she put her head against his chest.

N - Do you want me look into it? - he needed to know. Cause if she wanted him to, he would set the world on fire to see her happy.

A - No, Neil! I..I don't want to dig up those things again! - she spoke against his chest, pressing herself closer to him as she wafted in his smell.

N - That's okay. - he massaged her head. I understand. - I did understand. The ghosts of the pasts were too cruel & nasty. Some thrived on burning them alive, while some buried them in the past, right where they belonged. And as much as he wanted to avenge those who made her suffer, he was proud of how graceful and strong of a woman she was to seek her closer without revenge and to move on with life!

A - Thanks! - she kissed his arm as her fingers played with his.

N - Can I see the mark? - he asked, making Avni look up at him.

Avni watched how his eyes only held care & gentleness, she couldn't find any trace of pity for the poor little girl that people took her to be. No, Neil looked at her like she was one of the most precious things that he had ever come across.

Avni found herself nodding as she lifted her midi a little up so that he could see the mark that was there at the side of her waistline. Neil only looked away from her face when she gestured him to. His fingers slowly traced the scar and no ointment had soothed her so well, as his touch did. He bent down as he kissed the skin softly, peppered light feathery kisses that made her belly flutter.

N - I'm so proud of you. - he kissed her forehead. You're one of the strongest people I've ever come across, Avni. - he told her as he held her face in his hands. And you know what the best part is, you don't let whatever happened to you mess with the zeal to live that you possess. You refuse to give up on life. I can't even imagine how much strength does it take to deal with something like that so gracefully as you have! - he said sincerely, making her smile as her eyes turned glassy again. Not out of pain though this time around.

She blinked her tears back as she hugged him and he embraced her in his arms, putting light kisses at the top of her head.

A - Neil? - she called.

N - Yes?

A - Tell me something funny! - she looked up at him, the air had become too gloomy all of a sudden and she wanted out.

Neil looked amused at her demand but thought about something nonetheless. Avni pressed a quick kiss on his throat when he was still churning the wheels of his brain to come up with something funny.

N - Um, you remember that portrait that we have in the house library back in Hambledon? - he asked and she nodded. Isha was a bit cranky that day and we had taken the photograph in such haste that my sister hadn't made her wear any diaper or something. So, what happened was, Isha peed on me right after we had taken that photo! Dad, Didi & Jiju were laughing like maniacs while I & Isha were going crazy. - he told and Avni couldn't stop herself from laughing out loud. What in the pan-fried momos!

A - That is just so cute! - she placed an open mouth kiss on his cheeks while still giggling at the anecdote. And absolutely hysterical! Oh my god, you turning pink, Mr. Khanna! - she kissed both of his cheeks.

N - I love that little girl, Avni! - he smiled. You know how people always talk about the kind of love that they'll die for, what I feel for Isha is the kind of love that I'll live for her. And trust me, I hated living at that point of time. - his eyes looked distant, but full of love and life. He was probably thinking about his little princess.

A - I know, Neil. - she gave him a smile. I'm sure you already know but she loves you just as much. She keeps looking for you all the time. - she said and he looked back at her, a small smile on his face.

He pressed a kiss on her nose as he took in a deep breathe and pulled her closer, placing his chin in the crook of her neck.

A - Have you ever thought of adopting her? As in legally? - she then asked.

N - I mean I do want to be her father but I don't know if I should do it. - he had a thoughtful expression on his face. His eyes held confusion and his heart felt twisted. I don't want to keep her from her parents' identity, neither do I want my sister to be disappointed in me. I don't know what would be the right thing to do! - he bit on his lips as his eyes closed and he pressed his head on her shoulder, seeking comfort that only she seemed to provide.

People say that men shouldn't feel too much, or that they shouldn't be emotional. They say this is something what women are supposed to do. But Avni loved how Neil didn't shy away from showing his vulnerability and his struggles.

He was aware that he had his issues and he was willing to work on them. And the fact that he always thought over twice before every step & every decision that he took for Isha was just so beautiful. The man wanted to give the whole world to his little girl. She loved how selflessly he loved Isha.

A - How about you let her decide? Of course, she is too young to understand all this right now, but you know, when the time is right, may be you can have a conversation with her? - she suggested, brushing her hand up his back in an attempt to soothe him.

N - Yeah! - he sighed. I think I'm just gonna do that! I just want her to be happy. That's all that matters, honestly. I hope & pray that Dad & Didi would show me the right path! - he whispered to himself as he placed a kiss on Avni's shoulder.

She closed her eyes shut as she felt his touch linger on her skin. There was something so surreal in his presence that Avni felt her heart soothed.

She had always found it hard to open up to people about her childhood and the past about her parents, but with Neil, it felt like a conversation with self. And she felt so light once it was out. She was so grateful for the fact that he didn't stretch the topic too much and keep on talking about it because he understood that she wasn't comfortable talking about it. No complaints or demands, just simple understanding. He didn't make it an issue of his ego that why was she not talking about something so significant when he had literally given her all the details of his past. He simply understood that her past was something that she found difficult to talk about and he it let it be. He let her be.

The comforting silences with him, his unjudging eyes gave her the space that she needed, but the concern in his eyes and his soft smiles made sure that she knew that he wanted her, that he was there for her. Every time she would ask for him.

He made her believe that she wasn't alone. That she would find him standing besides her every time she would feel like putting her head on someone's shoulder for mourning, or every time she would feel like hugging someone for celebrating.

In that moment, lying in his arms, she knew that Neil Khanna, whenever he would love someone, he would love them with all his might & heart. A love like that of her parents'. They lived together & they died together! She wanted a love like that.

With that thought in the background & with all things Neil in mind, she let sleep take over.

Chapter 17

Avni woke up to a hefty breakfast as she found Neil drawing the curtains of her room, well the guest room, but Neil called it hers.

N - Good morning! - he smiled as he walked towards the bed.

Avni smiled as she watched him. Her sleepy eyes twinkling at his sight.

N - What? - he chuckled as he kissed her forehead. Why are you looking at me like that? - he asked as he sat next to her and passed her a cup of coffee.

A - When we had initially met, I would have laughed at the idea of you bringing me breakfast in bed. - she took a sip from her mug.

N - Well, what can I say, you swept me off the floor, Buttercup! - he teased as his hand wrapped around her thigh.

Avni rolled her eyes at his smug face but couldn't stop herself from smiling. Her heart fluttered at how sweet he was to her. Sometimes, she wished she knew the boy who he was two years ago, just the glimpses weren't enough. She needed more of him. All the time.

N - I've to go to office today. Have some work. Will you manage with Isha at home, or I can take her with me? - he asked as he passed the food to her.

A - No, we're good. Its been quite a long time since I've gone outdoors anyways. I guess we'll have our girls day, you can miss us, Mr. Khanna. Thankyou! - she fluttered her eyelashes dramatically, making him chuckle.

N - Um, I'm afraid I might not miss you! Sophia would be coming to London, actually! So, we might catch up! - he bit back a smile as Avni's eyes widened in shock.

A - Excuse me, you'll what? - she narrowed her eyes and Neil burst out laughing.

N - C'mon, we're friends. Friends do hang out together, Buttercup! - he spoke innocently.

A - What even! - she snorted. That girl eyed you like you're some juicy loaded sausage! And you say you want to hang out with her? - she was appalled.

N - But I am a juicy loaded sausage. Now, ain't I? - he winked notoriously.

A - You know what, go ahead! Have fun. I might invite my really close friend Adrien so we can hang out together! - she spoke haughtily as she munched on the toast.

However, a shriek escaped her throat when Neil grasped her thigh and pulled her on his lap.

N - You sure about that, Buttercup? - he whispered as his hand trailed down her arms, making her squirm on his lap.

A - You're not meeting Sophia! - she demanded against his lips as her hands wrung around his neck.

N - Is that an order? - he husked back.

A - Yes, Mr. Khanna! - she kissed his jaw.

N - What incentive do I get? - his hands caressed her waist, sliding under her night-midi dress.

A - What incentive do you want? - she bit on his earlobe, feeling a bit too bold in that moment. She could feel his firmness under her.

N - Pch! I bet you're too vanilla to reward me with what I want! - he teased, his hand snaking up to her soaked undies.

A - Is that a challenge, Mr. Khanna? - she jerked when his pressed the back of his hand against her clit from above the fabric of her undies. However, Avni held her ground strong, she pushed herself around his crotch making him groan at the friction.

N - What? - his mouth was just an inch above hers. Tell me will you let me do you dirty, Buttercup? - he spoke against her mouth as his hot breath tingled her skin and her core throbbed with want.

A - Promise me you'll render me breathless! - she pressed his hand against her warmth from above her dress and a smug smirk lifted his lips up. She could feel the ghost of it on her mouth.

N - Oh, I intent to give you fireworks, Buttercup! - he bit on her lower lip at the same time he tapped his fingers on her clit. I'll make your legs shiver, and your whole body will tremble with my name & my marks itched on every inch of skin. I promise I'll make sure you don't walk straight for the next few days! - his thumb pinched her clit making her gasp in pleasure induced pain.

Neil slowly let her lie down on the bed, making sure he doesn't hurt her back anyway in the process and his mouth never left hers as they fought for dominance.

He turned Avni around so that her chest pressed into the soft bed and a gasp left her mouth due to his sudden move. Neil pressed his crotch against her core as he leaned on her with both his knees on either of her sides.

He moved his hips against hers as he leaned down to place open mouthed kisses on the back of her neck. His hands wrapped her long hair around his fist while the other hand slid down the strap of her dress when he pressed deep kisses at her shoulders. The sloppy sounds of Neil's kisses and Avni's content hums filled the room as she held on to the bed stand to match his thrusts. Neil pulled back a little to run his hands down her body, descending from her back to her waist and then to her ass. Tugging at the sides of her undies, he pulled them off her in a swift motion before aligning his body with hers again. Avni moaned when the fabric of his jeans pressed against her soft skin, the zip of his pants pressing against her sensitive core as she felt his hardness through his clothes.

Neil rubbed his calloused hands against her skin as he kneaded the supple flesh of her ass cheeks, thus eliciting a moan from Avni. He then moved down on her body, pressing languid kisses all his way down to her inner thighs while Avni was left to be just a moaning mess as she pressed the side of her cheek into the pillow and let him pleasure her the way he wanted to.

He was at the edge of the bed now, cupping his clothed cock with Avni's feet, he bent forward to kiss her thighs, and then moved to her wet entrance. Her toes curled around his hardness when she turned her head to have a look at him. Her whole body shivered as he kissed and sucked on her wetness, just the perfect pressure and the warmth of his mouth setting every nerve on fire. Avni's feet moved on their own as she rubbed his already hard cock beneath his thick jeans.

Cursing, Neil pulled back as he looked up at her face. Innocent eyes hazy with seduction and want. He groaned as she turned around and pressed her hips into the mattress, baring her cameltoe to him. Sliding his hands up her legs, he bent them as he leaned down and put her foot on his shoulder while spreading her other leg as Avni watched him. He looked up at her as he licked her slit and their eyes met. Neil's grip on her thigh tightened as he slid his tongue up her slit before pressing a gentle kiss on her lips down there and Avni squirmed. She threw her head back as her foot slid down from his shoulder to his back when he began feasting on her.

Neil kissed her sensitive nub before sucking on it and nibbling in between while she whimpered under him. Her hands caught his hair as she pressed his mouth against herself while their eyes still refused to leave each other. His tongue mercilessly flicked her swollen clit as the hair of his stubble tingled Avni simultaneously, only heightening her sensitivity and pleasure. Tears pooled at the corner of her eyes as the pleasure became overwhelming when he thrust his tongue inside her and lapped up her heated flesh. She clenched her thighs around his neck as his face dug into her dripping core while he thrusted in and out of her in a maddening speed.

A - Neil, I'm -I'm so close! - she moaned, quivering under him.

N - Yeah? Come for me, Buttercup. Let me taste your sweetness! - he spoke against her clit and the vibration of his husky voice against her sensitive flesh along with the frantic movements of his mouth had her explode as she squirted on him.

Neil held her tightly as her whole body shook with pleasure and she panted for breathe. He licked her clean before leaning forward and capturing her mouth in a fierce kiss. It started off slow, then turned into a battle for dominance which Avni refused to give up on as Neil devoured her mouth, she returned the favour with as much fervour. Her shaky hands roamed around his back as she dug her nails in his skin while he sucked on her lips. He then trailed wet kisses on her jawline before proceeding to give her hickies on her neck while all Avni could manage to do was to let out moans of pleasure under his mercy.

There were layers of marks across her collar bone and chest by the time he reached her breasts and pushed her dress down her body, then came off her last layer of clothing with his skillful hands and Neil teased her sensitive buds as he circled his tongue around them both in slow circular motions. Avni's back arched towards his mouth but he refused to give her the pleasure she was whimpering for. Frustrated, Avni grasped his hair in her fists as she guided his mouth towards her pebbled bud and Neil finally gave her some relief as he wrapped his mouth around her luscious soft mounds and sucked on them.

An unhinged cry of contentment escaped her throat when he fondled with one breast while fervently sucked on the another, making her dive into pools of pleasure.

A - This feels so good! - she mumbled in between a moan as she ran her fingers through his hair while he pinched her hardened bud, biting the another one simultaneously.

N - Your body was custom made for me, Buttercup. Just so perfect! - he whispered in her ear as he fondled both her breasts making her come again due to the stimulation.

Neil then descended down her abdomen as he placed kisses on her soft skin, giving her tingles from the licks & swirls of his tongue and earning himself breathy moans from her when he bit on her delicate skin.

A - Neil? - she called when he swirled his tongue around her navel, making her belly shiver.

N - Yes? - he mumbled, looking up at her.

A - I want you. Inside me. - the voice was just above a whisper and Neil's cock throbbed at the demand.

N - Buttercup, are you sure you're ready? We can stop if you want me to! - he tested, needed to be sure because he didn't want her to regret whatever happened between them.

A - I am sure! - she gave him a smile as she blinked her eyes.

N - Come here. - he asked as he watched her.

Her dripping core clenched at the command. Avni took in a deep breathe before sitting up and moving to him as she sat on her knees right in front of him. Neil brushed her hair away from her face as he fisted them in his palm before giving it a gentle tug, making her look up at him.

N - Once I enter you, I'll make sure you don't walk straight for days at least. Do you think you could handle that? - he rasped as he kissed her jaw, descending down to her throat.

A - Ye-yes! - her breathe hitched at the thought.

N - Take my jeans off. - he said, pulling back.

She bit on her lower lip as her shaky hands moved down to the waistband of his jeans. Bending down, she kissed his hardness from above his pants as her hands fumbled with his button.

N - Fuck Buttercup! Such a tease! - she blinked her eyes innocently.

A - I don't understand? - she hid a smirk when he gave her hair a hard tug, making her hiss in pain.

She then unbuttoned his pants before pulling the fabric off his strong legs in a swift motion and crawled back in between his legs as she finally looked down at his crotch. Her chest heaved as she took in a sharp breath and her throat worked on a swallow when she registered his size.

N - Hey, it's alright. We can still stop if you're not comfortable! - he spoke softly.

A - No, its not that. Uh, do you think that will fit? - she heard herself asking, making Neil chuckle as she turned red.

N - Trust me, we'll fit perfectly well. Was made for you, Buttercup! And I wasn't lying when I said that you won't be able to walk straight. - he kissed her playfully.

A - Can I ho-hold it? - she asked as she blinked her eyes while he simply nodded.

Taking in a deep breath, she wrapped her delicate fingers around him as she swirled her thumb around his head. Neil groaned when she put her other hand on his thigh and leaned forward comfortably to stroke him in gentle motions. His grip on her hair tightened when she started moving her fist up and down his huge girth, fascinated how he twitched in her hand.

A - Do..do you think you'd like to..um, help me pleasure you? I, I've never-

And before she could complete the sentence, his mouth captured hers in a dominating kiss as he wrapped his hand around hers around his hard shaft. Neil guided her hand up his length and then moved it down in hard strokes as he continued kissing her softly. As she learnt the momentum and gained some confidence with his increasing groans, she started massaging him at her own pace and circled the pad of her thumb at the top of his head as she gave him wet open mouthed kisses on his jaw.

N - Fuck! This is the closest to heaven I'll ever get! - his voice was a guttural rasp.

A - Can you not swear, please? - she frowned. Isha picks up every word very fast! - she blinked and suddenly Neil was stupefied.

N - Are you for real? - he asked, the orgasm already waving away at the mention of his niece & she frowned more.

A - Uh, am I doing it wrong? - she blinked her eyes, referring to her hands around his cock.

N - God, Avni! You'll be the death of me! - he grumbled as he pulled her to his lap and pressed urgent kisses on her mouth.

Avni was quick to respond. Her hands kept massaging him, eliciting some more curses and groans from him in between the kiss and Avni made a mental note to work on his cursing thing.

N - I need to be inside you! - he whispered and Avni's core throbbed.

When she nodded at him, he made her lie down on her back as he slowly hovered over her, kissing her forehead while she kissed his shoulders. Neil placed his cock at her hardened clit as he moved it along her, flicking her bundle of nerves as Avni whimpered at how pleasurable it felt. A sigh left her mouth as her eyes drooped close.

Neil brushed the hair away from her face as he held her face in his hands while he brushed his tip at the entrance of her slit. Her legs trembled when he pushed the head of his cock inside her. Avni bit on his shoulder to stop herself from screaming and Neil invited the pain. Inch by inch, he slid inside of her, making her moan his name in delight. He remained still for a moment till the lines on Avni's forehead smoothened and she gestured him to move.

Neil gave her a few slow thrust, feeling the way her tiny muscles fluttered around him and the way her folds clenched him. In that moment, he could claim that he had felt heaven even without having been there. She felt heaven. Sweet, beautiful and godly.

Avni's hands rested on his cheeks as she pulled him closer while her mouth parted in a moan. Their lips hovered over each others', breathing & sighing & moaning & groaning in each other as they made love. Her toes curled when he picked up speed and drove her to the heights of both her sensitivity and sanity and the whole room was filled with their moans. The cool morning breeze entering the room through the window tickled them and the rustle of the blanket beneath them was soft to their ears.

Neil slipped his hands in hers and intwined their fingers together when he put her hands at either sides of her head. With every passing moment, his thrust grew harder, faster, rougher and Avni could feel them in her soul. Holding her hands captive in one hand above her head, Neil placed his other hand at her lower abdomen as he felt himself moving inside her.

N - You feel this, Buttercup? Me fitting so perfectly inside of you? - his voice was hoarse & strained and Avni was too deep in pleasure to put his words together and make sense out of them.

A - I feel so full, Neil. So surreal. You feel like a part of me! - she breathed out.

N - A piece of some puzzle that becomes such an integral part of your existence that you forget it is somebody else's! - he pressed a kiss on her forehead.

A - Just that. You're that piece to me! - & her orgasm hit her right at moment.

An animalistic moan escaped her as the knots in her stomach finally let loose and her whole body shook at the impact of her high while Neil still pumped her, overstimulating her clit with his thumb. He came shortly after her as a shot of raw beastly pleasure spread in his insides and his body felt like livewires of pleasure and satisfaction.

Avni kept peppering kisses on his forehead and the rest of his face when he rode his orgasm.

N - That felt so-

A - Ethereal! - she finished, pulling an effortless smile on his face.

N - This might as well become my favourite morning routine! - he chuckled, pressing a kiss on her cheek.

A - What is the time? - she suddenly asked when she registered his words.

N - What? - he frowned when he looked up at her.

A - What is the time, Neil? We need to go see Isha. She might have woken up! - she said and Neil could swear he felt his heart flutter.

For some reason, he was so grateful that these girls were so attached to each other and looked forward to spending time in each others' company.

N - I'll go take a quick shower & then get her ready for the day. You clean up as well, okay? - he kissed her forehead when she nodded.

The rest of the day passed in a blur for the both of them. Avni spent her time with Isha while Neil had a lot to catch up on work. Even though he was kept updated & worked from home, he still had to look over a lot in the various verticals of his business industries.

He made it home around dinner time only to find Isha & Avni waiting for him in the drawing room. Isha ran up to him as she saw him entering.

I - N-man, see I look like a ballerina! - she exclaimed as she twirled in her little ballerina outfit. Buttercup taught me dance! - she giggled when Neil held her up in his arms.

N - You look so beautiful, Ishi! - he kissed her cheeks. Can I see your dance? - he asked and she grinned as she exclaimed in affirmative.

I - But we eat food first? I am hungry and Peppa is hungry too! - she pointed to her Peppa pig plushie, making Neil chuckle.

N - Yes, Baby! Mama is hungry too. C'mon, let's eat. - he said as he walked inside with her in his arms.

Avni sat besides Isha as she fed her the mac n' cheese slowly, asking her to chew properly. Neil smiled as he watched them.

Once they were done with dinner, Neil cradled Isha in his lap while Avni sang her a lullaby and soon, she had fallen asleep.

It was only when Neil was sure that she was in deep slumber that he made her lie on the bed and covered her with the blanket while Avni slowly thumped her before pressing a kiss on her forehead.

A - She looks so precious. - she whispered as she brushed some of her hair back, just like a mother would do. I love her, my sweet little baby! - she said.

And in that moment, Neil knew that he was in love. Yes, he was still afraid that he might end up becoming someone like his mother, he was still afraid of getting his heart broken again, but he wasn't going to let his fears overpower the amount of love he held for this woman who was sitting next to him. In his bed, caressing his niece as she patched his heart up with a piece of her own.

He was so in love!

Chapter 18

Neil woke up to a complete checklist of things that he needed to get done by the end of the day. His secretary had mailed him all the details and he was sure that it was going to be a long day at work. After getting dressed up for the day, he quickly stepped into Isha's room as he got her ready and the both of them stepped down for breakfast only to find Avni there already.

N - Hey! I thought I'd get your breakfast in your room? - he said, that had been their routine for a week & a half now.

A - Actually, I have somewhere to be. Hazel, my friend has been asking to catch up since forever now! So, I woke up a bit early. - she said as she gave him a small smile.

N - Oh, okay! - he nodded. Ishi, baby would you like to go to office with me today? - he asked politely, hoping she would agree. With Rehaan going crazy at his attempts to get him, he couldn't leave Isha alone with the guards. He needed to be with her.

I - But I get bored. You have so much work, N-man and I don't get to play. - she pouted, clearly unaware of the dilemma of her uncle.

N - Ishi, Mama has some work to finish, please? - he requested as he fed her the waffle, wiping the crumbles away from the corner of her mouth while Avni could only watch the exchange without having any help to offer.

I - Can I go to Bry Aunty? I want to play with the fishies that they have! - she said as she licked some peanut butter off her waffle.

N - Baby, she might be busy! I'll have to ask. - he sighed but called Noah up anyways.

Fortunately, Bryer had a day off from her work and was more than glad to have Isha over and both Neil & Avni were at ease now.

Though Neil insisted to drop her, but Avni countered that she would be using the subway to travel as she had to go in the opposite direction. However, when Neil didn't give in, she ended up taking another car while he dropped Isha at Bryer's before heading to his office.

Work kept Neil busy. He had a few meetings lined up with various clients for his real-estate business, while had some documents to go through for the other industries that they catered to. By the time he was done with it all, it was evening. And to his dismay, he still had a business party to attend. Had it been for someone else, he would have skipped it, but the Raichands were a potential ally. They had been in the market since more than two decades and he could use some connections to kick start his intelligence service wing, and that was why he decided to go.

Leaving the office, he made a quick stop at Khanna Mansion as he showered and dressed in a tux for the party. He dropped a text to Avni asking her if she was having fun & asking her to take care of herself and video called Isha before leaving for the party.

The venue was just as grand as he thought it would be. Classic Raichand Fashion! Neil offered his greetings & pleasantries to some of the people as he constantly checked on his phone if Avni had replied to his texts. He couldn't wait to be at home, in bed with her. Also, he had to tell her about his feelings that he had finally admitted to himself. But he wanted to make it grand. He still remembered his Jiju had flown his sister down to Paris to propose her marriage and he still remembered the love struck look on their faces whenever they looked at each other. He wondered if Avni could see that he looked at her just the same. He was aware he did.

He had been thinking about the future a lot lately. About the life he will have with her & Isha. His Dad used to tell him that thinking about the future means that we have hope, something to hold on to. And Neil was tired living in the past. His present felt good, for once! And his future felt hopeful. A small smile graced his mouth as he thought about her.

However, the happy mood soon turned foul when he noticed the man walking up to him. Rehaan Qureshi. He gritted his teeth in anger as his hands curled up in fists.

R - Look whose here! Hello, Bhaijaan, how have you been doing? - he sneered & Neil had to control himself from creating a scene.

It's alright. Its just a business party and all the big names are present. He is just another guest, Neil. Don't get instigated! - he kept repeating to himself as he heaved in a deep breath.

N - Unfortunately for you, I've been doing good Rehaan! Apparently, your men aren't trained enough to kill me yet. Next time, try harder okay! - he patted his shoulder as he gave him a tight smile.

Before Rehaan could speak anything else, Neil turned around to move but collided with someone. The woman was probably coming to see Rehaan.

Neil wanted to be anywhere but here in that moment, however reflexively, he lifted his eyes up to look at the person who he had just bumped into.

And Neil wished he hadn't.

That was the last face he thought he would come across here. In this party, full of business delegates. How was a homeschool teacher invited? Did Raichands have any educational venture? Or were they acquainted with Mehtas? Neil had questions. A lot them as his gaze travelled down her before they settled on her face. He noticed she was wearing a beautiful pearl gown, looking ethereal as always but it was her eyes that caught his attention.

They looked alarmed. Like they had been caught off guard, she had a look of shock with a hint of fear in her eyes when she registered his presence.

N - I thought you were with Hazel? - he kept his voice soft, though the swirling questions in his mind were anything but calm.

However, before Avni could reply, Rehaan walked around them as he stood besides her. Neil's jaw tightened as did his fists when Rehaan put his arm around her waist and she let him. In fact, she looked just fine. As if, it was completely normal to her. He couldn't understand.

R - Meet Avni, my partner! - he said, making Neil frown in confusion. Oh, poor Bhaijaan! - he snorted at Neil's expense. Babe, did you teach his niece good? - he looked at Avni and asked. Neil could only watch as his throat ran dry and body felt colder than ever.

A - You bet! - she laughed as she winked at Rehaan and Neil felt like his heart would stop.

N - Wh-what do you mean? - he asked lamely, even when he could draw a picture of what it meant!

R - Oh c'mon, don't act dumb! - he waved his hand as if it was something funny. Or are you really dumb? Just like your father! - he said and Neil clenched his teeth in absolute fury.

He wanted to punch him in the face for speaking that way about his father. But that would only mean losing control. And Neil hated losing control. Not by the likes of Rehaan Qureshis.

N - Avni, what are you doing here? Weren't you supposed to be with Hazel? - he asked, keeping his calm.

A - Are you really that dumb, or do you want me to narrate exactly how we fooled you, Mr. Khanna! It was all a lie. I was a mole, to extract information out of you! - she said, and something in Neil told him she wasn't lying. She was looking into his eyes and neither her voice, nor her stance held any regret, or guilt or any other emotion for that matter. It was distant & emotionless. She was emotionless.

R - You know what, she is really good in bed. I'm sure you know it by now, but if you still want more, I might just send her over sometime! - the sick bastard whispered to Neil as he leaned towards him.

Neil didn't know how to respond. He wanted to kill him, but he didn't have the strength to even move his own hand.

R - C'mon Babe, let's go & meet the Raichands! - he said as he kissed the corner of her mouth and she smiled, snaking her hand around his arm.

It felt like someone snatched his breath away, and not in the way that he usually felt Avni doing that to him. This felt cruel. And inhuman. It felt like she not only tore his heart in pieces but also stomped on it until it ran dry of the last ounce of blood.

The fact that she didn't even look back at him even once was unsettling. How could it all be a lie? The club, the orphanage, the church, the attacks, Hambledon, the carnival, everything was a lie? It could not be. Neil refused to believe. And he was well aware how sly Rehaan could be, he must have something against Avni that made her lie to him. What they had couldn't be a lie. He was sure of it.

Neil watched them through the corner of his eyes. He didn't want to create a scene in front of Rehaan, so he waited till the time Avni separated from him and the moment he got a chance, he caught up with her.

She was walking into the corridor towards the restroom when he grabbed her by her arm and pushed her against the wall nearby, making sure that he doesn't hurt her as he kept his hand behind her head.

N - What is going on, Avni? - he asked, as he held both of his arms in his hands.

A - I thought Rehaan explained you all too well. Didn't you hear him? - she spoke, so distant as if she was bored talking to him while she tried to get rid of his hold.

N - Fuck it, Buttercup! You want me to believe that shit? You want me to believe that everything that we had was a fucking lie? - he gritted the words out. She was testing his patience now & God knew he had never been a particularly patient guy anyways!

A - Well, believing it or not is up to you, Mr. Khanna! - she pushed him back & Neil stumbled a step back at the force. But that's the truth. Everything was a fucking lie! - she looked into his eyes as she spoke.

N - Are there cameras here? Is he watching you? Please tell me something, Avni! - his eyes searched hers. Just one hint. That was all he asked for!

A - Damn it, Neil! - she ran her hands across her face. Why are you acting so clingy & desperate? - he couldn't believe that was his Buttercup speaking. Okay, if it's still not clear to you, let me break it down for you. Yes, its true that I'm Rehaan's partner and was plotted in your perfectly fucked up life. To fuck it up even more! To extract information about your moves and to give Rehaan an edge over you. We had thought that you'd not be attending this party and that was why I came here. Had a few deals to crack. - Neil felt his throat clogging as his eyes stung. She wasn't lying. He could tell that. But that's okay, I guess you really have nothing more to offer apart from that bullshit emotional drama that you literally grilled me with everyday. You're so melodramatic that way! - she rolled her eyes, as if his presence pissed her.

N - Avni, please! Why are you doing this to me? - he choked on his words as his hands tried to hold her.

A - Doing what? - she swatted his hands away. And stop touching me, pervert! Why are you making it sound like it was all my fault when you had your fun! Didn't you? - she gritted her teeth.

N - I don't believe this. Have you been threatened? Has Rehaan threatened you with something, Avni? Please tell me, I promise I'll make it alright. - he tried again, if she asked, he would be on his knees and beg her to tell him that she was lying, that what they had was genuine and that she loved him back.

A - Oh, poor heartbroken boy! - she couldn't stop the chuckle that escaped her, but her eyes were cold. You're so pathetic, Neil! It was just..what? A month? And you thought I could fall in love with you? You know, initially I had thought that it would be tough to get past you, to win your trust, but it was so fucking easy! You're just another man who one can win over a good fuck! You were so easy to manipulate that was shameful after a point quite literally! You were so stupid that you didn't even notice the small mistakes that I made. Never doubted the way I had the strength & agility of an athlete, something that a simple young teacher wouldn't have, never questioned that I could read just fine without my glasses but still chose to wear them. You remember you told me that my eyes speak of lost endings to you? Guess what, Mr. Khanna, they actually did. But you were so pussy-starved that you never made an effort to dig -

N - That's enough! - he didn't think he could take it anymore. Stop right there, Ms. Mehta. - he felt disgusted. Was that what she thought about him? She thought that he used her for his physical needs? Was it some sick joke?

A - Why, did I hurt you? - she pretended hurt as her hand flew to her chest and she whispered. Or are you upset that you won't get such pretty company anymore? - she gritted the words out. And honestly, Neil couldn't recognize her in that moment.

N - You're right, I was so delusional to think that I could find love being surrounded by the likes of you! - he spat. His pulse was wild and heart hammered against his chest. The noises inside his head made it impossible to hear his own voice. But you know what, I wish I could hate you, Avni. - his eyes softened for a moment before they turned dark, emotionless. All over again. He turned away but then looked back at her. Apparently, you're a better painter than I could ever be, cause the picture that you painted of yourself is just so far different from what you really are! Disgusting. - he had to clench his jaw & blink his eyes to stop the tears that threatened to fall from his eyes. But Avni didn't show any remorse.

She really was a liar! He hated how stupid he had been.

Chapter 19

Avni was a liar. She had lied when she had said that love would feel like catching a rainbow after rains, that it was a book that you can't stop reading, that it was home. When in reality, love felt like this. Shit. How Neil felt in that moment. Love was a pink coloured bubble, it was a book with all the pages torn out, it was a home with shattered walls, burnt & demolished. Wrecked. Love was cruel. And his stupid heart was too fragile.

Neil walked out of the venue and got straight into his car. His chest felt like someone had set him on fire and the pressure behind his eyes and ears was unbearable at that point. It seemed that all his dreams, all his hopes and all his wants came shattering down at his feet. Avni really did butcher his heart.

Trying to ignore the pain, he started driving towards Khanna Mansion as he texted Noah to drop Isha over. But then his vision became foggy and his body refused to cooperate. When it reached the limit of his endurance, he parked the car at the side of the road and it was then that tears fell down his eyes like some avalanche. The same way his life fell down like a card house.

He wanted to scream, he couldn't utter a single cry. He wanted to laugh, the tears won't stop. He wanted to set the sky on fire, this rain of melancholy swarmed everything in vision. He wanted to find God, look him in the eye & tell him that he was unjust. And that he hated how much he wanted her.

His throat felt dry and his eyes stung and his body felt numb but he couldn't succumb to it. Neil had always been an understanding child. When his mother left him, he consoled himself saying that it was okay. He could make it alright. When he lost his father & sister, he told himself that he had to look after Isha. He could make it alright. He had always thrived on solving the problems, made him feel like he was needed and wanted. So now, when he sat in his car, with a broken heart and hopeless future, he told himself that it was all a mere nightmare. He could make it alright.

Wiping away his tears harshly, he started driving again and was fast enough to get home & change before Isha reached. Noah didn't take a minute to know that there was definitely something wrong but Neil told him he wasn't ready to talk yet. Understanding that he might need some time to figure his feelings out, Noah didn't pester him much for the night and took his leave.

N - Hi, Baby! Did you enjoy? - he put a smile on his face.

I - Yes! - she grinned as she kissed both his cheeks. Did you miss me? - she then asked as she held his face in her little hands.

N - Of course, Princess! I missed you a lot. - he kissed her forehead as he carried her to her room.

I - Where is Buttercup? - she asked sweetly and Neil drew in a harsh breath.

N - She had some work, Baby! - he said as he put her in her bed and sat besides her. Its time for bed. Now shall we get you ready for bed? - he tried to divert her attention.

I - Okay! - she smiled.

Neil put her in her night suit before he combed her hair and Isha rewarded him with a sweet kiss on his cheek. Sitting besides her, he thumped her forehead gently as he read her a story book to put her to sleep. Tired as she was after playing the whole day with Noah & Bryer, it didn't take Neil much effort before she was in deep slumber.

He took in a deep breathe as he kissed her hair and covered her fully with the blanket before moving out the room. Thoughtlessly, Neil found himself walking towards the attic just above his room where he used to paint. He turned the lights on and simply stood there, observing the various canvases that were placed there. Each reflecting a different emotion. A version of him.

It was almost funny how it was the same house, the same room, the same colour palette. But it was not the same anymore. She was not there, and no one asked him "Why do you paint, Mr. Khanna?".

Neil stepped inside as he took hold of some of his brushes and the water colours. Mindlessly, he painted some strokes of black just like her eyes, then some pink with a hue of red just like her lips, and some other colours he failed to keep track of but when he stopped, she was staring back at him. Smiling at him. Neil wanted to laugh at the predicament. Could not.

He snatched the canvas off the stand and crumpled it before throwing it away. Putting on a fresh one and he couldn't help but think how his life used to be a black canvas. She painted it white. And now that was it. Blank. His life was blank without her.

After some time of futile attempts to paint, Neil resigned to his room but couldn't catch any sleep. Tossed & turned for hours but didn't find a single moment of relief. It was around three in the night when he finally went to Isha's room in an attempt to get rid of that ringing headache. And he did find some ease as he held his little princess in his arms and slept for a while.

Avni on the other hand, had quite a happening night. She had left the party with Rehaan and she willingly agreed when he asked her to sleep over at his place. It had been quite some time since they last did it anyways.

A - Did you know he would be coming? - she asked when they reached his penthouse, referring to Neil.

R - No, I didn't. - he shrugged. But trust me the look on his face was so gorgeous. - he snickered. Poor guy looked wrecked and betrayed. For a moment, I thought he would pass out. - he commented as he poured some whiskey for himself. The colour of the drink reminded Avni of Neil's eyes, she shrugged the thought off.

A - How do you plan to go ahead? As in, what now? - she asked as she took the seat besides him on the house-bar.

R - What comes now is, we kill him, Sweetheart! - he said, Avni smirked at him. But, I want him to see his whole life crumbling down to ashes. Now that his heart is broken, I need to take his business empire down. - he thought out loud while Avni listened to him silently. Well, on second thoughts, Babe, I think we can sketch that out tomorrow, cause right now, I'm gonna have some fun with you! - he looked at Avni suggestively as he downed his drink.

She didn't need to be cajoled though, giving him a flirty smile, Avni got down the bar stool as she stood between his legs and took his bow off. Rehaan put his hands on her waist as he pulled her closer and bit on her neck hungrily. Avni let him.

She yanked him by his collar as she led him towards the bedroom. It was going to be a long night.

Avni woke around eight in the morning and slipping into Rehaan's shirt, she made her way to the kitchen to get something to eat. She made herself a cup of coffee and two toast. Sitting on the platform of the kitchen, she sipped on her coffee as she took a bite of her toast.

"Is that you, Avni?" - a voice asked and Avni had to get down to the floor as she turned around to look at the early visitor Rehaan had.

A - Yes. And who would you be? - she asked the lady standing in front of her. She was probably in her late fifties but the way she carried herself in that chanel suit and pearls was impressive.

S - You can call me Mrs. Qureshi! - she said and it didn't take Avni much to figure that she was Rehaan's mother. Mrs. Shweta Qureshi, previously Khanna of course! Well, heya! Neil's Mom. You suck! So, we finally meet. Have heard a lot about you! - she said.

A - All good things , I hope! - she threw an insincere smile Shweta's way as she took a sip of her coffee.

S - Are you in love with my son? - uh, which one, lady? Avni would've asked but chose not to, as it didn't really matter.

A - No, I'm not. - she confessed.

S - Then what makes me come across you at his place this early in the morning? - the older lady asked as she put her purse on the table and looked at her.

A - Well, I spent the night here. I guess, we're just having fun, Mrs. Qureshi. - she shrugged, not really understanding where was this conversation heading. God, she couldn't care less.

S - Here is a piece of advice, Avni. Rehaan has always been a difficult child. He had always got what he wanted and gets bored very easily. So, you might not want to get too involved. - she spoke cautiously, as if testing Avni & she couldn't help the chuckle that escaped her throat.

A - Is that your parenting mantra, Mrs. Qureshi? When you can't control your son, you go around controlling things & people around him as per your convenience? - she mocked and she was sure that hit a nerve because Shweta's jaw ticked in displeasure.

S - I believe I don't need parenting guidance from you, young lady. - Avni wanted to give her a shoutout for still maintaining her composure.

A - Of course, not! - she gave a tight smile, hoping that she would take a hint and dismiss the conversation.

S - By the way, is that how you usually talk? I think your parents could use a parenting tip or two! - she smiled tightly and Avni's teeth clenched.

A - I think you want to go see your son, Mrs. Qureshi? - she spoke sweetly.

Shweta turned around as she started to walk toward Rehaan's room, however was stopped by Avni.

A - Uh, just a minute, Mrs Qureshi? - she called, making Shweta turn back to look at her.

S - Yes? - oh, she sounded like Neil! Avni wanted to laugh at the irony.

A - Is it true that your second husband killed your ex-husband Mr. Prakash Khanna? - her eyes were lethal and she made sure Shweta heard the venom in her voice.

S - Excuse me? - she was appalled at what Avni said, as if the thought was something so far from the south that she would laugh out with disbelief.

A - Is this where we play the game of pretending? Or you really don't know that your husband was a criminal? - she spat, not beating around the bush, or trying to sugarcoat her words anymore. She was tired of it.

S - Listen, that's enough! You're standing in my house & accusing my dead husband? - she reminded her but Avni couldn't seem to care enough.

A - Dead doesn't mean innocent. - she smiled. But I guess, you're too blind to see the truth, & too heartless to give a damn about it, Mrs. Qureshi. - she gritted her teeth. Afterall, what can one expect from someone who chose to leave her own little kids & run away! - she placed her mug in the sink before she slowly walked up to Shweta. Each step holding the intent to destroy & ruin. Next time you want to give parenting tips to someone, - she spoke in a low voice. Dangerous. kindly start with your own self. God knows you could really use some. - and with once last glance at her, Avni walked away.

She made her way to the guest bedroom to get changed into her clothes so that she could leave already. The placed suffocated her. And she was so done dealing with the shit people threw her way.

If someone had the audacity to talk about her parents, dead parents, they should also have the capacity to handle it when life bites back at them. Avni didn't care if Shweta loved Zain Qureshi, or about the fact that why did she leave Prakash Khanna & their kids, but she couldn't let her slide away before giving her a piece of her mind.

The lady seemed to be in a bubble of her own and Avni felt a strange sense of triumph to burst it out for her to see the truth. This was what she got for toying with her loved ones. And no one spoke about her parents that way.

However, even when she felt nothing but repulsion towards the woman, she couldn't shake away the feeling that she had in her gut. Avni felt like Shweta really had no clue about Zain's involvement in the plane crash. She could read it in her eyes. Was Zain really innocent? Did Neil lie to her?

She needed to find out.

The day passed in a blur as she worked on the various things that were going on and Avni needed to mitigate damage. She was supposed to attend a meeting with Rehaan, with some drug dealers that were interested in supplying drugs to them.

Opting for a casual blue jeans & black silk spaghetti top, Avni finished her look with pencil heels as she made her way to the club. It was a filthy place. The club was in the outer suburbs of the city and reeked of alcohol & drugs. The cheap neon lighting gave flashes of the sweaty bodies that danced on the floor and the way most of the people were eating each other's mouth.

Avni made her way inside the club, and the more she went deeper, the more the smell lingered. She found Rehaan sitting in a corner as he talked to two men who looked like wrestlers to say the least.

R - Hi, Babe! You look amazing. - he eyed Avni down as she sat next to him. Want me to fuck you after this? - he whispered in her ear while she simply winked at him.

A - Only if you get this deal! - she pressed her hand on his thigh, making him grin sickly.

R - So, gentlemen, do we have a deal? You supply us the drugs & we give you more market for alcohol? - he asked & it was then that Avni noticed the two men sitting across from her.

One of them had a nasty scar on his face while the other looked like he had just escaped jail.

How about we get to share this sexy fuck over here? - one of them spoke & Avni could feel bile rising in her stomach.

R - Sure. But only once I'm done with her! - Rehaan laughed animalistically while Avni chose to ignore them.

She needed to get done with this as soon as she possibly could, or else she might end up shooting the two of them!

Chapter 20

It was her parents' death anniversary. Fifteen years ago, she lost her happy little family. And everyday since, she had missed them, wished that they were at a happier place now, hoped that she would unite with them in afterlife.

Avni allowed herself one day to wallow at her fate & in self-pity once a year. That was the day. And that was why she was sitting at the bar in a club and drowning the bitter liquor to numb her pain. She was beyond rationality at that point. The way the freak standing next to her was eyeing her didn't matter. Neither did the fact that he was now touching her, his slimy hand was hiking up her thigh but Avni couldn't bring herself to care anymore. At least the creepy & disgusting feeling that she felt in the pit of her stomach told her that she was alive, still feeling.

He used to keep his thumb on her wrist to feel her pulse. To see if she was alive, with him.

Avni found it funny, a laugh slurred out of her mouth as she downed yet another shot of vodka and the next was already placed in front of her. She looked around the club with her blurred vision and was surprised to find a hazy figure of Neil in her line of sight. A laugh bubbled up in her chest.

Said he was heartbroken! Liar. - she thought as she watched him.

Avni noticed he was sitting around a small round table in the corner with two men. The three of them spoke in discreet tones & nodded their heads in between. Neil looked calm. Authoritative & commanding nonetheless. She needed something strong to drown herself in and thus ordered a stronger drink.

By the time she was done with her drink, the men shook their hands & separated. Neil was making his way out of the club, didn't even spare a glance at her. Did he not even notice her? Avni frowned at the thought. Was he already over her?

Her fist curled up around the glass in her hand when she saw a girl colliding with him and she could swear it was on purpose. Her jaw clenched in sheer anger when Neil passed her a polite smile and attempted to walk away but the woman didn't take a hint.

She grabbed his hand and said something with her eyes fluttering in a flirty notion and that was the undoing. Avni slapped away the man's hand on her leg and the next second she was standing besides Neil. Pushing away the woman he was talking to, she stood in front of him. His eyes widened for a minute, in shock & surprise, but he then replaced them with his standard cold eyes. Oh, she had had enough of them! What was he even trying?

A - What are you- - she couldn't complete her sentence as Neil walked past her and to say that her mouth hung open in bewilderment would be an understatement. What the hell, Neil!

Why are you walking out on me? - she slurred the words out as her wobbly legs tried to yank him back.

Neil was shocked how drunk she was, could barely keep her eyes open and her legs couldn't even take one step without stumbling. He sighed when he turned to look at her. No matter how much he wanted to stay away from her, he couldn't leave her there in the club like that. And he couldn't even hate himself for being so concerned about her. He loved her, and a single night wouldn't change that fact. Moreover, he had just come to terms with the fact that he was so ill-fated that he always loved what he couldn't have. As much as it was Avni's betrayal that caused him a heart-break, it was his own damned destiny too. He couldn't bring himself to hate her.

He was just going to try to get over her, and keep all the happy & positive things that she gave him. Even though a lie, she still had restored his faith & shown him the right path to go around life. He was going to follow that. Obviously it sucked that he would be alone in that journey, but he'd have to learn to deal with this longing because he couldn't have her. Did he even want her? The woman he fell in love with was an illusion, wasn't even real. Guess, people were right when they said that love was blind. People in love only saw what they wanted to see and Neil must be mocked his wits off. Apparently, Buttercups really were poisonous & he had been so stupid to feed himself on it.

A - Do you like that chic? Huh, Mr. Khanna? - she blinked her eyes to focus on him, her head was swirling as she held his shoulder to stand straight.

N - That's none of concern, Miss Mehta. - he took in a breath. You're wasted, come, I'll drop you at your place. - he said in a distant voice.

Avni didn't particularly like how he was treating her like an annoying responsibility but she smirked at the girl who was eyeing Neil as she grabbed his hand and made her way out of the club, stumbling & fumbling, knowing that he wouldn't let her fall.

She slipped in the passenger seat and when she struggled with the seat belt, Neil simply tied it for her. She noticed he had tightened his jaw as he refused to look at her.

A - So, what were you doing at the club anyway? - she tried to get his attention.

N - So that you could go & tell your partner about it? - he said as he kept looking at the road.

A - Oh c'mon, Neil! Were you looking for a rebound? - she smirked as she ran a finger down his arm and suddenly, Neil felt suffocated in his own space.

He couldn't help but glance in her direction once. He couldn't believe she was the same woman he fell in love with. His throat gulped as his eyes turned glassy but before he could show any visible emotion, he stopped himself as he focused on the road.

Thankfully, Avni stayed quite for the rest of the ride. Neil had gone to the club to meet some of his delegates that he needed on board for launching his intelligence services. Since he was already acquainted with them & the meeting was an informal one, they had done it at the club one of them owned. However, he didn't feel the need to clarify himself. Neither did he dare to ask her why she was so wasted on a weekday. That was so unlike her. Okay, that went too far! He didn't know what the real her was like!

Neil stopped the car when her house came into view and Avni sheepishly smiled at Neil. Oh, she was so drunk & out.

A - My feet hurts. Can you take me up? - that was yet another lie she told him. She didn't want to stay alone that night.

Neil heaved out a long breath but obliged nevertheless. Getting down, he walked around the car as he help her step out and held her by her arm before he locked the car. He then put his arm around her shoulder as he helped her walk towards the porch and Avni felt disappointed. She had thought he would carry her inside.

After much hussle, they finally made it inside and Neil made her sit on the couch of her living room.

N - I'll pull the door, it has auto-lock, right? - he asked and Avni thought just how much he loved her that made him care for her even after knowing her truth.

A - Why don't you stay here? - she got up from the couch as she stood an inch away from him. And make sure that I'm safe, hm? - she whispered as her finger traced his lips.

Neil took a step back. She took one forward as she fisted his sweater in her hands and kissed his jaw. Slow, soft, feathery. Neil's eyes closed shut as his heart thundered against his ribs.

N - Avni, stop it! - he said, clenching his jaw but couldn't find the strength to push her back.

A - Why? Do you not want me anymore? - she spoke against his skin as she kissed his neck and Neil fisted his hands.

She took his sweater off as she let it fall on the floor and grabbed his hand as she led him inside her room. Neil knew he should stop it. She wasn't in her senses and going any far with it would only prove her claim that he was using her for his physical needs. But in all honesty, it had never been about just sex for him, he had always looked for a connection of soul with her.

Neil drew in a harsh breath as he yanked his hand out of her hold and stepped away from her.

N - I need to leave! - he whispered to himself as he turned around.

However, he had only taken one step ahead when she pulled him back and pushed him on her bed. Neil was astonished for a whole minute and before he knew it, she had already tied his hands to the bed stand with a tie.

N - What the hell, Avni! What the fuck are you trying to do? - he gritted his teeth. Wasn't she the one who wanted him gone? Wasn't she the one who told him to not touch her?

Avni did not answer. She simply leaned over him as she kissed his throat and made her way down to his crotch. To his shock, she undid his belt before taking his pants off as she placed a kiss on his cock from above the fabric of his boxers. Pulling a little back, she took the boxers off him as she looked at him.

She fisted his hard cock from the base as she wrapped her fingers around his huge girth. Keeping her eyes stuck to his, she bent down to swirl the tip of her tongue around the head of his cock. Despite everything, a ripple of pleasure ran through Neil's body as she teased him with her tongue.

Avni then took just an inch of his rock hard shaft in her hot mouth as she sucked on his pre-cum deliriously while her hands kept fisting his length in their firm grip. Neil's breathing turned erratic as she sucked on him feverishly before sliding her tongue up on him, learning his texture and shape.

In that moment, Avni could swear that God was a woman, cause who man could make something so beautiful and ecstatic. Every groan that escaped his mouth as he had thrown his head back in pleasure, made Avni hot in her core. Fascinated, she peppered kisses along the length of his thick shaft before she reached for his balls. She covered them gently with her palm as she massaged them and then sucked them. Neil's hips pressed deep into the mattress and his face was a representation of what pure unadulterated pleasure looked like.

Gaining confidence from his reaction, she started running her fingers up & down his thick cock as she kept sucking on his tightening balls. She pulled back when she felt him twitching in her hands. Keeping her palms on his strong thighs, she sat on one of his thighs as she started rubbing her dripping core against his thigh at the same time she leaned forward and took his whole length into her mouth. Neil groaned as he tried to free his hands from the tie when his balls slapped against her chin as she bobbed his twitching cock in & out of her mouth. Gagging and drooling all over it.

Her lace cladded breasts jiggled over the side of his v-line as she tried to find pleasure for herself at the same time she stimulated him with loads of it. Avni slid up & down on his thigh to find her release as she swirled her thumb up & down the slit of his head, edging him more & more. She then again took him in her mouth as she sucked on him. She didn't know if it was the alcohol or the courage that she got from his pleasured moans, but she had not felt so powerful ever. She didn't know what took over but she grazed her teeth with his rock hard cock as she sucked him, at the same time finding herself close to her own release.

A deep groan left Neil's throat as she started sucking him at a maddening speed together with playing with the delicious weight of his beautiful balls. She gave him one last powerful stroke and he shot loads of hot cum as did she. Her juices dripped down his thigh as she kept rubbing herself, overstimulating her clit. Neil basked in the sight of absolute pleasure when she gave him a half dazed smile as she wiped her mouth from the back of her hand.

A - Do you think anyone else could pleasure you so well? Hm? - she asked innocently, but Neil couldn't unsee the sadness in her eyes.

N - Avni- - he started to explain how it was all so wrong.

A - No! Listen to me. - she threw a tantrum like a child. You're mine, Neil! - she blinked, suddenly feeling sobber than ever. Why in the stupid soggy french-fries do you not get it, dammit? - she was tired now. All she wanted was to be held by him close to his heart.

N - You're drunk. - he ignored the way his heart bled in pain and agony. You should rest now! - he tried to yank his hand off the tie but she had tied it really tight.

A - No way! - she announced. I know that you'll push me away once I'm sober. So, I'm just gonna make full of it when I am drunk. - she established the fact as she looked at him in the eye. I'm gonna bury you so deep inside of me that you wouldn't know how to get out! - she whispered and Neil could feel his heart picking up speed.

N - Avni, listen to me! We can not-

And she bit on his lower lip. Avni sucked and nibbled his lips as she undid the buttons of his shirt.

A - You talk too much! - she mumbled before moving down on him and all Neil could do was to watch her in shock & disbelief. He talked much and she was one to say that? Huh!

She trailed kisses across his broad chest as she licked and sucked on his skin all the way down to his abs and then finally reaching his gorgeous v-line. Avni spread her legs as she put her knees on either of his sides while Neil just watched her, anticipating what her next move would be. As much as he had always loved being the dominant one in a situation, he definitely enjoyed the feisty side of Avni. She had always been so sweet and amiable with him that he was surprised at how demanding and authoritative she could be when drunk. But then, to think about it, how much he really knew about her? As much as he did was all a lie. She wasn't what he had taken her to be. And that shit hurt. Bad. More than he had imagined it would.

Unaware of his dampening thoughts, Avni took his semi-hard cock in her hands as she aligned it with her entrance. She fisted his cock as she tapped it twice on her wet core before running it up & down her swollen clit. Neil hardened under her ministrations and all the thoughts left his mind as he dove deeper into the pits of pleasure.

She slid the head of his cock into her hole as she squirmed in delight and light-headedness. Slowly, she slid him inside her, inch by inch, feeling every vein of him inside her. Both of them moaned in pleasure once Neil was fully inside her and her folds clenched around him, so tight that he thought she would consume him whole. Avni squirmed around him as she jiggled herself around his thick hard shaft inside of her and Neil wanted nothing but to rip that fucking tie from his hands and have his way with her.

Placing her hands on his abdomen, she began riding him slowly, letting him feel and stretch every inch of her while she felt him throbbing inside her. Avni slowly increased her pace as she jumped on his dick, the dirty sound of him sliding in & out of her along with the sound of his balls slapping against her skin filled the room followed by her moans & his groans.

Neil thrusted into her as he lifted his hips up to slam into her dripping entrance when he felt her movements turning sloppy because of exhaustion and stimulation. Avni met his thrusts with equal fervour as she leaned down against his chest to kiss him. He grabbed her mouth in a ferocious kiss as he pounded in & out of her in strong powerful thrusts, edging her close to her release.

A - Could you please smile at me like before? - she whispered as she looked at him. Her face holding hope and desperation in equal measures.

N - This won't happen again, Butterc- Miss Mehta! You were drunk and I was not thinking straight either, but I'll make sure that it never happens again! - he said as he gave her one last hard thrust and both of them came at the same time.

And it was the same exact moment when a tear fell from Avni's eye, followed by another and another. Her body shook from the intensity of her orgasm but her heart hammered against her chest for a different reason altogether.

She had really lost her chance with him. Hadn't she? Did he really hate her so much?

Avni couldn't put together what happened after that as she threw herself in his arms and let sleep take over.

Chapter 21

Avni woke up cold. Even though she was covered in blankets and sunlight filtered in the room through the balcony, the blankets felt cold and the sun was blinding. A sharp pain shot up in her head the moment she sat up, her eyelids felt heavy and her clothes were sticky. She looked down at her body to find that she was wearing a party dress, the one she had worn to the club the night.

Club. Alcohol. Neil. Well, fuck!

Her throat worked on a swallow when she tried to remember the events of the last night in detail. A loud groan escaped her mouth the moment snippets of last night flashed through her memory. Embarrassment and guilt came gnawing its claws down her chest and she wanted to bang her head to a wall for how much it was aching. But there was another emotion that she felt. Hurt.

She was aware that she was in no position to feel hurt at the fact that Neil left even before she woke up, she knew she didn't deserve him in the first place. But she couldn't deny that she felt hurt not finding him in her bed. She had wanted to wake up in his arms.

With her head throbbing and her whole body aching with pain while her heart felt numb, she got down the bed as she made the sheets. She should wash them, but she didn't. Of course, it was creepy but the sheets faintly smelt of him and she wanted to gather as much of him as she possibly could. She didn't want to shower either, cause she had remains of him on her for obvious reasons, but she literally reeked of alcohol and her head hurt at the nauseating smell.

She prepared herself a hot water bath and after almost half an hour of staying in there, soaking herself in the water, trying to bring some peace to her heart and well, failing miserably, she decided to get dressed & get to work. She hated it. Every bit of it. She hated how she couldn't run back into his arms and cry herself to oblivion. The water had felt warm to her body, but her heart was still numb. Whatever warmth she had felt in his presence, he took it away with him. London felt chillier this February than it ever had been and she hated winters.

Throwing some loose clothes on herself, she sulkily walked to the kitchen to make herself some breakfast. But what she found there surprised her. Her eyes turned glassy when she found a plate of breakfast arranged for her. Baked beans, scrambled eggs with two slices of fresh loaf bread and a bowl of chia pudding topped with her favourite fruits. She even noticed he had placed a glass of some tonic which she believed was for her hangover because besides it lied a strip of saridon tablets.

Her throat clogged up as her mouth filled with an acrid taste when she carried the tray that he had neatly placed on her kitchen counter to the dining table. A lone tear fell from her eye as she ate the first bite, and then another followed when she chewed the food and her chin wobbled. Soon enough, Avni was breaking down in hysterics as her whole body shook and her heart bled for her beloved.

She loved him. She loved him so much. He was right, whatever happened between them wasn't a lie. What she had told him was a half-baked truth. It was true that she indeed was plotted in his life by Rehaan, but whatever happened after that was not a lie.

How do I tell him? That I can't find it in myself to breath when he is not around. That he is the sun that my earth orbits arounds. That he is the life that he had thought I refused to give up on. That he is what I think my forever should be. That he is what I think love would be.

The food tasted bland on her tongue, but so did everything else without Neil & Isha being there. But she had to continue this drama. She had to make sure that he doesn't find out that she was lying. This time around, she really was lying. Cause she loved him so much and she felt pathetic & miserable how she couldn't see him, or have him smile at her. Not until she finished what she was there for in the first place.

She was selfish for treating him like shit when all he deserved was love, but Avni had her reasons. And now that she knew his side of the story too, she was all the way more determined to finish what she had started.

Wiping the tears off her face, she finished her breakfast and the tonic that Neil had prepared for her. The moment she placed the dishes in the sink and washed her hands, there was a knock at the door. Avni frowned, who could come to her place without even intimating her before.

Sighing, she walked up to the door as she opened it & was confused to say the least when she found Shweta standing in front of her.

Really? Does this woman has someone spying over me or does she possess some kind of sixth sense? How in the stale thai green curry does she show up whenever I've been with her sons? God, couldn't you just spare me some time to cry over Neil and swoon at the same time at how sweet he is? I miss him. And I miss Isha. My babies!

A - What do I owe the pleasure for, Mrs. Qureshi? - she put on a fake smile.

S - Aren't you too discreet about your hatred towards me, Avni? - she smiled & Avni stopped herself from rolling her eyes.

A - I just like to keep it natural! - she said, dropping the smile.

S - Can I come in? - she asked.

Woman, no! But your son can. I would kiss him senseless the moment Neil steps in.

A - Sure. - she said.

Avni led Shweta inside as she made her sit on the sofa in the living room. Though reluctantly, she poured the coffee that Neil had prepared in a cup and offered it to Shweta. Giving Avni a small nod, she took the mug as she sipped on it.

Avni stood opposite to her as she leaned on the armrest of the sofa and Shweta's eyes snapped up to hers the moment she drank her first sip of the coffee.

S - Did you make it? - she asked as her eyes held surprise and a weird emotion Avni couldn't name.

She simply shrugged, insinuating that she had prepared it, not wanting to divulge any details about Neil to her. She still wasn't sure of Shweta's intentions yet.

S - It tastes oddly familiar. Reminds me of someone! - she said as her lips twitched and she looked down at the mug, her fingers grazed the handle as she darted her tongue out to brush her lips. She looked regretful. Almost sad & guilty.

A - Why are you here, Mrs. Qureshi? - she asked, not wanting to beat around the bush.

S - Can we sit & talk? I can tell that you're not really fond of me but you always listen to everybody, Avni. Give me a chance? - her voice didn't hold any pretense and Avni was actually surprised how genuine she seemed. Her eyes had that look sometimes Neil gave her when he was tired of fighting.

A - What is it? - she asked sincerely as she sat on the sofa opposite to her.

S - I & Prakash Ji had an arranged marriage, it was more of a family alliance. I didn't want to get married at that time, I had wanted to be an actress but my family didn't support. Nevertheless, I got married as per my family's wish and I'll be honest, Prakash Ji was everything that a woman could ask for in a man. He gave me respect, loyalty, care, freedom & love. And eventually, I reciprocated all his feelings, apart from love. Not because he lacked something, but because I was still adamant that that marriage had cost me my career. Prakash Ji had even asked me if I wanted to work or do something after marriage, but I was clearly forbidden by my parents to take any of it up. Along the years, I tried to love him, tried to love the life I was living, but couldn't. We had kids and even then I wasn't happy.

In my heart, I still felt like something was missing. Like I wasn't where I was, and the thing missing where I was present, was me! - she took in a deep breath as she circled her finger around the rim of the coffee mug. She shook her head as she closed her eyes before looking up at Avni. You must think that I'm probably the worst mother out there, and you would be right in thinking so. I really didn't deserve to be a mother to those two little kids, Ishani & Neil. Neither did I deserve Prakash Ji. But it became too heavy, Avni! Every time I was with the kids, I felt like something is wrong, like that was not what I wanted. I could never be the mother that they deserved & they could never be the life I wanted, or wished to see myself in. - she paused for a moment as she fumbled with her words & a sad smile spread on her mouth. I am not particularly proud of what I did, but I did it anyway. I ran away. Leaving my kids behind. Leaving Prakash Ji behind. Started working for a modelling company, a few shows here & a few shows there. That was when I met Zain. Somehow, we just clicked. He was tall, dark, handsome, mysterious, and he loved me. We got married and I had Rehaan. Now that we're doing it, I'll be completely true to you, there were moments in the past twenty three years of me being with Zain that made me think that he was involved into something that wasn't right. But I was too blinded with love. And I really had no clue about his involvement in Prakash Ji's accident. Zain did inform me about it, but it was like a general thing, as if someone would talk about a random news. It never occurred to me that he really was quite envious of the Khanna Empire. And yes, needless to say, of course it was failure on my part when I didn't reach out to Neil. Was never there for him. When I got know about the plane crash, - she gulped and Avni saw her eyes turning glassy. I was unsettled. - she bit on her lip as she blinked her eyes to stop her tears. I felt like a failure all over again. It was my child who died in that crash. My blood. But I could do nothing about it. And I was so ashamed that I didn't know how to show up even for their funeral. The past two years have been really miserable, Avni. First the plane crash, then Zain's death. It felt like my world came crashing down. Rehaan was never really close to me. He was always close to his Dad. - she told. You know, yesterday, when you said all those things about Zain being involved in the crash, it was then that I really saw all the lies and half-baked truths that I had been fed all these years. I..I looked into it all & you were right. It really was Zain Qureshi, my dead husband who killed my ex-husband and my child. - she said and Avni couldn't help but grab her hand as she gave her a comforting squeeze. I'm ashamed of what I did and I know that I don't deserve even Neil's apology, his approval of me as his mother is a far fetched dream. - she took in a deep breath as she wiped off the tears that had fallen down her face. But I want to make it alright. This time, I want to do the right thing. - she said.

A - What do you mean? - she heard herself asking.

S - I know who you are, Avni. And I know exactly why you've associated yourself with Rehaan. - she said, and Avni felt her jaw ticking. I'm his mother, and even though I know that I gave birth to a monster who trades with little girls to make money, I can't bring him to an end with my hands. - she exhaled harshly. But, I can help you with it. You've been searching for the evidences in his office, his dungeon and his penthouse for the last two years, right? - and Avni was surprised at what she just spilled. The woman really knew what she was doing. You won't find them there. If there is one place where you can find those evidences, its in the Qureshi Villa. Zain kept all his dirty secrets in his library. - she told as she kept the empty mug on the table and clasped her hands as she looked up at Avni. But it requires a passcode to enter, and there are only two people who know it. - she paused for a moment. Rehaan & me. - oh, Avni knew that look. All too well!

A - What do you want in return? - she asked, it was obvious that she wouldn't help her without any benefit of her own. Avni just had to know how deep the shit was.

S - Aren't you a smart girl? - she remarked as she smiled while Avni just shrugged. She couldn't wait to get it over with. The headache that had been subdued by the tonic, seemed to return back with full force. I want to see Neil once. Just..just one look, that all I ask for.

What? She didn't really say it, did she?

Well, lady! He refuses to see me either. - a sick voice sneered inside Avni's mind. She really wanted to bang her head somewhere.

Chapter 22

Fortunately for Avni, it was Friday, which meant that Neil would take Isha out for a park-date. It was their weekly ritual. Netizens would say that she was a toxic stalker who was lurking behind the bushes in that black cap to cover her stupid face from Neil's sight while she hid herself in the park & waited for them to come. But Avni believed that the said netizens could shove their opinions up their asses because she was literally dying to see her little girl. As much as she was doing it for fulfilling her part of the deal with Shweta, she was also doing it because she wanted to see Isha. It had been three long & agonizing days that she hadn't seen her. And she was already afraid that Isha might forget her. The thought alone made her stomach churn and the food that she had had for lunch threatened to make a reappearance. Avni batted the thought away.

Shweta was waiting in her car which was parked outside the park and Avni was supposed to text her to come & get a peek of Neil when he seemed to be unassuming. She exhaled a rough breath. Why was he not coming already? She wanted to see him.

But when he really did come, Avni's breath hitched. He wasn't wearing his usual browns or beiges or blues, they were his go to choice of outfits. Rather, he was wearing an old rose sweatshirt with white pants while he held Isha in his arms and walked into the park. Isha looked like an extension to him, a part of him, as she wore the exact same sweatshirt and white jeans shorts. Avni was stunned how pathetically she had missed those two and their cute twinning selves. A soft chuckle escaped her throat at the same time a tear fell from her eye when she figured that Isha must have asked Neil to put her in matching clothes.

She wiped the tear from the back of her hand as she hid herself from his line of sight when he made Isha sit on the swing and slowly swinged her in the air. The little girl giggled. A small smile found home on her face as she watched the two of them.

A sigh left her as she remembered the reason she was there. Avni took her phone out from her jeans pocket and dropped a quick text to Shweta. 'You can see them now.' - the text read and soon enough she saw Shweta getting down from the car.

Avni's heart thundered in her chest, she felt herself gripped by a strange fear. What if Neil spotted his mother? What if he thought that she (Avni) was doing all this to hurt him? What if he never allowed her to see him again? She dreaded the consequences.

She took in a sharp breath when Shweta started walking towards them. Panic surged through Avni and her pulse went into a frenzy. It wasn't supposed to be like this? Shweta was supposed to see him from a distance. No. No! NO! She should have known it was going to backfire. How could she be so stupid to trust Shweta? She was going to tell him that she was his mother, wasn't she? Neil would hate Avni for this. He had clearly told her that he didn't want to see his mother.

Avni's heart pounded in her chest as she watched Shweta when she stood next to Neil and smiled at Isha.

S - You've such a lovely kid, young boy! - she said as her eyes turned glassy.

N - Thanks. - he smiled back politely.

Isha had always been a happy baby, so there were people who always stopped to wave at her, or say hi, or exchange pleasantries. It wasn't something that was new to him, but when the lady kept standing besides them as she watched him & Isha, Neil was confused. She looked like she knew them.

N - Do I know you? I'm sorry I don't recognise you. - he blinked his eyes, raking his brain if he had seen the lady before. On thinking hard, he did find her face a bit familiar, but he couldn't pinpoint. May be they had met at some business gala? He couldn't seem to remember.

Avni thought her heart would leap out of her chest when she saw them conversing but couldn't hear anything from the distance. She moved a bit deep into the bushes in an attempt to hear them but no use.

S - Uh, no! We don't know each other. - she said with a small smile on her face as she tried her best not to cry in front of her first born son. You look lovely, little girl! - she patted Isha's cheeks who gave her a smile in return and in that moment Shweta knew what she had missed out on. Take care, son! I wish you all the happiness in the world. - she caressed his face before she turned around & walked away.

Neil was confused at the way she became so emotional. He couldn't understand why would some stranger behave that way, but what did he know? He knew nothing about people & the struggles that they went through. Moreover, he was done thinking & over-analyzing every thought & every gesture that people showed. It never turned out to be fruitful for him, rather left him broken & shattered when people dropped their masks and revealed their true identity. He was done! But he also couldn't deny the way his heart seemed to sink a bit when the lady walked away from him. It felt like he was being left alone. Stranded. Again. The way she left him behind and walked ahead to disappear from his sight felt almost too familiar and sad. Why did it make him sad? She was a literal stranger!

I - Mama, I want ice-cream. - she said making Neil break his trance & focus on her.

N - C'mon Ishipie, lets go get some ice-cream! - he smiled as he carried her in his arms.

Avni hid herself amidst the bushes as Neil walked outside the park, and thus walked towards her, however before he could pass her, a cluster of ants bit on Avni's legs and she yelped in pain, thus stepping out of the bush in hurry. Only to regret it the next moment.

I - Buttercup! - Avni closed her eyes shut in fear when Isha spotted her and squealed for her. Neil was definitely going to be mad.

Slowly blinking her eyes open, she bobbed her head up as she looked in their direction. Isha had a bright smile playing on her face while Neil was confused before she saw a look of anger taking over his eyes.

The moment Neil's eyes followed Isha's hand and his gaze landed on Avni, he was, once again reminded of the fact that all things beautiful were sin. And sin brought punishment. Just like the one he was suffering.

His jaw ticked as his teeth clenched when the flashes of her betrayal crossed his mind. It came in waves. Huge, dark, dangerous waves of grief that toppled his life over, tussled with his heart and left it to bleed in agony.

Last night, when they were together, there were many moments when Neil wished that he never went to that party. That he never knew about her lying to him. He wished for that sweet floating cloud that ignorance brought with itself. He felt so sorry for his own self, he couldn't hate her even after knowing her truth. By the time he had finally gotten rid of the tie she had tied him with, she was fast asleep and as much as it crushed his self-esteem, Neil was sick enough to stay there for the night as he watched her sleeping. She had looked so peaceful & innocent.

An actress so good, didn't even leave character in sleep. - he wanted to laugh at the thought.

Neil drew in a sharp breath when Isha wiggled in his arms and requested him to put her on the ground. Apparently, she wanted her Buttercup.

N - Ishi, we need to go! - he spoke with his teeth clenched but Isha didn't seem to listen.

Avni bit on her lips as she tried not to cry out loud, she couldn't show him yet but she yearned to hold Isha in her arms. Her nails dug crescents in her palms as she curled her hands up into tight fists. Her heart hurt when Isha started crying in his arms when he didn't put her down.

I - I want Buttercup! Please Mama - she cried as precious tears fell down her beautiful eyes and her nose turned red.

Fuck Rehaan. Fuck the truth! I can't see my baby crying.

Avni stomped towards Neil as she took Isha in her arms and cradled her slowly, brushing her hair away from her then wet face.

A - Calm down, Baby. I'm here. - she cooed in her ears and Isha seemed to relax a bit, though she was still weeping.

I - I missed you! - she sniffed and Avni could swear she would die for her.

A - I missed you more, Baby! - she kissed the top of her head.

However, the calm Avni felt was short lived when Neil snatched Isha away from her, making her cry all over again.

N - Next time I see you anywhere near my niece, I swear to God, Avni, I'll forget that I ever lov- - he inhaled a sharp breath and looked away. You know what, I wish I had never met you! - he gritted his teeth as he furiously walked away with a wallowing Isha in his arms.

Avni could only watch, as she stood there and Neil moved on. Her eyes welled up and her limbs quivered physically at the way he had just brushed away her whole existence. Her heart sank to her knees and all Avni wanted was to run up to him and tell him how much she loved him. But she couldn't. Not yet.

So this is how it felt! This is how it feels to be left alone. This is how Neil must have felt when I told him my truth. And it was only fair that I go through the same pain too. - Avni thought.

She always thought that she was an unfortunate child. Yet she always abided by what her parents taught her when they were there. Haarna nahi hai mujhe jeet ke liye, jeetna hai mujhe preet ke liye! - her mother would say to her ten years old self as she used to repeat after her. But after her parents', the only person that had shown her love was Neela, who Avni loved more than she loved her own self. She had thought that she would never fall in love because it only brought destruction with itself. But then life took over & Neil happened. He became her preet. The one she fell in love with. The one she was to fight for.

But how does someone fight the one they loved? And all the revenge be damned, she was tired of fighting now. If anything, she just wanted to sleep in Neil's arms.

She had grown up lonely. Of course, Neela was there and she found a friend in Hazel too, but the time just before she went for sleep, it was in those times that she used to sit by the window of her room and stare at the deserted roads. They used to be so silent and spotless, as if abandoned. Just like she was. By life. Early on in life, Avni had learnt how to put smile on faces, on her own too, but what she missed was the feeling of belonging. She never really belonged. To anywhere. Anyone.

But then she met Neil. For the first time in life, she felt like she belonged. To him. With him. What she felt for Neil was an all-consuming fire. It was like one day she was unaware of his existence, and the other day she was in love with him. Theirs wasn't the kind of love that progresses slowly & breaks down the walls around the hearts in slow thumps. No, Neil crumbled her guards down the moment he looked at her with those gorgeous hazel sky eyes, and in that moment she was already in love with him. He welcomed her sunshine, embraced her silence, assured her insecurities and batted away her fears. And for the first time in life, she had planned a future. With him & Isha. Avni wasn't sure if she wanted to laugh or cry at her fate. Probably the dream she had woven was too big, she had to pay the price.

S - I'm sorry you had to-

A - The evidences, Mrs. Qureshi! - she spoke in between before Shweta could finish herself. Avni didn't need to hear it from her to know that even if Neil still cared for her, he would rather die alone than ever let her in again. All that was left was to finish what she had started and get done with all that trash for once & all.

Shweta nodded as she led Avni to her car.

The drive was silent & Avni was just looking out of the window as she tried to brush away the hurt she felt at Neil's seclusion.

S - You love him, don't you? - she broke the eerie silence & Avni just shut her eyes close.

A - I do. - she simply confessed, there was no point hiding it from her anymore.

Avni was glad that Shweta did not speak anything after that, and she was left to her Neil-filled thoughts, then she wasn't in the car anymore. She was on a capsule of a giant wheel & opposite to her sat Neil. In all his gorgeousness. He would then tug her on his lap and touch her closely, making her lose her senses and dive deep into their own world. "I love you, Buttercup!" - he would then whisper in her ear and she would bite a smile back. A kiss on her shoulder, one on her neck and then he would-

S - We're here, Avni! - Shweta said, breaking Avni's reverie. She shut her eyes close as a deep sigh left her mouth.

Avni rubbed her hands across her face as she took a few deep breaths in before stepping out of the car. She looked around as

Shweta led her to a staircase and then turned left and stopped only when they were standing in front of a large vintage door.

S - This is the study where Zain used to work and keep all his documents. You might find what you're looking for. - she said, a sad gleam present in her eyes.

Shweta then entered the passcode and the door opened. She gestured Avni to move inside while she turned to look at Shweta in confusion.

A - You're not coming in? - she asked.

S - He was my husband, Avni. And Rehaan is my son! - she gulped as she looked away.

Avni nodded her head in understanding. She could understand it was tough for her. Even if they were monsters, they were still her family and the fact that Shweta knew what giving Avni access to the study could cost her & she was still doing it anyway was a clear indication of the fact that she wanted to make amends. If that didn't mean that she was seeking redemption, Avni wasn't sure what else would.

A - Thankyou, Mrs. Qureshi! - she said genuinely and Shweta simply nodded.

S - I'll be in my room. You go ahead! - she said.

Giving one last glance to Shweta, Avni stepped inside. Her heart pounded in a frenzy as the nerves took over. This was what she was working for the last fifteen years. Lies, betrayals, fights, blood. She was past all of them. All for this one moment, where she finally gets to bring an end to the people who caused her & her loved ones so much misery & agony. She gets to seek her revenge.

Avni took in a deep breath as she started going through the many drawers that were there in the room. Her heart raced with every file that she fumbled with, went through all the pages and papers in the hope to find what she was looking for, but no luck yet.

She then opened the cupboards and scanned all the shelves, all the books, all the folders, but they were either about Qureshi Industries or, the news articles about the Khanna Empire. Avni lost track of time but she was sure she had been searching up the space for at least an hour now.

Disheartened, she sat on the sofa that was placed in the corner of the room as she looked up at the ceiling and exhaled a harsh breath. Her hands rested on the sofa and it was then that she felt it.

Avni immediately stood up from the sofa as she yanked the seat off it. She had heard Rehaan talking about it once when she had spiked his drink in order to obtain information out of him. The sleazy man couldn't even notice that she had mixed his drinks & everyday when he thought that he was having sex with her, he was actually knocked out of his senses to even remember what really happened the last night.

As if I'd ever sleep with that piece of shit! - Avni scoffed at the thought as a triumphant smile spread on her lips.

There it was. A hard-disk labelled with a red tape and something in Avni told her that it was what she was looking for. She took the hard-disk from the makeshift sofa and quickly grabbed her laptop from her bag. Connecting the hard-disk with her laptop, Avni tried to transfer the data so that she could make use of it. But the disk was password protected. Of course!

'Rehaan' - she tried.

'Shweta' - wrong again.

There was only one gamble left, or else that disk would corrupt itself and Avni's heart threatened to leap out of chest. Her pulse drummed and she could feel beads of sweat at the sides of her forehead.

What could it be? She didn't even know Zain to predict how his mind worked and what the password could be.

Zain Qureshi had always envied my father's empire of business. He wanted to be on the top and for him to achieve that, he had to remove NK Constructions from the market, my father's company.

Neil's words ringed in her mind and a thought popped up. Could it be? She didn't know, but had to take the chance anyway. With clammy hands, Avni typed.

'destroynk'

What a despicable man, Avni thought. How can someone keep a password like that, but the fact that now she had access to the hard-disk shot a boost of adrenaline through her veins.

She bit on her lips as she clicked on the folder and her screen flooded with a number of small folder icons.

Two of them stood out though.

Khanna, and Mehta.

CHAPTER 23

Avni was startled when the door of the study opened abruptly and before she knew it Rehaan stormed inside the room with a furious rage evident in his eyes.

Avni's heart beat went haywire as fear engulfed her and within the blink of an eye he grabbed her as he fisted her hair and pulled her up from the sofa that she was sitting on. A painful hiss slipped out of Avni's mouth as he dragged her to himself, making her drop her laptop and the hard-disk on the floor.

A - Leave me, Rehaan! - she hissed in pain. What are you doing?

R - What the fuck are you doing, you filthy slut? - he spat as he yanked her hair harshly. What did you think? I won't find out that you accessed my study? Bloody bitch said that you loved me, huh? - he grabbed one of her arms as he twisted it behind her back, making her yelp in pain. Tell me? Who are you? - he gritted out.

Avni did not answer. Instead, a shriek left her mouth when Rehaan slapped her cheek hard but she didn't let a word out.

Avni had been working for this since the last fifteen years. She had trained since the age of eleven like a wounded lion waiting to attack. She had learnt how to fight, fire & fucking win. After Neela had adopted her, she had trained herself as a professional fighter, boxer & shooter for ten long years, at the same time she worked on finding who the real culprits behind her parents' death were. Neela had backed & supported her at every step as she provided Avni with the means & power to dig into the truth. It was when she had turned eighteen that she found out that her grandparents hadn't killed her parents. It was Zain Qureshi who had. The year Avni turned twenty, she started mingling with the inner circle of the Qureshis. Rehaan had always been a spoilt brat, and thus was an easy goat to scrap. Avni met him at bars and caught him in her trap. Her words honey, & intentions lethal. By the time she got his trust, he had already started divulging information to her once she got him drunk after a long evening of partying. She gathered the information about all the safes, lockers, properties, businesses, dungeons that Qureshis possessed. The more she got to know, the more the Qureshis disgusted her. And she had swear to bring them down. It took her four painfully long years of patience & intelligence to finally get her hands on the evidences she was looking for. She couldn't let it go to waste. At no cost.

She just needed some time, so that she could grab the laptop back & take a backup. If only Rehaan loosened his grip on her. But just as all victories don't come easy, neither did hers.

Rehaan dragged her out of the study as he twisted her arm in his vile grip. Avni loathed his touch, it made her skin crawl in disgust. From the periphery of her eye, she saw that some of his men had held Shweta captive too.

Shweta was unaware of the development, but Rehaan had put an alarm on the lock of the study. If anybody opened the door, he would get a notification and that was how he got to know about Avni intruding in his space. The moment he got to know it was her, he saw red. The woman had paused herself as an innocent poor girl who he had bedded so many times, he couldn't remember the count. Apparently, she had double-crossed him. Rehaan doubted if she was a mole, planted by some of his enemy.

The thought was a clear reminder of the fact that he had committed a mistake. If Avni had found out about all the illegal activities that he was neck deep in, be it sex rackets, or trafficking, or drugs, or the many business frauds, Rehaan would be in deep trouble & he couldn't afford that. He needed to get Avni off his back and the only way was to kill her. But he needed to find out who had planted her & who all were involved with her.

One of them certainly being his own mother. The bitch had let her in his study, where she knew all his secrets lied. It was a shame that his father was so pussy-whacked that he married someone who had literally fled her own family like a plague. He could never come to respect his parents. If anything, they felt like a burden, and the moment Rehaan got hold of all the power after his father's death, the first thing that he wanted to do was to uproot Neil Khanna. The only remembrance of how his father was a failure. Rehaan didn't want to be one. He was aware that Neil was smart, very smart & intelligent. He had single handedly flourished the Khanna Empire no team of the best delegates could ever have. But Rehaan refused to let him win.

Feeling a ball of anger coursing through his nerves, he dragged Avni down the stairs and then on the floor as he threw her in his car.

Avni groaned in pain the moment her head landed against the metallic handle of the door and blood oozed out in a stream. She felt light headed as she felt dizziness washing over her when she lost a considerable amount of blood. Rehaan's men had tied her hands behind her back as he drove her to some unknown location while Avni could barely keep her eyes open.

The moment they hit the road, Rehaan had gone into a frenzy. He flew the car & stopped it in abrupt motions, making Avni shake & hit her head around the car, causing pain & there were moments when she thought she would pass out.

Avni thought her brain worked funnily. When she thought she was going to die, with her wrists hurting so much that they might fall off her body and her throat running dry, her eyes stinging and blood dripping down her head, in that moment, the only thought that crossed her mind was if she could just get to see Neil & Isha once. No revenge. No pain. Nothing. All she wanted was Neil. Just once.

She groaned when Rehaan stopped the car abruptly and Avni had to struggle to keep her eyes open. Swallowing, she slowly rose on her knees when he didn't start the car again to look around. They were in the middle of nowhere. With her hazy vision, she could only make out that they were in the outskirts, no one or nothing was around except for some large containers. She figured they were somewhere near the port, or some warehouse of some sort.

R - Did you call your lover here, you bitch? - he pushed her back, making her tumble across the seat and hit her head on the door. A muffled cry escaped her mouth and the tape that he had put on her mouth hurt. Tears oozed out Avni's eyes in pain.

But then she registered his words. Lover?

Could it be Neil?

Avni swallowed the thick lump down her throat as Rehaan ignited the engine again but before he could have started the car, the door of the driver seat burst open and there he was. The one she was dying to see. Neil.

Neil yanked Rehaan out of the car as he smashed his head across the windshield. Avni flinched as she hid behind the seat. From the corner of her eyes, she saw Neil throwing punches over punches on Rehaan's face in a fit of towering fury.

Neil had promised himself that he would never resort to violence again. But the moment his eyes fell on Avni & he noticed the blood dripping down her head, he couldn't stop himself from succumbing to his desire of causing as much pain to Rehaan as he had caused Avni. His vision turned crimson as he threw a punch in his gut and blood sprew out of his mouth but the bastard still laughed like a maniac.

R - Hitting your own brother for that slut, huh Khanna? - he spoke in between coughs and with every word that left his mouth, Neil found the rage in him growing more intense than it was the last second.

Rehaan tried to punch Neil back but his steps fumbled and he punched him on the face, giving him a black eye.

R - Was she so good in bed? C'mon, I'm your own blood! - he spoke disgustingly.

And the mention of their mother seemed to only enhance Neil's fury ten folds. He pushed him back on the bonnet of his car as he mindlessly punched his face and the blood Rehaan spat splashed over Neil's face. Neil's hands had become numb and Rehaan had stopped fighting back. The sound of the cracking of his nose sent a comforting sensation in Neil's bones. He knew he was sick for feeling it, but he knew no other way. The Neil who had promised himself not to resort to violence again seemed dusted beneath the weight of all the atrocities that the Qureshis had committed against him & his family, and also under the weight of a certain someone's betrayal, that hurt Neil more than he could ever fathom.

N - The next time you lay your hands on her, or on any other woman for that matter, remember that you'll have to go through the same pain in this very world, Rehaan! I don't know if heaven & hell are real, but life gets back at you. Some way or the other. - he spat as he left his collar and stepped behind. Not wanting to see his unfortunate face anymore.

Avni saw Neil walking around the car as he made his way towards her but stopped when Rehaan called him.

R - This is life getting back at you, Khanna! - he said as he pulled the trigger of his gun which he had pointed towards him and Avni's heart stopped beating.

A gunshot. A thud. A body fell down.

Tears poured out of Avni's eyes at the sound of the gun-shot. She felt like she was ten again. Scared. Lost. Weak. Helpless. Flashes of her mother being dragged by the masked men crossed her vision and her body shook in fear as sweat formed on her whole body.

Avni flinched when the door of the car opened and more tears poured out of her eyes when she saw him. He stood there, with blood splashed on his clothes and on his face. But his eyes were soft. She let him carry her out of the car as he made her sit on the top of one of the container boxes that were placed there.

She swallowed in order to give some relief to her dry throat when he silently undid the ropes that she had been tied with and then slowly took the tape off her mouth. A hiss of pain escaped her lip when he scratched it off but then he brushed her hair back gently and Avni felt like it wasn't the end of the world. That may be things could still get better.

A - Neil-

N - I need to go see the cops. Just wait here, okay? - he spoke and she found herself nodding.

Avni had been so lost that she failed to notice that about a small trope of officers were dragging Rehaan to their car while he coughed blood out of his mouth and he had been shot in the leg. The gun shot had hit him, the cop had shot him. A sigh left Avni's chest, Neil was okay!

She watched as Neil talked to the cops who informed him that Rehaan had been charged of kidnapping and human trafficking. The kidnapping part was obviously proved as Avni was right there but they still were looking for the evidences to prove that he was involved in other illegal stuff. Neil pursed his lips in a thin line as he nodded his head & silently listened to what the officer said. He then shook his hand before the officer walked back to his car and Neil sighed a long breath out.

Turning around slowly, he walked up to Avni and carried her in his arms as he took her towards his car and made her sit on the passenger seat.

He fastened her seat belt and without uttering a word to her, settled in the driver seat. Neil drove in silence while Avni simply watched him from the corner of her eyes. Her head felt dizzy and she was quacking in her boots thinking how he would react to it all.

Neil stopped the car and Avni noticed they were in front of a private clinic. Wordlessly, Neil carried Avni inside and asked the doctors to treat her wounds. He waited outside while the doctors checked & treated her wounds.

His silence irked her. It felt eerie & unnerving. She needed him to let her in but couldn't gather the courage to speak. Once they headed out of the clinic, Neil was focused on the road and it was as if he had pledged not to spare even a glance at her.

The drive was as silent as Neil's nights used to be before meeting Avni. Even the sound of breath was audible in the compact space and he felt suffocated. On the other hand, Avni soaked in the smell of him as much as she could, cause she was too unsure of their future from that point onwards. Would Neil ever trust her again?

The car came to screeching stop and Neil looked straight on the road, while Avni waited for him to say something. Anything. He had never been so silent, not even when they had just met. She hated how he refused to acknowledge even her presence.

When Avni figured that Neil was in fact not going to say anything, she tried to initiate a conversation.

A - Would you, um, would you like to- - she had meant to ask him to come inside but he didn't let her complete the sentence.

N - No, Miss Mehta. - he gritted his teeth. He curled his palm around the steering wheel when they itched to reach out to her & hold her, to ask her if she was alright. I would not. You may leave now! - he exhaled sharply.

Tears welled up in her eyes and her throat hurt as she tried to bite her sobs back. He wasn't even looking at her and she contemplated if she could just beg him to hold her once.

A - How did you..ah, - she cleared her throat as it had started feeling dry & choked. She wanted to cry. How did you know that Rehaan was, you know, was about to harm me? - she asked, gathering all her courage.

Now that made Neil turn to look at her. In confusion. His forehead showed frown lines as he looked at her. Avni blinked her eyes, the cut at the side of his face looked painful. A hiss of pain brushed past her lips. Her fingers twitched to hold his face but she fisted them tightly, turning her knuckles white.

N - What do you mean how did I know? You sent me your location! - he told as he showed her the text on his phone.

Her brows drew together in confusion. She had left behind all her stuff back in the Qureshi Villa, then who could send Neil the text. And it was then that it hit her, the cops. How did they reach them?

A - Did you call the cops? - she asked, in order to confirm her doubt.

N - No! - he simply stated.

Okay? That made no sense. If not Neil, then who? And who would send her location to Neil? Shweta couldn't.

N - You didn't send me the location? - he asked, making Avni snap her attention back to him.

A - Doesn't matter. - she shrugged, actually too tired to think it through. You saved me anyways! - the words slipped her mouth even before she could rethink them.

Their eyes met. Avni gulped as he held her eyes for a second but then looked away the next. Her chin wobbled as she blinked the tears away, it was getting tough to breathe. Neil clenched his jaw as his grip on the wheel tightened till the point he couldn't feel his knuckles anymore. He swallowed a lump down his throat as his eyes stung with unshed tears.

A - Neil, I..I am sorry. - her voice cracked when she tried to hold his hand but he flinched away. I love you, please at least- - tears were falling freely by then, she couldn't hold them back anymore. It was hurting so much. She felt like her lungs were giving up on her.

N - Fuck you, Avni! - Neil had to physically stop himself from shouting. Just how low do you plan to stoop, god dammit! - she could see the rage in his eyes, it made her tremble. Now that Rehaan is arrested, you want to come back to me? What do you think I'm? Some shitty back up plan? - and he hated how he knew he would willingly be that back up plan for her. He would get his heart broken all over again if it meant he could get some time with her. He felt pathetic.

A - No. No, Neil. - she wiped her tears from her wet face. Her voice was merely a plead now. Its not what you think. I can...I'll explain. What I told you that day was only half the truth, I had my reasons, I am so sorry. Look, I- - she was ranting in a breath as she felt this urge to make things alright between them coursing through every fibre of her being.

N - Were you plotted by Rehaan, Avni? - Neil cut her in between as he asked her what really broke the deal for him. As expected, she didn't say anything as more tears poured down from her eyes. Neil loathed the sight. Answer me? - his voice was shrill and a sob escaped Avni's mouth as her shoulders shook with disdain, exhaustion, pain & everything else that Neil had promised he would never let her feel.

A - Y-yes, but-

N - But what, Avni? But what? - he was being too harsh. Avni didn't know how to handle. She was accustomed to his soft side, where he only showed her love & care. She was aware that the setting that they met in was not idol, but couldn't he just give her one chance to at least explain herself? Did he not love her anymore? Well, she knew she did.

A - I love you! - she told truthfully. That was all she could muster. She was fifteen years tired, and all she wished was for him to hold her in his arms. To provide her some of his warmth. Only he seemed to possess it.

However, her seemingly truthful confession only aggravated Neil's anger further more. He was fed up of the lies she had told him. It had been a good amount of time since the party, yet she never reached out to him to even clear her stance. To tell him that she was being threatened, or under any pressure, or that she had her reasons, anything for fuck's sake! But now that Rehaan was arrested, she suddenly was in love with him? Neil indeed was a fool & desperate for love, but he wasn't fool enough to commit the same mistake all over again. May be he was still committing a mistake by choosing this longing that he had for her, rather than giving up on his pride and let her in when she was willing to. But Neil was done playing those sick games.

A - Please say something, Neil. - her voice quivered when he did not say anything for a while, just stared into the space with a blank face. This moment probably held her future, her heart race in anticipation.

N - What is even the point, Avni? - the exhaustion was evident on his face. His shoulders slumped and eyes were downcast. What is the point even if I tell you how I feel? Would you change how wrenched I feel right now? - he met her eyes while tears flew down her face in endless streams. Even if I do tell you that you broke my heart and that I lov-! - he shook his head as his eyes shut close and a he exhaled sharply. Avni was a mess now. Tears straining her face, nose clogged, chin wobbling, throat choked. It hurt so much to see him slipping away from her life. This is so stupid. - he mumbled under his breathe as he ran his hands across his face. The truth Avni Mehta, - he looked at her. is that you're a liar and I am a fool. And I refuse to be one in the coming future. So its best that we part ways. - he said in a tone of finality.

A - Neil, you're being too harsh. - she choked. Please at least let me explain-

N - Leave, Miss Mehta! - he whispered as he leaned forward and opened the door of the car.

Avni felt a shiver run down her spine as the chilly wind hit her and her vision blurred with her tears, but neither did she know what to say to him anymore. No matter whatever she tried, he wasn't going to listen.

Sucking on her quivering lower lip, she bowed her eyes down as she watched her twitching fingers.

A - I loved you. I love you. I didn't lie! - she whispered before stepping out of the car.

With his own eyes turned glassy, Neil swallowed the lump down the back of his throat when he shut the door of the car while she was still standing there. Exhaling a long breathe out of his mouth, he drove ahead while she watched him leave.

Chapter 24

The chilly night felt like freezing her to bones as Avni forced her legs and dragged them inside her house. It was hurting everywhere, her head, her arms, her legs, her eyes, her heart.

However, she had to look past it when she found the lights of her house open when she entered. Curling her hands in a fist, she tip toed inside the house but then instant relief washed over her when she saw that one human who could provide her some relief apart from Neil or Isha. She found Neela standing in the kitchen as she stirred something on the stove.

A - Maa! - her chin wobbled as she called her and Neela turned around.

Her heart broke to see her daughter in such a distraught condition. Her head was wrapped in a bandage and there were cuts on her cheeks & hands & legs. Neela quickly turned the flame off and engulfed Avni in a hug who broke down in her arms.

A - Maa, its hurting so much! - she cried while Neela stroked her hair.

Neela - Calm down, Avni! It will be okay. - she whispered as a tear escaped her own eye at her daughter's pain.

A - It will not, Maa! How can anything be okay when he doesn't want me anymore. He hates me. And I failed my parents too, I couldn't avenge my little brother who was not even born. The cops won't find a thing & Rehaan will be left to his devices all over again! - she cried, it was unjust. Her heart bled in pain.

Neela - You did not fail anyone, Avni! - she patted her cheeks as she tried to make her look up. And Rehaan won't escape this time. He can't. You'll provide the evidences to the police. - she said and Avni frowned.

A - I lost my laptop, and I am sure even if I do get to Qureshi Villa, his men would have destroyed it all by now. - she whispered, feeling a flux of bile rise in her stomach.

Neela - No Baby! - she wiped Avni's tears away. When you texted me this morning that you're going to Qureshi Villa, I had immediately left for London, and it didn't take me much to reach here from Cambridge. - she told as she had been staying in Cambridge since the last few months to remain out of the sight of Qureshis. They didn't want to risk someone identifying Neela & this getting Avni's cover blown. I had a spare key to your apartment & when I got in, I just activated the tracker that you had put on Rehaan's car. Sent the live location to Neil through your number once I logged into your account. - that answered some of Avni's questions. I called the cops too, reported about the kidnapping & human trafficking. - she said and Avni listened as things finally made sense. And, about the data on the hard-disk. - she said & Avni could feel her heart race in anticipation. The mail that you had sent to yourself had been successfully uploaded before Rehaan could do any damage to your devices. I logged in your email & downloaded all the files. Have backed them up in a pendrive. So you can check the files & submit it to the cops. - she finished and Avni felt relief & gratitude washing over her.

A - I don't know where I would be without you! - she said as she hugged Neela.

Neela - You would just be fine, Avni. I've raised you strong enough! - and Avni was grateful.

A - How did you figure the passwords? - she asked.

Neela - It was an easy guess! - she chuckled. Neil's birth date was the password. People in love were really stupid.

A - He hates me! - she mumbled as a tear fell from her eye.

Neela - Do you love him? - Avni simply nodded. Like really love him, Avni? Not the fleeting kind of love! - she needed to be sure.

A - Nothing about him is fleeting, Maa! - a chuckle escaped Avni's mouth. I love him. Truly, deeply, madly. There are no two ways about it. - she told truthfully as a sad smile spread across her face.

Neela - In that case, my dear daughter, love sometimes spells as patience. - she said, making Avni frown in confusion as she tried to decipher the meaning behind her words. One needs to be patient when in love. And Avni, you'll have to give him some time, to process things. One day you tell him that everything was lie & the next day you want to get back with him. It is tough for him too, right? - she said softly.

A - But he doesn't let me explain! - she cried.

Neela - Okay! Then you try to explain again. - she said and Avni blinked her eyes. She could do that? Would Neil listen? Neela chuckled as her daughter now had a mistic look in her eyes. How about you go freshen up, eat dinner & get some sleep. We'll think about this tomorrow? - she said & Avni found herself agreeing. She felt burnt out & could really use some sleep.

Neil walked into the shower the moment he reached Khanna Mansion. Blasting the shower at full, he stood under the steaming hot water until his skin burnt and he was forced to feel something. The passing week had been exhausting to say the least. With finding out Avni's truth & dealing with the aftermaths, and working on the launch of his business, and handling Isha when she had been so emotional on not finding Avni around, all of it had been a torment.

He was still in his office when he had got that text from Avni, she had sent her location. Initially, Neil had found it weird & had decided to ignore it but on second thoughts, he couldn't shoo away the dreading feeling he felt in the pit of his stomach. He would rather be a fool to her vile means than to be a coward who would regret not reaching to her in case she needed him.

She had sent him her live location & thus Neil chased her. The moment he had seen her bleeding with her hands tied & mouth shut, something in him snapped and he had again transformed into that monster that he was trying to bat away.

He was being too harsh, she had said. But what about the heartbreak that he was going through? Didn't she feel how cruel it was on her part to leave him alone to deal with the mess that she drew him in? For the life of him, he couldn't figure what was the truth & which parts were the lie? Or was it all a deceiving beautiful dream? He couldn't tell. And it was frustrating.

Drying himself with a towel, Neil stood in front of the mirror. He had bags beneath his eyes, two cuts on his face, one slightly deep, while the other was more like a scratch. His eyes held no emotions and his lips didn't know how to lift up in a smile. Basically, he looked exactly how he had looked for the past two years minus the last month. When he was with Avni.

Neil felt his head hurt as it throbbed in pain and he groaned out loud. Dressing up quickly, he made his way to Isha's room who was colouring in her drawing book.

N - Hi, Baby! How are you? - he kissed her forehead when she hugged him, dropping her colour pens.

I - I missed you, Mama! - she mumbled and Neil held her close to his chest.

N - I'm sorry, Ishi. Mama had some work. But I'm here now. - he said, brushing her hair back.

I - Did you fight monsters? - she asked as she narrowed her eyes at the bruise on his face.

N - There are no monsters, Ishi! But you can put a kiss here, will you, please? - he asked sweetly and the little girl nodded.

Isha pressed soft kisses on his whole face, pulling out a small smile on his face.

N - Did you eat your dinner? - he asked, stroking her hair.

I - Yes! - she nodded.

N - C'mon then, its time for bed, Baby! - he pressed a kiss on her forehead and she cuddled against his chest.

Neil cradled Isha in his lap as he tried to make her sleep but the little one didn't seem to be in the mood.

I - Mama?

N - Yes, Ishi.

I - Where is Buttercup? - she asked.

N - She is busy, Baby! I told you how old people have to work, right? - he spoke softly.

I - But she can work here. I will help her too, Mama! I'll be a good girl. - she objected & Neil felt his heart sink.

N - Okay, how about you grab some sleep now & collect some energy. Then you'd be able to help better, right? - he suggested, stroking her head gently.

I - Yes! I love you, Mama! - she said, hugging his stomach.

N - I love you too, Ishi! - he kissed her forehead.

Once Isha was fast asleep, Neil laid her on the bed as he covered her with the blanket and moved out of the room to distract himself from his constantly swirling thoughts.

Noah - Bitch, will you please stop ignoring my calls? - Noah screamed as Neil entered the living room.

N - Pch, its dead. I forgot to charge it. Besides what are you doing here at this hour? - he asked, feeling irritation sipping in.

Noah - What have you done to your face? - he asked as he pressed his thumb on his cut, making Neil hiss in pain.

N - You're such a skunk, Williams! Stop irritating me. - he barked, sitting on the sofa.

Noah - Fine! Help yourself. - he said as he passed him the first aid box from the drawer & sat opposite to him. Now tell me what is wrong? - he asked and Neil knew there was no way out.

N - Its about Avni! - he sighed. She..she was.. fuck, she was planted by Rehaan to whisk information out of me. I don't know what happened, the both of them must have been at some disagreement or something, but Rehaan was taking her to one of his dungeons. That fucker had hit her & I lost it. Somehow, the cops arrived & they arrested him, saying that someone had filed a report against him on the grounds of trafficking. - he told while Noah listened to him patiently.

Noah - I don't understand. Avni...why would she do any of it if she was working for Rehaan? - he was confused, just as Neil was.

N - I don't know, Noah! I'm just tired & exhausted. - he groaned, making Noah sigh.

Noah - I understand how you must be feeling right now. But, before reaching to any conclusion just...what I mean to say is just don't rush it okay. Ask your heart if it really thinks that Avni was lying all this while? - he spoke calmly.

N - Does it really matter? She wasn't saying the truth either! - he couldn't get over it.

Noah - Neil, you're being overly emotional right now. Just think it through. She might have her reasons, you can't reach a conclusion even before listening to her. - he tried again, well-aware that his best friend could be quite dense at times. He knew Neil was vulnerable & hurt, & that was why he couldn't let go of the fact that Avni was lying to them all this while, but even Noah could swear he had seen love in Avni's eyes. Moreover, nobody saved you from a bullet if they were not in love with you.

N - Funny! She said the same thing. - he chuckled humourlessly.

Noah - Bro, just listen to your heart. I am not asking you to run after her & let her in in your life again, but at least try to find the truth before giving it all up. - he put his hand on Neil's shoulder. Neil, its the first time in the last two years that I've seen you happy for your own self. And its the first time in the last twenty three years that you've ever believed in love & hoped for a future for yourself. So, just give yourself a chance & try to find the truth. - he urged & Neil found himself nodding.

He didn't know if Avni really was innocent or was just trying mess up with him, but at least she deserved benefit of doubt. Neil had been so blinded by his own emotions that he just couldn't see & hear anything else. Everything else apart from the fact that he was feeling pain was white noise to him. But he had to refocus & restart. And in fact, he deserved to know the truth.

So this was what he was going to do. He would ask Avni to explain what she did & why did she did so. And only then would he decide if he wanted to give themselves another chance, if they had a chance to begin with.

I loved you. I love you. I didn't lie! - Neil shut his eyes close as her voice ringed in his ears.

N - For all your bitchiness, - he focused on Noah. you do know that I am glad to have you, right? - he really was. Noah & Bryer were one of the very few people that Neil could trust his life with.

Noah - Oh, don't worry about it. - he waved his hand in mock dismissal. I do know that you would be a sad ass oldie without me! - he snickered.

N - Fucktard! - he rolled his eyes as a small smile spread on his mouth.

Noah - I've ordered food for you, so eat before you sleep. I'm gonna go home, Bryer must be waiting. - he then said sincerely & Neil smiled as he nodded.

Neil woke up in a fairly better mood the next day. For once, he was not thinking about what was going to come next, or how was his fate going to unfold. For once, in a really long time he breathed as he sat in his bed without any thoughts chasing him. Soaking in the morning sun, he walked in his balcony as he stretched and let the sleepy laziness leave his body.

It was still winter, but spring was to come soon. He wished that his life would bloom too this spring.

As much as Neil thrived on control and made sure he was always on time, that day, he strangely didn't want be on time, or take charge of anything. He wanted to let loose. He wanted to live. Freshening up, Neil made his way to Isha's room as he woke her up & after brushing her teeth, they headed downstairs.

I - Is it no shower day today? - she asked, brushing away her untamed hair.

N - How about we go play in the pool today? - he suggested making Isha exclaim in excitement.

Neil walked them to the pool & made Isha wear the inflatable rings before he asked her to jump into the water. Excited as she was, the little girl jumped right into the pool and splashed water on Neil as the sound of her giggle vibrated in the air. Getting into the water, Neil made Isha swirl around the water and they splashed water on each other for a while before he thought that she might catch a cold. Though Isha wanted to stay more, Neil persuaded her to take a warm bath so that they could make some hot chocolate & Isha was sold at that.

He got Isha ready for the day before he himself took a hot shower & then they had their breakfast.

It was when Isha was lying on Neil's stomach as they were sprawled on the couch while watching a new episode of Peppa Pig that a house help came up to them.

Sir, Miss Mehta is here. Shall the guards let her in? - she asked to confirm as Neil had asked the security not to let anyone in without his permission apart from Noah & Bryer.

Neil's heart picked up speed as his throat worked on a swallow. He nodded his head as he gestured her to let Avni in. He didn't know what it would bring, neither did he know what was he hoping for her to explain, nor did he know what was she there to save by a supposed explanation, if that was why she was there in the first place. But he was doing it anyway. He was going to try once, but at the same time, he couldn't let Isha suffer. He knew she would become emotional again if she saw Avni, so he moved to his study & asked the maid to bring Avni there.

In a really long time, Neil was nervous. He felt fidgety as he tapped his fingers across his desk and his foot drummed on the floor as he waited for Avni to come. He didn't know what to expect.

Was there anything true between the two of us? - He thought he would ask.

The door opened slowly and she stepped in. Their eyes met and Neil frowned when he watched her. The bandage was there on her head, her eyes looked swollen and cheeks looks patchy, as if she had cried endlessly for the longest of time. A strange pain gripped his chest when she didn't move, kept standing there at the threshold, as if too afraid of how he might react.

N - Take a seat. - he said in a low voice & he saw her swallow before she started walking inside.

Avni felt like she was taken a month back when she had entered the Khanna Mansion for the first time. It was the same way the guards had asked for Neil's permission to let her in, yet it was all so different. It was wrenching in a way that Avni could hear her heart shatter when he didn't address her as 'Buttercup'. She bit on her lip to stop herself from throwing herself into his arms.

N - What brings you here, Avni? - he knew very well, yet didn't know how else to approach the matter.

Avni blinked her eyes as she pushed her tongue to dart out & wet her chapped lips. She then fumbled through her jeans pocket as she took a pendrive out and placed it on the table between them. Neil's gaze travelled from the pendrive to her while she was just staring at the table.

A - Whatever I told you about my parents was the truth. - she started and Neil's heart pounded in his chest out of fear & anticipation. And, just like you, even I had thought that my grandparents had got them killed. - she said as she swallowed before looking up at him. My father worked in one of Zain Qureshi's companies. Software Development. - she told and Neil had already prepared himself for the worst. While working for him, he had come across the various scams & frauds that he had committed and..and that Zain used the data of his customers to threaten them to give him more business. My father objected to it & was planning to quit working for him. I was too small to understand all this stuff when they..they were...when they were alive. - she fumbled, a sharp intake of breathe and Neil's hands itched to reach out and provide some relief somehow. When I had seen their dead-bodies, I had swear to myself that I will bring justice to my family. That I will bring all those people down who had taken my family away from me. Neela Maa helped me through out it all. Till I was eighteen I had believed that my grandparents had done it & did my work to find out who had hired those goons, who had kidnapped my father on his way to his office and all those stuff. But nothing made sense, absolutely nothing or nobody that was under my radar indicated the involvement of my parents' families. Instead, they all indicated towards one man - Zain Qureshi. - Avni gritted her teeth as she spat the name out. I then tried to dig up more information on him, talked to my father's colleagues and then - she breathed. Finally. One day, I finally came across one of my father's friend, I had got his number scribbled on my father's diary and I made a call. The only identity that the man knew me by was that I was my father's daughter, but he helped me through & through. He told me how Zain had attempted to bribe my father, even offered a partnership in his business to get him to shut up about the discovery of his vile ways, but my father refused. When Zain was actually afraid that he might end up in prison, he did what he did. - her breath quivered. Killed my family. And then, the only goal of my life was to take that man down & do the impending work that my father had left. Expose him. - she looked at Neil. The fire in her eyes told Neil that she was telling him the truth. For two years, I worked to gather information about him, to reach him. And that's why I befriended Rehaan. - she told as she bit on her lip and Neil felt his skin crawl. But, unfortunately, by the time I won Rehaan's trust, Zain had already died in a heart attack. - she looked up at Neil as understanding washed over his face. It must be after the plane crash. I still had to expose Zain Qureshi's doings, and honestly Rehaan was even worse. There is not one immoral or illegal work that he has not committed. So, for the last two years, I've been fooling him into believing that I'm his ally, when in reality all I wanted was to take him down. - her eyes then softened, as if in hesitation. She took in a lungful of air through her mouth as she focused on Neil. Two months ago, he asked me to escort you, he had..he had wanted to kill you. And, to be honest with you, I agreed to play along only because I wanted to keep Rehaan's trust, because I needed him to know how & where to find the evidences of his crimes. - she told, digging her nails in the back of her hands to stop herself from shivering under his gaze. She didn't know if Neil would believe her, but she was going to tell him the truth anyway & let him decide thereon. Obviously, I wouldn't have let any harm to anybody innocent even if it wasn't you, but well, we were supposed to cross paths like this, I guess. - she blinked and Neil looked away. His jaw looked tense. Yesterday, I finally got my hands on the data & that is in this drive. It contains details of all the private information that the Qureshis had stolen from people to blackmail them. And, they are fool enough to store data of the gun-men that they used to kill each of them. There is a folder named Khanna that contains the bills of the air-craft that Zain had purchased, the one in which your family was. - she told softly & Neil's eyes snapped up to hers. And there is a folder named Mehta that contains details of all the snipers that were used to kill my family. As well as, it contains the audio recordings of the various meeting that Rehaan had with drug dealers & all those people who were involved with his rackets, I had recorded them when I had attended them with him. - she told while he simply listened, not able to decide how to process all that. I leave it you, Neil. I'll accept whatever you choose to do with this drive. And with us. - she swallowed while Neil bit on his lips. It was too much to take. He didn't know what to do. So he asked the one question that was the easiest for him to ask, but the toughest for him to process.

N - Any-anything that happened between us, was any of it true? - his voice was a whisper. Or was it you keeping Rehaan's trust? - he blinked as his fingers felt sweaty & clammy. This anxiety was killing him. He knew what he wanted her answer to be, but would that be?

A - I wouldn't have saved Isha that day if it was for Rehaan, Neil. - she told simply, her face clearly reflected the pain that she felt at the words that he used. Did it feel like an act to him? It is true that I was planted in your life, but whatever happened after that was the real me. Initially, I had thought that I'd keep a distance between us because I didn't want to get distracted, but hearts are slippery, I guess. Mine happened to fall for you, so deep & hard that I don't really think there is a way back. - she swallowed as her throat felt choked. Moreover, you saw parts of me that nobody noticed. You saw parts of me that I wanted to hide, yet you noticed them, & loved them. You made me love those parts about myself. You make me feel so complete, Neil. I can not even begin to explain. I belong with you! - she told truthfully.

N - Why didn't you tell me earlier? The truth. - he couldn't help but ask. It was getting tough to draw enough oxygen in.

A - I didn't want you to get hurt. Rehaan is an animal, Neil. He would have done everything to kill you, but because he thought that he was above you by breaking your heart using me, he was sailing high in his false sense of victory. I simply took advantage of that to distract him and stab him at his back, just like he deserved. - she gritted her teeth & that made sense to Neil. In fact, he felt a sense of pride washing over him for the woman sitting in front of him.

N - I don't know what to say. Or how to feel in the first place. - a sigh left him as he rubbed his hands across his face. It really was getting difficult to breath. He tugged at his collar.

Now that he knew what the actual truth was, the only dilemma was if was willing to trust Avni again. It was not a question of love anymore. Of course, he loved her & it seemed that she loved him back. But he couldn't be too sure. And he didn't know if he was ready to take the risk. If he was ready to get his heart broken again.

A - I know, I can understand. - she nodded. Just if it make things any better, that night, the club. Our first meeting really was destined. I really was out with Hazel to enjoy myself, it wasn't planned. - a small smile spread on her mouth as she looked at Neil. And you know what the funny part is, I never thought that you'd be the man I was supposed to escort. I had thought that it would be some sleazy man, someone just like Rehaan. But you turned out to be the exact opposite. - she chuckled as a tear fell down her eye & acrid taste filled her mouth. Neil, since the last fifteen years, I've been so busy thinking about revenge, betrayal & hatred that I had no time for love. Neela Maa says that I don't know how to show affection, but then I met you. And now I know how to. I don't have a fancy vocabulary, neither do I know poetry so I'll just tell you the truth as raw as it is. - she gulped as Neil's heart raced. I love you, Neil. When I met you, I was not looking for love, but you didn't just give me love but so much more. You gave me concern, you gave me loyalty and you gave me this fierce sense of being protected & looked after, something that I had yearned since my parents. - she sucked on her lower lip to draw a breath in when her throat felt clogged. You remember when you told me that you'd be leaving the Mafia, I had felt that it was so unnecessary, I'd have been okay even if you had just held me close & offered me a smile. But you did so much more. Neil, you're like one of those paintings that you paint. Beautiful & mesmerizing. But may be I was the rain that threatened to ruin! - she chuckled humorlessly as her chin wobbled. I know that you don't want me back, and I'm sure you're right in doing so, but I just want you to know that if, if ever you feel like you want to settle down, or have someone by your side, please give me a chance. - she wiped her tears as she offered him a smile. I'll wait. - & with that she walked out.

Chapter 25

Neil felt an eerie silence following him everywhere he went the moment Avni had left his study. He didn't know how to deal with the information she had provided him with. Of course, not the Rehaan part, he had already deposited a copy of the pen drive to the cops and was sure that Rehaan won't have an escape this time. With things settled on that front, he still was confused how to deal with things between him & Avni.

He felt confused, unsure, afraid and guilty. Confused if he could trust Avni when she had said that whatever unfolded between them was real. He knew what he felt was genuine but how does he bring himself to trust her when he still couldn't leave behind the visual of Rehaan kissing her and her smiling back at him. She had looked so convincing, he couldn't seem to look past it. He understood that she was doing it for avenging her parents, but Neil needed some time before he jumped to conclusions & made hasty decisions. Suddenly, he was unsure if he could let her in completely all over again. If there was one thing he knew about relationships, it was the fact that they required complete faith & trust. One couldn't have half a faith in a person & trust them with their hearts & lives for the rest of their lives. Neil wasn't sure if he could give Avni his heart just yet. He was afraid that all of it might just not end well. What if they weren't meant for each other. What about the possibility that Neil really was just a means to her destination in the grand scheme of things. Now that she wasn't obliged by anything, she might actually notice that how insecure & ugly he really was as a person. What if she didn't like him, or want him then? And, he felt guilty for feeling all these emotions. Instead of being with her in the time that she actually might have needed him, he was trying to push her away & maintain distance. As much as it was unfair to him, it was unfair to her too. Neil understood it, but still was selfish enough to need more time before he submitted to this madness that he felt for her. Love!

Love, Neil figured, was similar to a rope. It could hang you, or it could save you from a fall. It was just him who needed to decide if he wanted to hang himself with it by letting it go, or if he wanted to save himself from holding it close & tight. But that was the catch, he was too tired to do any of it. He couldn't fathom letting it go, letting her go at the same time, he couldn't figure how to hold on to her when he struggled to understand his own self.

Growing up, he had fed himself with the theory that love wasn't for him, meeting Avni definitely changed that and he believed that may be, he could have his forever too. But the five years old Neil was too terrified of being left alone. He was still that five year old at heart. If only Avni could tell him that she was willing to stay.

Two days had passed & Neil still hadn't given any answer to her, but he needed time. He wasn't sure for what, yet he did. In an attempt to distract himself for his Avni-haze, he engaged himself in work, once done with it, he took up cleaning. Isha's room had been a mess.

Neil picked up all the scattered toys and put them back in the basket while Isha dutifully helped him clean.

It was beneath the heap of her toys that Neil found something. A sparkly little object. An earring. Avni's. His heart skipped a beat. Was it some kind of hint?

I - That's Buttercup's! - Isha provided what Neil had already figured.

N - Yes, baby! - he attempted to smile.

I - Shall we go, give it back to her? - she blinked her eyes up at Neil.

His heart skipped a beat again. Shall they go?

N - I think manners tell us to go, Ishi! - he bit on his lips. May be it really was a hint? Hell, he just wanted to see her. This could be the perfect pretext.

I - Up, N-man! - Isha opened her arms as she asked him to lift her up.

Neil smiled as he carried her in his arms & walked to his car. Guess they were going to return her earring to her. Gentleman! & Little lady, of course!

Reaching Avni's place, Neil secured the earring in his pocket as he got down the car & carried Isha in his arms. Locking the car, he took in a deep breath before he started taking hesitant steps towards her house.

With fumbling hands, he rang the bell. At that point, Neil could count the throbbing beats of his heart. Could hear the roar of blood in his ears.

However, his heart fell when someone other than Avni opened the door. Was that her mother?

N - Uh, Can..can I see Avni? - he asked politely, throat working on a swallow. Neil felt nervous, a little short of breath.

Neela - She left. - she simply said, her eyes holding concern.

Neil couldn't understand. He didn't want to understand. Blinking his eyes, he shrugged, as if telling Neela that he couldn't comprehend what she was saying. She left? To the grocery store? Or to the nearby library, may be? Or she left - as in left him? Was it so easy to give up & leave?

Neela - Neil, she was miserable! - she sighed. Said that she couldn't stop seeing you every time she closed her eyes, couldn't stop thinking about you! - Neela told.

N - Is not that reason enough for her to wait for me? - he flinched at his own tone. Neil wanted to scream & cry. Failed. He wanted to scratch her name off his life. Failed. He wanted to keep her to himself for the rest of their lives. Failed.

Neela - She is waiting for you, Neil! - she told a bit sternly this time. But I was done seeing my daughter wailing & crying every second of the day. - she said, and suddenly Neil felt guilty. There is a week long trek starting from tomorrow. I just wanted Avni to take her mind off things, so I pushed her to go there. She didn't want to go. - she told & a sigh left Neil's mouth.

N - I..I am sorry, I didn't mean to- - he sighed, shoulders slumped down while Isha too was on the verge of crying.

Neela - Her flight takes off at 2 pm. You still have two hours left. - she spoke discreetly and Neil looked up, his eyes determined this time.

I - Let's run, N-man! - she whispered in his ears and he smiled at her.

Turning to leave, Neil shook his head and turned back.

N - Thankyou so much, Neela Maa! - he spoke genuinely and a small smile found home at Neela's face, Her daughter really had found the best man for herself. She knew it in that moment.

Neil started his car once he had made Isha settle in her baby seat. His heart was racing just as fast as his car did. Which was beyond the speed limit.

Neil couldn't brush away the feeling that had coursed through him when Neela mentioned that Avni had left. It felt like all of his fears coming alive. In that moment, he knew that he couldn't let her go. Agar woh saath de, toh main uss par bhi yakeen karna sikh lunga aur, shayad khud par bhi. Par uske bina zindagi mushkil hai. And he really was too tired already. The woman knew how to dress demons as angels, she had not only taught him how to live in his present, but had also taught her to be happy. Truth or lie, he couldn't let go of the fact that she was the first breath he took after two long years.

Suddenly, Neil felt like all his battles with the dark were put to rest, the fog of doubts was clear and he could see now. In his reflection, in his eyes, he could see her. And all of it led to one thing. He couldn't live without her. He didn't want to.

They'll figure things out, work on them. He would learn to trust again, both her & himself. With that promise to himself, he drove to the airport as fast as he possibly could.

Once the security check-in was done, Avni had locked herself up in a washroom as the tears refused to stop falling down her eyes. Popular movie culture suggested that Neil would come to stop her, and thus she would have her iconic romantic airport proposal. But she had no hope left.

Two days had passed since she last saw Neil in his study & she hadn't heard anything from him since then. There was nowhere, not even for a single moment that she didn't picture Neil around, or could think about anything else apart from him & Isha. He was there in her bedroom, he was there at her favorite window, the one where they got the most of sunlight, he was there in her porch with his car, his voice ringed in her ears as he asked her to tell the moon about him, or as he called her Buttercup!

But it was all a lie. A lie that Avni told herself. The truth was, that Neil wasn't there, with her. Neither was he going to be. She was left to live like this, with him imprinted all over her life but was unfortunate enough not have even a glimpse of him.

Her heart felt so fragile in that moment, as if it would give up on her and crumble down if she didn't see Neil soon. Hoping to see him was like she was hoping for something that was against all odds.

She needed to go away, be somewhere where she couldn't see Neil. Subconsciously, she knew the attempt was futile, but Avni had always been a bit delusional when it came to love.

But who decided the odds?

So, against all odds & against all the shattered hope, carrying Isha in his arms, Neil made his way inside the airport, purchasing the only ticket that was available. For God's sake, he could have purchased a ticket to Antarctica & fly with fucking penguins if that meant he could stop Avni!

He dashed inside the airport as he made his way towards the announcement room.

I - We need to rush, N-man! What if she flies away. - Isha expressed her concern and Neil fastened his speed.

N - Don't worry, Baby! We'll make it. - he assured though his own heart pounded in his chest with anxiety & fear coursing through his nerves.

Once he was standing outside the announcement room, Neil asked the guard to let him in who looked at him in return as if Neil was some terrorist asking him to be his shield. Neil almost rolled his eyes. He didn't have time!

N - How about I let you talk to the aviation minister? - he scanned his contacts & was quick to dial the number. Here! - he handed his phone to the guard and he was dumbstruck. Was this man fooling him?

He narrowed his eyes at Neil as he took the phone from him & pressed it against his ears.

Yes sir. Yes sir! - he said as he fumbled with his words & nodded furiously as if the minister could see him through the phone.

Please come in, Sir. - he said as he gave the phone back to Neil and escorted him inside the room.

A number of heads turned up from the screen in front of them as they adjusted the microphone away from their mouth and stared at Neil & Isha. Ignoring them, Neil looked for the microphone that was connected with terminal Z12. Avni's flight.

Standing in the queue for boarding, Avni couldn't help but feel her heart race as a single thought overpowered all her fears & doubts.

What if she just tried once more? What if she asked Neil once more? One more time. One more chance. She would do anything to win his trust back. Just one more chance.

Wiping the tears from her cheeks with the back of her hands, Avni stepped out of the queue as she walked back, however halted with a jerk when she heard the voice that came from the announcement portals.

N - Uh, Av-Avni? Can you hear me, Buttercup? - there was a pause, some shuffling. Yes, yes Ishi! - he mumbled somewhat away from the mic but everyone could hear him anyway. Avni, what I want to say is, uh, look I know whatever happened was...I mean the circumstances we came across weren't the best. - Avni's heart raced as her eyes turned glassy again. And I know I did my share of mistakes by not reaching out to you earlier. I..I am sorry. - and tears fell from her eyes. Could you please, hey! You hear me, right? Can you please wave your hand so that I can be sure? I see you! Over here, in the announcement room, you know! - he motioned his fingers around as if she could see him. Neil felt like he really was horrible at expressing himself. He had been so anxious & afraid, he never really put a thought about what he was going to say to her. And no, I didn't use any violence to get in here. Just made a call. - he clarified instantly and Avni chuckled despite the tears. She wiped them as she waited for him to continue. I swear. Anyways, what was I saying, uh yes! Buttercup, I want to-

There was an abrupt pause and some shuffling before another voice came through. Avni had been dying to hear that sweet little voice.

I - Buttercup, what Mama wants to say is that please take us with you. Wherever you're going. Can we please come along?- Isha spoke with confidence. That sassy little princess! We love you. And Mama is being shy, but I'm telling you I even saw him talking to your painting. He painted it. Uh, am I talking too much, Buttercup? - she then asked sweetly. Neil had always taught her to be polite. I don't want to take away Mama's moment of shine, so I'm giving the mic back to him, but please don't leave! - she pouted as she gave the mic back to Neil who only smiled at his little girl.

N - Yeah, pretty much what she said. - he paused. We- I love you, Buttercup. Can we give this a chance? - he asked hopefully.

Not only Neil's, but the hearts of all the passengers & crew members who heard the announcement raced the moment the question was let out. Avni felt like all the eyes were on her and time seemed to pause for a moment. Neil really was there. Asking her if she would like to give them a chance. Or was it one of her dreams again?

She didn't know, couldn't tell for the life of her. But after what felt like centuries of pain, agony & wait, Avni raised her hand up in the air & waved.

Fuck, yes! - Neil cursed under his breath just above the mic but then immediately covered Isha's ears.

N - Meet me at the domestic departure gate! - he said into the mic before rushing out as he carried Isha in his arms.

Avni literally ran her way to the departure gates while the crowd at the airport burst out in hoots & howls as they cheered for her. She saw Neil rushing to her from the opposite direction while Isha swayed in his arms & Avni couldn't help but chuckle as tears fell from her eyes in a frenzy. Happy tears.

Neil was nearly out of breath by the time he reached her.

N - I love you! - he said, and Avni took wobbly steps towards him as she wiped her tear strained face. Please don't cry, Buttercup. - he said as he smiled at her.

A - I thought you wouldn't come! - her lips puckered out but she smiled the next moment.

N - Couldn't let you go! - he whispered as he brushed her hair back from her teary face.

A - I love you! - she confessed.

I - I love you too, Buttercup! - Isha said, making Neil & Avni laugh through their tears.

A - I love you more, Baby! - she took her from Neil's arms as she smothered her face with kisses.

N - Let's go! - he held his hand out for her to hold.

Avni smiled as she slipped her hand in his and they walked out of the airport.

N - I'll get your luggage picked up by someone! - he assured her while she simply nodded as she tucked her seat belt after making Isha sit in her baby-seat.

The drive was silent as Isha fell asleep and so did Avni. Neil shook his head in amusement, both of them had this weird habit of napping when he was driving. Reaching Avni's house, he stopped the car as he woke her up.

N - Avni? - he called and she squinted her eyes open.

Adjusting to the light, Avni looked around and couldn't stop the disappointment that she felt on noticing that they were outside her house. She had thought he was taking her to Khanna Mansion. Neil could read the questions on her face.

N - Buttercup, I love you but, - Avni felt her heart sinking. I..I want to do it right this time. Its not just about who you are, or about the whole Rehaan fiasco, but Avni, I'm still dealing with my own insecurities. I've trust issues and I do want to work on them. - he said, and Avni listened with her utmost attention while her pulse drummed in anxiety & anticipation. I want to take things slow between us, do things the traditional way! - he bit on his lips. Lets just go on dates & get to know each other. The real us, you know! The people we are when we are not dealing with shit & trauma. Let's find our own selves while we pave our way to each other. I..I hope I'm making sense to you! - he fumbled, his stance was nervous.

And in that moment, Avni loved him more.

She understood what he was saying. In fact, she understood him too well. And she agreed to what he was saying. She was sure that they were going to find each other at the end of it all.

A - I understand, Neil. Let's take it slow. I'm willing to stay. - Neil's heart skipped a beat. I'll let you steal one heart beat at a time! - she smiled, making him smile back.

N - Go in, rest for a while. I'll pick you up in the evening, Buttercup. For our first official date. - he smiled.

A - Our first official date! - a smile graced her own mouth as she whispered to herself.

And sure enough, there were many more dates to come.

Chapter 26

It had been two years since Neil & Avni had been officially dating. Two years since he had asked her to go on their first official date. And to put it briefly, the last two years had been absolutely blissful to the both of them. Initially, they had struggled with the changed dynamics of their relationship, but the bond & connection remained the same, in fact strengthened over the period of time.

Both of them had agreed to take things slow & not rush into anything, that was why Avni had been staying at her place for the first one year of their relationship. She only moved in to Khanna Mansion after a year when Neil had proposed to do so at their anniversary, making sure that she was comfortable at all steps in the transition.

Isha was growing faster than ever & as sad as it made both Neil & Avni, they were also happy to witness their little princess grow up. It was, hands down, the most beautiful thing that they had experienced.

Avni had joined as a teacher in a renowned school while Neil enlarged the various vertebras of the Khanna Empire.

On other fronts, they had turned in the evidences to the cops that proved the involvement of Qureshis in various scandals & illegal activities. The case went on for the larger part of the first year of them dating & in the end Rehaan was convicted of numerous murders, human trafficking, sex rackets, & corporate frauds, the court had ordered him to serve death sentence.

Avni was still in touch with Shweta, who had opened her own NGO and was mostly kept busy by work. Avni had told Neil everything about how Shweta had helped her find the evidences and she even insisted him to let go & meet his mother once, but he kept refusing. God forbid, Avni just didn't want Neil to regret not making amends with his mother when he still had the time. Cause having absent parents was one thing, but not having them at all was another. And, especially when the said absent parent was trying to redeem themselves, then the least they deserved was a discreet meet with their child once in a while. However, she had had no luck yet. Neil could be really thick-headed at times when he wanted to.

One thing that came as a surprise to her was that how quickly Neil & Neela had grown fond of each other. Neela Maa had become the mother figure Neil never had & Neil had successfully become one of Neela Maa's favourite people to exist. Whenever Avni & Neil had a fight or argument, Neil would immediately resort to Neela Maa for help & she would very obviously make things easy for her favourite child. Sometimes, Avni thought Neil had snatched her mother from her, but the next moment she would feel her heart flutter at how adorable they looked together.

They celebrated all of their holidays in Hambledon, where Noah, Bryer, Mrs Brown & family joined them and they were this strong pack of wolves together. They were a big happy family. Life had been good the last two years. They had been happy and it was only the beginning.

In the moment, Avni was sitting in her room as she dialed Neela to ask if Isha had eaten her food on time. Isha had been wanting to spend some time with Neela since a long time now & Neela had been more than happy to hear that.

A - Hi, Maa! How are you? - she asked once Neela picked the call up.

Neela - I'm good, Avni. How are you, Baby? - she asked.

A - Yeah, I'm good too. Has Isha eaten? She usually gets hungry around this time. - she asked & heard Neela chuckle, making her frown.

Neela - My baby now has a baby! - she laughed & a small smile spread on Avni's face. Don't worry, she has eaten. She is colouring in her book now. Do you want to speak to her? - she asked.

A - No, its okay. Let her be! I just missed her. - she said as a sigh left her.

Neela - Gosh, Avni! Just come over tomorrow & bring Neil along. We'll have dinner together? - she asked and Avni smiled at the idea.

A - Sounds like a plan, Maa! See ya! Love you! - she said before putting the line off.

Once disconnecting the call with Neela, Avni looked around to find Neil, only to find him in his attic studio where he was busy working on his painting. Suddenly, wanting to mess with him, she walked up to him as she slowly sat on his lap, making a good show of her ass in front of him.

Avni sighed in delight as she shuffled in his lap, subtly rubbing his crotch with her plump rounds making him groan but he had to get the painting done. He had already been working on it from quite long now. However, Avni had been feeling quite playful lately, and more than anything, she believed it was only fair that he paid back for the embarrassment that she had to face when he fingered her under the table while they were out on a dinner with Isha's friend with her family present there too.

She turned her upper body to the side as she placed open-mouthed kisses on his jaw at the same time as she moved herself against his crotch. She gasped when he snaked his arms around her waist and turned her around so that she was now straddling him.

N - Holy cheese dumplings, Buttercup! You leave no means to drive me nuts! - he groaned as he gave her thighs a firm squeeze.

His hands fiddled with the waistbands of her undies as he bunched her sundress up and leaned forward to kiss her. Avni's eyes closed on their own accord when he pressed his lips against her mouth and one of his hands snaked up to her back while the other still fiddled with her waistband. Their mouths worked in sync when Neil sucked on her upper lip while she sucked on his lower lip and their upper bodies shook as they devoured each others' mouth.

The moment his hands found the zip of her dress, he undid it with a rough tug and she moaned still in the kiss. The dress loosened and fell down her body, bunching up around her waist as she still had her legs wrapped around him. Neil's fingers dipped in some of the colour that he had on his colour palette and he smeared it on her arms, watching as he painted her red. Avni shivered at the impact while he simply kissed her shoulder blade, his hand following his mouth as he left a trail of red all across her chest.

Avni hastily took his shirt off as she placed urgent kisses all across his chest and abs while he grabbed her hair in a fist. She was surprised when he bent her down so that her back was against the cold floor and he removed her legs from around his waist. Avni watched him with hazy eyes as he dragged her dress off her body and next went off her undies.

She squirmed suddenly feeling shy as he watched her with his heated gaze. Neil slowly, torturously slowly took his clothes off as he smirked hearing her heavy breathes.

N - As much as I'd love to paint you with my colours, I bet my cum would look even better smeared all across your tiny little body, Buttercup! - he whispered in her ear and Avni felt heat wafting off of her at his dirty comment.

A - You think so highly of yourself, Mr. Khanna! - she teased as she narrowed her eyes at him while he just smirked at the little challenge.

N - You wanna test that theory, Baby? - he rasped out as he spread her thighs while still having his eyes locked with hers.

Avni shivered when he gave her hardened clit a rough lick as he watched her watching him. Her back arched and hips bucked up when he flicked her hood with his tongue while his hands massaged her thighs. Latching his mouth on to her sex as he sucked her, Neil emptied a bottle of red paint on her abdomen and his hands slowly spread it across her body. The coolness of the paint did little to help the fire that the man was setting her on.

Neil toyed and played with her like an instrument, heightened and lessened the pressure as he pleased, earning delicious moans, whimpers and protests from her. Every time she was about to get the sweet reward, he would take it away from her, snatching away her relief, heightening her need, bringing her to the edge, making her lose her mind with need. For him. All for him.

A - Stop torturing me, Neil! - she whined when he didn't lick her where she wanted him to.

N - Or what, Buttercup? - he teased. And Avni had had it. She wasn't going to back down just because he was looking like an incarnation of Adonis himself with that sculpted body of his.

A - Or else, Mr. Khanna, you're going to sleep in the balcony for the next week! - she threatened but that only made him chuckle.

The sound vibrated through her core as he was still sucking on her clit and her whole body shook as the aftereffect.

N - You look cute when you try to sound mad! - he chuckled as he look up at her from between her thighs and Avni thought that was it. This was how she was going to die. Because her boyfriend wouldn't give her the release she so desperately needed.

Neil further laughed at the way she eyed him in half annoyance and half anger, but anyways decided to end the torture. His mouth worked on her like an expert when he flicked, licked, sucked, and devoured her clit and she came undone without much resistance, provided how much he had edged her.

Avni's eyes rolled back as she moaned his name in variations of tone and rhythms while he kept massaging her thighs to soothe her even more when she rode the waves of pleasure.

Avni frowned when he stood up and extended his hand for her to hold. She raised her brows in question but followed nevertheless. Neil walked her up to the wall opposite to them and it was then that she noticed that he had a white silk cloth tied on the wall. It reached down till the floor and she turned to look at him in question.

N - I want an imprint of you when you're mine in the rawest sense one can be someone's! - he said and Avni could picture what he meant.

He was going to take her against this wall and have her imprint on this cloth. That's why the paint! Oh, now she got it! The man was so full of surprises. She never thought he would ever do something like this! She was speechless.

Her pulse spiked when he pushed her against the soft cloth and her body pressed against it. Soaking the paint of her body on the cloth. Neil stood behind Avni as he slowly traced his knuckles along her back, making her shiver and then slowly traced his palms along both of her shoulders and descended them down her arms. Her whole body felt erogenously sensitized. His chest brushed against her back before it pressed it into her, crushing her under his gorgeous weight.

Avni felt her curves being encased by his strong muscles and frame. Her softness moulded perfectly to his hardness and a sigh of content left her mouth with the first thrust that he made inside her. Her eyes dropped close in delight when he stayed still inside her and let her adjust to his length and he only went deeper inside once he was sure that she was relaxed and ready.

Tiny muscles spasmed around Neil as he started moving in & out of her warmth while both of them moaned at the sensations. Avni's soft ass cheeks were pressed against his thighs and the sound of flesh slapping against each other vibrated in the room every time Neil pounded into her. Her moans grew louder and the guttural sound that left Neil's throat became rougher with every thrust that he made inside her.

Neil's hands grabbed her hair in a fist as he pushed her body into the cloth while he took her against the wall and Avni was floating in pleasure. With every thrust, Neil hit a nerve that set Avni on fire & promised to burn while she clenched around his thickness, making him throb inside of her. Soon enough, their bodies crashed onto each other as they welcomed the sweet relief and drenched in its glow.

Once Neil was sure that he had gotten the imprint of her that he wanted, he turned Avni around as she wrung her arms around his neck and gave him a dazzling smile. She pressed herself against him making his firmness press against the smooth skin of her belly at the same time her pebbled buds pressed against his chest. Neil engulfed her mouth in his as he snaked his fingers in her hair while he ravaged her mouth.

Avni trailed her hand down his chest before she caught hold of his hard cock and started stroking it in slow motions, making him groan in the kiss while she simple giggled at his torment.

They explored and consumed each other in different places & positions until they found themselves in the shower but still couldn't take their hands off each other. All they remembered was that when they woke up the next day, Neil was still inside Avni & she had a gorgeous smile of ecstasy on her face.

Getting dressed, both of them busied themselves in work and hardly saw each other during the day. It was around evening that both of them got ready to head to Neela's place.

Avni played the music in the car while she noticed Neil being a bit nervous as he drove the car in silence.

A - Is everything okay, Neil? You look anxious! - she asked.

N - Uh, no! Everything is fine! - he smiled but Avni wasn't fully convinced.

However, she didn't press the issue much as she didn't want to pressurize Neil into talking about something he didn't want to talk about. After a few more minutes on the drive, Neil stopped the car abruptly and Avni frowned.

A - What happened?

N - I think the car broke down. We'll have to call a mechanic! - he said.

A - Not right now, Neil! I'm hungry. - she almost whined.

N - Um, Neela Maa's place is just five minutes away. How about we walk till there & then I can get a mechanic after the dinner. - he suggested.

A - Aren't you so sweet? - she exclaimed, kissing his cheek.

They got down the car and Avni walked merrily while Neil followed her behind.

The moment they turned left, a loud gasp escaped Avni's mouth as she observed the way the whole lane of her mother's house was lit up. There were hundreds of candles lined up on the road and a pavement was made with flowers. All of it looked like stars were twinkling on the ground.

A - Neil, what is- oh my god! - a whisper of surprise left her mouth when she turned around.

N - Miss Mehta, I love you! - he said while he was sitting on his knee. Will you allow me to tell the moon & the stars about you for the rest of our lives? Will it be okay if Buttercups can be all my firsts & all my lasts? Will you, please, marry me? - he said as he held a ring in his hand for her to accept.

Avni felt her throat clogged as her vision blurred and tears fell down her eyes. She couldn't believe he was proposing marriage. Neil had always being a bit repulsed by the idea because of what had happened to his parents, but here they were. He was proposing her. Marriage!

N - Avni? Why would you cry? Am-am I doing it wrong? - he asked, feeling scared & confused altogether.

His scared face made her laugh as his innocent eyes made her swoon.

A - I'm afraid you really are doing it wrong, Neil! - she shook her head, hiding a smile.

N - That Bitch Noah! He said this would be a great way to propose. Stupid fucker! - he whispered under his breath. Um, would you tell me how to do it right, Baby? - he asked, trying to smile but he felt awkward to say the least.

Avni laughed as she pulled him up on his feet.

A - Just kiss me already! - she whispered hastily as she pressed her mouth against his in an urgent kiss.

Neil's eyes widened in surprise but once he recovered, his arms snaked across her waist as he pulled her closer and kissed her passionately. She still had not answered his question but he was hoping the kiss meant a yes!

"Oh, let her breath, you pervert!" - Noah's voice ringed in their ears as it followed a series of laughter.

Caught off guard, Avni jolted back in surprise as she turned around to look back. Neela Maa was holding Isha in her arms as she covered her eyes, while Noah, Bryer & Hazel stood besides her.

Feeling bashful, she hid her face in Neil's chest while he simply rolled his eyes at Noah.

N - Uh, Avni? Will you marry me, please? - he asked again, now feeling uncharacteristically nervous.

A - What even in the sweet creamy mango custard! Of course, I will! - she smiled as he slid the ring on her finger.

They had celebrated the night. Neela had prepared a scrumptious dinner and they had sent photographs to Mrs. Brown. By the time they had reached back home, Isha had already dozed off in the car & Neil had carried her to her room in his arms.

On the contrary, Avni could grab no sleep in excitement. She was getting married!

A - Hi! - she said, pressing a kiss on his cheek when Neil woke up.

N - Hi! - he said, a small smile on his face.

A - What's wrong? - she asked, sitting up as she looked at him.

N - How do you always know it? - he sighed. Its like you can read my thoughts or something! - he sat up, tugging her closer to himself.

A - Not your thoughts, but I can read these eyes! Quite fascinatingly, these mesmerizing hazel orbs have a language of their own! - she whispered as she dragged her finger down his nose gently and then to his mouth before she trailed it down his chin, making him shake his head in light laughter.

N - I was just...thinking! - he shrugged.

A - Do you want to talk about it, or do you want to drop it? - she asked softly as she looked at him.

N - No, its just...do you think I should meet Mo- uh, Mrs. Kh- - he shook his head. Mrs. Qureshi. - he finished, his beautiful eyes were silent for a while, sad & confused. Avni wanted to fill them with happiness & love.

A - Do you want to see her? - she asked.

N - I don't know! I was just thinking...now that we're getting married. Is it...is it okay that I want her to be there? Do you think I am betraying Dad? - he asked, seemingly lost in his own thoughts.

A - No, Neil! - she kissed his cheek. Why would you think that way, Baby? In fact, I think your Dad would be proud that you're finally leaving the past behind & moving on with life. The one who forgives is always the one with a big heart, Neil. - she hugged him while he held her back. A sigh left his mouth as he pressed his forehead against her shoulder.

N - Will you come with me? - he asked making her smile.

A - Wherever you want me to! - she answered making him smile.

Neil felt jittery as he got down the car and looked around with nervousness radiating off him. His toes felt itchy and his hands had turned clammy.

N - Buttercup, I think we should go back, it was a bad idea. I don't think- - he went on with his rant while Avni listened to him.

Sighing, she slipped her hand into his as he kept on talking, making her put a finger on his mouth.

A - Neil, relax! - she said, squeezing his hand gently. Calm down, its going to be okay. - she assured with the blink of her eyes but Neil was still fidgety, though the way she was holding his hand did seem to provide some relief.

It was a Sunday, two days after Neil had mentioned meeting his mother, that they had come to the NGO to give Shweta a visit & to inform her about them getting married.

Taking in a few calming breaths, Neil walked inside as he intwined his fingers with Avni and looked for Shweta. When they asked for her on the reception, the receptionist had greeted him with a full blown smile, as if she had been waiting for him to come. Gleefully, she had led them towards Shweta's cabin while she told them all about the activities that the NGO conducted.

Neil felt himself breaking out in sweat the moment they reached the cabin, but he pushed back the panic and asked himself to act cool. It was just one meeting, he could handle it.

Neil knocked on the door softly as he waited for some responce to come before entering inside.

"Come in" - a soft voice said.

Taking in a deep breath as Avni smiled up at him encouragingly, Neil pushed the door open and stepped inside. A lady was sitting in front of him, across from the mahogany desk.

S - Please, sit. - Shweta said, unable to cover the quiver in her voice. She was as nervous as Neil was. Avni had already informed her of the visit.

Neil swallowed as he nodded and sat on the chair opposite to her. The room was painfully silent. Neil needed a distraction, he tapped his foot on the floor as he looked down at the desk. Read the nameplate - 'Shweta', no last name was written.

S - How- how are you, Ne-Neil? - she gulped the moment his name escaped her mouth. It tasted like a sweet memory. But haunted her dreadfully.

N - I..I am good, M- - he wasn't sure how to address her. How are you? - he asked, collecting the courage to look up at her.

S - I'm good too, Beta! - a sob escaped her mouth and Neil fisted his hands on his thigh.

Avni concernedly placed her hands on his tightly curled up hands, and Neil's fists loosened a bit.

S - I'm so sorry for everything, Neil! I am just so-

N - Please. Please, don't. - he spoke painfully. Avni held his hand tightly. Naa hi toh main maaf kar paunga, naa hi aap kuch badal payengi! Let's just agree to not hurt each other anymore. - he said and Shweta stilled for a minute.

What did that mean? Was this the last time he was seeing her? Her heart sank but she nodded anyways, wanting to give him whatever he wanted.

N - I..I am getting married. Will you...attend the wedding? - he asked hopefully as he looked at her.

Shweta took in a deep breath before she wiped her tears with the back of her hand and smiled at him.

S - Thankyou for letting me attend, Neil. - she spoke genuinely while Neil simply nodded.

Either of them were at a loss of words & Avni didn't want to intrude. She understood that it was difficult for the both of them to navigate through something so complicated & delicate at the same time. But she hoped & prayed that it would get better with time. Some day, they would share a close bond hopefully.

S - I am so happy that you chose Avni as your life partner, I'm sure she'll proof to be the best partner one can have! - she smiled as she patted Avni's cheek.

N - Thankyou! - he said with a small albeit genuine smile on his face.

S - Would you like some tea? Or coffee? What would you like to eat, Beta? - she then asked and Neil shook his head politely. Have some snack at least? Do you like almond cookies? We had baked them in the NGO yesterday. - she told.

N - May be next time? I just had lunch before coming here. - he spoke politely and Shweta couldn't stop the way her heart soar at what he just said. There would be a next time. She eagerly nodded.

S - Uh, do-do you think you'd like it if I pack some cookies for you? Isha might like them too? - she asked hopefully.

N - Isha is allergic to almonds. - he told & Shweta's face fell. She really was terrible, wasn't she? There was no way she could make things right between them. But, I would like some, Mom! - he said and Shweta could swear her heart stopped for a second.

S - I'll just go get it for you! - she said, wiping some tears that fell from her eyes and Neil just smiled.

Avni smiled at Neil while Shweta had gone to get them the cookies.

A - How do you feel? - she asked softly as she brushed her thumb at the back of his hand.

N - Lighter! - he confessed. I know it would take time for us to gel up, but at least I can try. - he said thoughtfully.

A - Do you have any idea how much I love you, Mr. Khanna? - she asked, astonished yet not surprised at all with the man sitting in front of her. Avni loved the way he was always trying to make things easy for others. She loved the way Neil never possessed any form of ego or some twisted sense of pride. He accepted it when he was at fault & tried his best to work on himself. And he always allowed others second chances when they committed mistakes. Not everyone could have a heart to forgive. He did. Avni felt proud as well as strangely protective of him.

Pookie deserved all the happiness that dear universe could give him in exquisitely blended chocolate syrup tiramisus.

N - Um, I could use a reminder. - he pressed a quick kiss on her cheek as he laughed when her ears turned pink.

A - On second thoughts, I don't think I'll have the time to give you a reminder, Neil! - she sighed dramatically.

N - Excuse me? - he frowned.

A - We have a wedding to plan, Mr. Khanna! And I want everything grand. - she nearly exclaimed.

N - Big deal! Its just some vows! - he spoke nonchalantly on purpose to rile her up as he bit back a smile.

A - You're so going to sleep in the balcony for the next week. - she finalised. And, no touching! - she narrowed her eyes.

N - You think you could stay away, Buttercup? - he whispered, suddenly feeling bold as he trailed his hand up her thigh.

Avni jumped in surprise as she chided his hand away.

A - We're in an NGO! Would you please behave? Your Mom might come in any minute! - she shook her head in exasperation.

N - God, your antics only turn me on more, Buttercup! - he groaned while she laughed.

And this was pretty much how life was going to be. They were going to argue, they were going to make up, they were going to stand by each other in all things happy & in all things sad.

They were going to love each other till the stars have fallen! And beyond that.

Chapter 27

Neil & Avni had been married for a week. They had been so busy the last month with all the preparations and work that they had hardly got any time to spare, and so decided to spend some quality time with their little munchkin, Isha.

After having dinner, Isha had insisted on watching a movie. When Neil switched the TV on and surfed through the options, Isha had caught eye for 'Finding Nemo'. Pressing a kiss on her cheek, Neil played the movie while Isha sprawled on his stomach and Avni sat besides them on the couch, her hand stroking Isha's hair gently as the film played.

On screen, when Nemo called Marlin 'Dad', Isha couldn't understand. What did 'Dad' mean? Did fish have two names? Was Marlin & Dad both its name? Why did Nemo had only one then? Blinking her eyes in confusion, she looked up at Neil who was watching the film.

I - N-man? - she called.

N - Yes, Baby? - he paused the film and Avni too, brought all her attention to Isha.

I - What is Dad? - she asked as she looked up at Neil with her exactly same light chocolate brown eyes.

And Neil was at a loss of words. He hadn't put a thought to it when the film was playing.

Fuck, I should have known what this film was about! - he thought & Avni too, looked concerned.

But they couldn't escape it all the time. Isha was obviously growing each day & she was a curious child, asked Neil about everything & anything that came across. Moreover, with Qureshis out of the question, Neil was a bit less paranoid about the security of his family and was even thinking of putting Isha into a school just like all her friends instead of home - schooling her anymore. He wanted her to talk to people & make friends. Usually, siblings made up for more ways than one, but Neil & Avni had already had this conversation. They had decided not to have their own kids because it might impact Isha when she grew up. They wanted her to know that she was a part of them & they would love her with every breath that they inhaled. It was probably time that they had this conversation with Isha.

I - Mama? Do you not know? Buttercup, do you know what is Dad? - she asked Avni.

Avni bit on her lips as she struggled how to explain her while Neil took in a deep breath.

N - Ishi, Dad is someone who protects you, takes care of you and loves you with everything that they have. - he told softly and Isha squinted her eyes as she tried to understand Neil's words.

I - So does that mean you are my Dad? And Buttercup is my Dad? - the five years old asked. Of course, Neil was her Dad, wasn't he?

A small smile graced both Neil & Avni's faces as their hearts soared & raced.

N - Will you accept me as your Dad, Ishi? - he asked and Isha was confused.

I - But you're already my Dad, N-man! You carry me on your shoulders and take me to parks and get me ice-creams. And make my braids and cook my favourite food, and sing me lullabies. This is what Dads do, right? - she asked innocently and the adults couldn't help but chuckle at her little questions.

N - Yes Baby, this is what Dads do! - he answered as his eyes welled up and he kissed Isha's forehead.

A - Can I be your Mumma, Baby? - she asked.

I - Mumma? - she tasted the word. Is it the she-word for Dad? Like lady is for lad? - she blinked her eyes and Avni almost laughed.

A - Yes, it is! - she kissed her cheeks.

I - Okay, Mumma! - the little kid grinned and Neil & Avni couldn't have been prouder.

Five years old Isha didn't know, but she had given the world to Neil & Avni. This was what they were - Isha's Dad & Mumma!

I - Dad, Mumma! I want to ask you for something! - she then exclaimed.

A - Baby, no more ice-cream. You already ate today. - her tone was strict but soft, Isha frowned.

I - Not ice-cream, Mumma! I want a baby-brother! - she told, making Neil & Avni shocked at the demand.

N - Where did that come from, Ishi? - he asked, recovering from the shock.

I - All my friends have brothers or sisters. I want them too! He would be my little baby. - she smiled as her eyes shone at the thought.

A - Do you not like it with us, Baby? Do you feel lonely? - she asked, suddenly worried at the possibility.

I - No, Mumma! I love you, but I want a little baby brother too! I want to play with him. - she insisted.

N - Okay, Ishi! But you do know that babies aren't just to play with, right? They grow up & need attention too. What would you do when there are times when Mumma & Dad can't give all of their attention to you? - he asked slowly, he needed to know how she processed things.

I - But you'll still love me & still help me, right? - she asked.

N - We will always love you, Ishi. You're our baby! - he kissed her forehead.

I - So we can love baby brother together. I'll be a good big sister, Dad. I promise. Please! - she drew out the most compelling puppy eyes and Avni's heart skipped a beat realising just how much she loved this little girl.

N - Okay, we'll think about your baby-brother later. How about we finish watching this movie now? - he asked and Isha agreed.

Isha went back to sprawling over Neil's stomach as she engrossed herself into the fish-world while Neil & Avni held hands as they watched their little princess smile.

Some years later, when Isha would chase a little Neav around the house, Neil would smile looking at them and think just how much they looked like his younger self with his sister. Neil would live his childhood through his kids. And Avni would know that her parents were smiling down at her from heaven, knowing that she was living the life they couldn't have. She would live her childhood dream through her kids.

Khanna Family would be a happy little family. Forever!

Chapter 28

Avni had called Mrs. Brown to ask her what dishes Neil liked to eat while growing up. The time that she had spent with him, he was usually the one who cooked, the man had a bunch of house-helps and hardly had any work left to do but he used to cook Sunday dinners for Isha & her. He had been quite busy since the last week, the real-state business was soaring and the intelligent service vertebrae had been swarmed with clients.

Of course they still saw each other everyday but it was much less than Avni would want to. She was still looking for job in schools, had always wanted to be a teacher. So in order to take a break from the never ending adult life chores, Avni took a day off as she prepared all of Neil's favourite dishes for lunch while she went around the whole hog of the recipes & instructions Mrs. Brown's gave her.

Packing the food in a lunch box, Avni left her house in a pretty floral dress as it was spring and Neil loved her in dresses. She picked up a bunch of buttercups from the florist before she booked a cab to Khanna Industries' headquarters.

Greeting the receptionist, Avni made her way inside as she took the elevator to Neil's floor and soon enough, she was knocking on his door.

N - Come in! - came his voice, Avni could figure he was engrossed in work by the way he sighed just after calling her in thinking that it was some employee.

She gave him a bright smile as she walked inside and Neil looked pleasantly surprised to find her there.

A - Hey! - she said, placing the lunchbox on the table while she still carried the flowers in her hand.

N - Hi! - he smiled with amusement reflecting in his eyes. Are those flowers for me? - he asked tilting his head to the side.

A - Uh, no! I got them for your secretary actually! - she gave him a tight smile.

N - Um, I believe she likes roses more! - he hid a smile as he ducked his face behind his laptop & was sure that Avni would be fuming in a minute.

A - How generous of a boss you're, Mr. Khanna! Know your employees so well! - she gritted her teeth as she sat on the chair opposite to him and nearly slammed the poor buttercups on his table.

N - I mean- what do I say? I am just a loving person, you know! - he smiled like Cheshire cat.

A - Hahuh! How funny! - she fake laughed. Not really! - she glared and Neil broke out in fits of laughter. Riling her up had become his favourite pass time.

N - Okay, at least give me those flowers! - he then sobered up. Avni just rolled her eyes but handed them to him anyway.

A small smile spread across Neil's face when he brushed his fingers along the flowers and smelt them.

N - What do I owe the pleasure to? - he asked, referring to both the flowers and her surprise visit.

A - You've been working so hard these days. So, I just came for moral support! - she grinned making him smile wider. And you're so pretty, I thought I could just watch you for sometime while you work & look sexy. - she chirped making him laugh again.

N - Were you always such a pervert, Buttercup? Or are my good looks messing up with your brain chemistry? - he teased.

A - Um, its a mix of both I believe! - and he laughed harder. Avni loved the sound of it. He had been smiling more often now, it felt so good. I brought lunch. Shall we eat? - she then asked.

N - Yeah! I'll just call in the canteen so they can bring some cutleries. - he nodded while he dialed the intercom & asked for two sets of plates.

Avni unpacked the lunch box as she served the food in their plates while they sat on the couch.

N - This is so delicious, Buttercup! It tastes amazing! - he smiled while he scooped another bite in his spoon.

A - I cooked for the first time. I was so nervous if you'd like it or not! - she mumbled while biting her lips.

Neil just blinked up in a smile as he held her hand and put a soft kiss on the back of it.

He could figure that she had done some research before cooking all this food. It could not be coincidence that she prepared all his favourite dishes and exactly the particular way he liked them. May be she asked Noah, may be Mrs. Brown. He didn't know, but he definitely saw the efforts she was making all this time.

They had been dating for a few months and Avni had not done even a single thing wrong. She was there for him in all things up & all things down. She supported him when he felt unsure, comforted him when he felt distraught, corrected him when he needed guidance, covered for him when he messed up, and loved him through it all. Life was doing so better with her in it. He was working on his business - his father's legacy, he was working on his relationships, he was working on himself, and he could see the positive changes that she had brought him. He was happy.

Until he was not. Until the heartbreak didn't rear its ugly head back in his gut. Until the pain didn't stir him up in the middle of the nights. Until the thought of people leaving him all the damn time didn't mess with his head every passing second of his being. It came in patches, he wasn't always horrified of her leaving him, but the fear of it happening and the subtle lack of trust on both himself and her was still there. He was still afraid. Of being left alone.

And that was why when the subtle touches became a bit more obvious and passionate, Neil freaked out. Avni was holding his face in her hand while she had her other hand resting on his chest and their mouths were inch away. His eyes dropped close when she traced her finger down from his temple to his nose and then dragged it down his lip, making her way to his chin as she tugged his lip out.

A - Neil - her voice came out as a whine, as someone starved of touch and intimacy when they were going crazy for it. Please! - a moan, a whimper.

But Neil could do nothing to relieve her. If he was being truly honest, he ached to touch her, to have her under his mercy. He missed the physical intimacy and the feel of her, but at the same time he remember clearly well the hurtful words that she had thrown his way.

You had your fun! Stop touching me, you pervert! Another man who one can win over a good fuck! So pussy starved that you couldn't see the mistakes that I made.

He wasn't going to make the same mistakes again. No, he was better than that. Neil fisted his hands as he pressed his eyes shut when Avni kissed his jaw. It was a soft feathery kiss, but it burnt Neil. His teeth gritted and jaw locked as he took in a deep breath and pulled back.

N - Av-Avni, I-

Avni blinked her eyes open when she felt him moving away, taking his warmth away. He looked pained. Betrayed and conflicted. And she knew why. She had failed again. She had failed yet another time to gain his trust. She knew he was trying. She could see it in the way he tried to open up about his emotions and thoughts in front of her. He had proved himself to be the most amazing boyfriend to her. He was patient, and calm, and understanding, and supportive, and everything that one could ask for. But there still seemed to be a distance between them. There was still a wall of glass between them & he refused to let go of its confinements. No matter how much Avni tried to break it down, Neil couldn't bring himself to let go of it.

She understood that he was hurt and had gone through a very bad phase but couldn't he see her trying? Couldn't he see her literally breaking down every time he pushed her away. Of course, he was not doing it on purpose, Neil was not someone who held grudges, and she knew that he still loved her. But why was it so tough to trust her again?

A - Its- its okay. - she mustered up a smile. I understand. - she really did but that didn't mean it hurt any less.

That broke Neil's heart even more. He was not only hurting himself, but he was hurting her too. Though unintentionally, but he was. And it broke his heart to see her gathering up a smile when all she wanted was to cry. He could see it in the way her shoulders shook & her eyes dimmed every time they ended up like this. It felt like he robbed her of the light that she always carried around herself. He was feeding on it. Yet, she never complained. Not even once.

N - Its not like I want to paint you this villain & dump it all on you but - a ragged breath left him. I just can't bring myself to-

A - Its alright, Neil. - she cut him mid-sentence. It would have hurt so much to hear him say that again. That he can't bring himself to trust her. Yes, she fucked up bad but didn't she deserve a chance now that she was trying so hard? I..I should go. You must have work to finish. Don't think much about it. I'll call you in the night okay? Take care! - she said and got up as her throat stung & eyes brimmed with tears.

Avni turned around and started walking out but just when her hand was on the door-knob, Neil pulled her back to himself as he grabbed her arm and yanked her back in a hug.

Neil put his arms around her as he engulfed her petite body in his embrace and buried his face in the crook of his neck. A tear fell down Avni's eye as her breath hitched when she held him

back. It had been so long that he had held her last time. It felt like a life time had passed since then.

Their chest pressed up against each other as their hearts beat in sync and pulse drummed in a wild fashion. No one spoke for a while, they just stood there in each other's embrace while Neil collected the fragments of his healing heart back together and Avni basked in the warmth of his presence.

N - I am hurting you, ain't I? - he asked with his face still buried in her neck.

A - No! You're simply trying to save yourself from getting hurt! - she blinked her eyes, hugged him tighter.

N - I'm sorry, Avni! - he spoke honestly. I really am so sorry, its just tough! - he closed his eyes shut, sniffing her up close, trying to calm himself.

A - I know! - she rubbed her hand across his back to provide some comfort while her own heart bled.

N - Why don't you ever complain? Why don't you give up? I know I'm being too difficult! - his voice broke twice in between and so did Avni's heart.

A - You did not give up on me when things were tough for you! - she pulled back as she held his face in her palms, looking into his eyes. You chose me over your life, over the way of living you were familiar with. So, now I am choosing you, Neil. - tears slipped past Neil's eyes and she simply kissed them away. He let her.

N - Just give me some time, I'll get over it. - he pressed a soft kiss on her lips. I promise, I'll love you right!

A - I know! And I am willing to stay.

And both of them fulfilled their promises till the last breath that they took.

Epilogue

Sometimes, all Neil wanted was to rush back home and hit the bed. That night, he wanted to run away from home.

Or may be what felt home wasn't just Khanna Mansion anymore, may be home was Khanna Mansion with Isha & Avni in it.

A deep sigh left his mouth as Neil stretched his arm out and brushed it across the other side of the bed while he lied on the left side of it. It felt cold. It was beyond Neil's comprehension how a hotel room in a different continent altogether had felt like home to him but his own room felt cold now that Avni wasn't sharing it with him.

He rubbed his hands down his face before he picked his phone up from the nightstand and scrolled through his camera roll. Pictures of Isha, Avni & him smiling, laughing, enjoying flashed through his screen and an inadvertent smile graced Neil's face as he swiped through them. Pausing at every picture a second more than necessary, zooming on Avni's & Isha's faces to catch their smile, imbibe it in his memory.

They had gone to Disneyland for vacation to celebrate an year to their relationship. Avni had laughed and Isha insisted him to call it an anniversary & not an year to their relationship, but Neil could hardly see a difference. Honestly, he had found the whole anniversary idea a bit cliche but he chose not to act upon it because Avni had been really excited. He had proposed they take a trip to New Zealand as Avni had really wanted to visit but she suggested Disneyland as Isha wanted to go there. It had warmed Neil's heart to know how much she cared for their little girl. The both of them had been like two kids left to their own devices while they roamed through the theme park & insisted on trying every ride that they came across. Though Neil had acted like a strict parent, he secretly enjoyed how beautiful and heartwarming they had looked enjoying themselves.

He & Avni had made quite a lot of progress in their relationship, and simultaneously, Neil was doing good working on his issues. He had gone for therapy for a while and it did help a little but he had soon figured that the more he spent time with family, the more he was letting the clutches of his fears go. One of the very root causes of his trust issues was his insecurity, the sense of not being enough & thus losing people he loved. Avni had shown him so much love and care, that he had started believing that may be he wasn't that bad after all.

In the earlier phase of their relationship, he had been quite cautious and controlling about his feelings. He didn't want to get his heart broken again, but Avni was a slow intruder. She had slowly but surely managed to win his trust. She never questioned his reasons for holding himself back from giving in to this fire that they felt for each other. She understood him when he tried to protect himself when it felt too overwhelming and scary to give his heart away for a free fall into the pits of love. And that patience & delicacy that she had shown to him, had him tumbling over in love for her all over again!

Avni had left no scared part of his heart unattended, no piece of want & assurance unfulfilled. She had loved him. In all the meanings of the word. And this time around, he knew she wasn't pretending to care, or love. No! She wasn't acting, she simply did care & love him. And so did he.

Growing up, seeing his father so torn & distraught, he had given up on the notion of love for himself, but apparently life had its means to prove one wrong. And what he felt for Avni was a clear testimony. He was so thoroughly in love with her, not because he wanted her to love him back, but because she taught him how to love himself on his own. That is one skill not many people can teach you. She helped him grow & love & care & flourish. And he was willing to do all of that for her as well. For the rest of their lives.

When Neil figured that he wasn't going to get any sleep, he sat up & climbed off the bed before walking up to his closet. Opening the drawer where he kept all things Avni, Neil fished out a small earring. The one he had found an year back while cleaning Isha's room.

He had kept it as a backup in case he ever needed a pretext to see her at her place. But he didn't want it anymore. He didn't want to drive about half an hour to get a glimpse for her, or find excuses to linger more in her porch so that he could talk to her a little more.

After one year of working on his issues and being smothered by her love, he only wanted more of it. What Neil wanted was to wake up next to her, to come back home to her after a long day at work, to cook dinner for her & Isha while they watched some show, to have a long soothing hot bath with her when it was too cold to endure, to have her snuggling up close to him because she couldn't sleep otherwise, to have her tickling him while he tried to get his painting right, to have her turn to him for the slightest of inconvenience & the greatest of problems because she trusted him just as much as he trusted her, to have her smile at him when he brought her flowers for no reason. He wanted all of her. And he couldn't wait anymore. As much as he loved going out with Avni, he couldn't wait to come back home with her, to her.

He slipped the earring in his trouser pockets before checking up on Isha and then making his way to his garage to take his car out.

He was going to ask Avni to move in with him. He was going to have the life he always thought he could never have, but had yearned for all this while. Hopefully, she would say yes!

And, she did say 'yes!'